Other works by Eric Michael Craig

Atlas and the Winds
Book One: Stormhaven Rising
Book Two: Prometheus and the Dragon

Shan Takhu Legacy
Book One: Legacy of Pandora
Book Two: Fulcrum of Odysseus
Book Three: Redemption of Sisyphus
Box Set: Shan Takhu Legacy

Wings of Earth
Book One: Echoes of Starlight
Book Two: Dust of the Deep
Book Three: Chains of Dawn

Short Story
Ghostmaker

WINGS OF EARTH: THREE

CHAINS

OF

DAWN

ERIC MICHAEL CRAIG

Cover Design: Ducky Smith

PUBLISHED BY
Rivenstone Press
ISBN: 978-1-7337283-4-8

CHAPTER ONE

Mir'ah akCha'nee squatted on the low hill, staring down through the narrow pass toward the open grass covered ela'rah. She could see the girls of the Ar'ah tribe spreading the glowing zo'mar utel and she knew Ekan would soon slip his way up to their usual camp. Since they first met three seasons ago, he snuck out every night when his tribe reached the northern end of their migration. They loved each other, and now that they were old enough to lay claim to the right of coupling, they would be bound.

She waited on the edge of her own zo'mar and stared into the darkening sky. Tonight she changed her stars.

Walking back over to the center of the ring, she sat down on the damp grass and pulled out her scribe-stick and a fresh piece of hide-sheet. She'd thought about what she would say to the Tuula. Not all children became Tuula, but her grandmother had always favored her as special. It had been a long tradition that the Tuula picked a chosen one to follow. To lead.

Mir'ah was soon to be the Tuula of the Cha'nee.

Except that she wasn't.

She planned to join the Ar'ah and would leave with them at the next dawn when they moved off to encamp at their next kana'shee. It would break her grandmother's heart, but she could not bring herself to give up her love, as she must, to be the Tuula herself.

Ekan's tribe would welcome her, as all tribes welcome those who are lost from their homes. The world was full of enough dangers, and it was only together that they survived above the beasts of the sharrah. They had once forgotten this and almost vanished to dust. The tribes of Ut'ar lived in peace now because they knew they must, although the reason was long into the darkness.

Before she could join her new tribe, she had to tell Tuula that she was never returning home. It would be hard for her to accept, since no chosen one had ever left the Cha'nee tribe in all the remembered generations.

Moktoh, her wakat companion, shuffled up beside her and pressed his head under her arm, waiting for her to rub behind his ears. He knew she was leaving, and even though she would take him along, he needed reassurance. He was nervous about carrying the message back to her home and leaving it for Tuula to find in the morning.

"Gramma no happy Mir'ah go," he said.

"Tuula no happy," she said, speaking to the wakat in his language. "Mir'ah must."

"Mir'ah love Ekan more big than Tuula?"

"No. Gramma first love," she said.

"Moktoh first love," he said, pushing a big ear against her breast and listening to her heart beat. He was trying to hear the truth in her thoughts.

"Moktoh more big love," she said, laughing. "Always big love."

"Why you leave to Ekan?" he asked, still listening to her heart." You stay. Make Gramma happy. Make Moktoh happy."

"Ekan makes Mir'ah happy," she said. "Moktoh go too, we both happy."

He leaned away from her and held his eyes closed for a long time. *I trust you.*

She ran her palm over his nose ridge, around behind his

ear, and rubbed until he squirmed. "Moktoh good friend forever. Mir'ah make words on hide-sheet and Moktoh take and put on Mir'ah sleep-mat. Then Moktoh come back and we go with Ekan. Gramma find in day."

The wakat sat and stared at her as his simple mind sorted out the long instructions and then chittered a slow agreement.

Mir'ah crushed the stain-bulb over the end of her scribe stick and scribbled a message on the hide-sheet while Moktoh watched her. When she was satisfied that she had said what she needed, she waved the note around to dry the message into the skin.

"What words say?" he asked.

"Words tell Gramma, Mir'ah love Tuula big," she said. "Moktoh take now. Go fast. Ekan coming and Mir'ah wait."

He chittered again, snatching the hide-sheet out of her hand and pushing it deep into his pouch before he scampered up the nearest tree and swung off toward the Cha'nee village.

It would take some time for the wakat to return. She settled back in the grass and watched the stars. They would have plenty of time before Moktoh came back and so she luxuriated in the sensation of the wind whispering over her skin while she waited for Ekan to arrive. When he reached her, they could couple again and she tingled inside at the thought.

Tonight both night-sisters were still below the edge of the world and the sky was dark. The New Star hung low over the trees and she wondered again what it was. Brighter than most of the other lights, and colored so that it was not like any of the others, it hung where it always was.

New Star appeared in the sky long before she was born but she knew that something in its presence held her destiny.

She had always considered it a beacon, given to her by the Lights of Guidance, that her path was single and unwavering. Unlike the other stars that marched across the night, New Star never moved against the sky. It gave her confidence that her journey was set into the future. With a certainty, she would ascend the mount and lift the Arak Ut'ar.

Yet tonight as she watched, a spark broke free from New Star like an ember from a fire. As she watched, it fell toward the sharrah and vanished over the mountains across the ala'rah beyond the Ar'ah camp.

"The Lights of Guidance bind Mir'ah to this path," she whispered. She felt joy, even stronger than the sense of loss from leaving her entire life behind. She wanted to jump up and dance, but held herself to sitting up and looking down the pass to see if she could see the glow from Ekan's zo'mar arak.

Mir'ah stared for several minutes before she spotted the faint bobbing motion of his arak as he held it above his head to ward off any korah that might lurk in the trees. He was still far down the trail and she thought about running to meet him, to tell him of the binding she had just seen. But again, she could be patient. They had their entire future to share.

Behind her a sound like the rustling of the wind pulled her eyes away from watching Ekan in the distance. It was strange and she sniffed at the air. A korah never moved in silence, but it wasn't the only predator in the sharrah. She reached into her pouch and pulled out her edge. She was well inside the ring of her zo'mar utel so she should be safe, but a beast driven mad by hunger might still try to cross the glowing stones. Mir'ah rolled over and pushed herself into a crouching position, facing the wind noise.

Stretching her eyes, she brightened the dark and scanned

4

the trees. Nothing moved.

Beside her, a crashing in the brush like a charging boar korah and she spun, ready to launch herself toward the sound. She felt no fear, only sadness that if a korah came for her this night, Ekan would never know she had decided to couple with him. To bind to him. To nest and child for him.

Instead of facing the wild beast and its thousand teeth, she saw the entire edge of the sharrah light up like a hundred zo'mar shattering at once. She hesitated, covering her eyes with her free hand and holding her edge forward while her vision returned.

What demon is this? No creature on the world other than the Ut'ar used the zo'mar.

A sound like a lightning flea's scream pierced the night and she clutched at her naked breast in pain. Again the hissing sound, and another tear of agony on her leg as she staggered back. And a third time she felt the sizzle of lightning flash across her stomach. Gasping hard to swallow enough air to remain on her feet, she realized she was falling.

Her eyes focused up on the stars and she blinked in rage. "How could you betray the Mir'ah ak'et Tuula akCha'nee? It is my path," she whispered.

A voice, strange, not wakat and not Ut'ar, spoke from the trees in words she could not understand. Another voice answered. Struggling with all her heart she turned her head and looked over into the sharrah.

Three Ut'ar stood at the edge of the clearing. Their skin shining brighter than the zo'mar beneath their feet. *Marat akUt'ar?*

One of them walked over to her and knelt, saying something else that she could not understand. He opened a pouch in his skin, pulled out a small flat stone, and placed it on her chest. He moved it and it grew warm, glowing faintly.

He jerked his head up and down and spoke again.

Another one walked over and bared his teeth at her. He didn't look angry like he meant to attack, his eyes gazed at her with gentleness that confused her. He dropped to the ground on the other side of her. "Mir'ah ahhhkChaan'ney Tu'ullah," he said, speaking slowly and with a strange tone to his words. She wanted to chitter at his funny voice but couldn't move. He said other things in those words she did not understand, and bared his teeth again, but she wasn't afraid of him even though she could not have moved to protect herself.

The two Marat akUt'ar grabbed her arms and pulled her over face down onto her stomach on the grass. She could feel hands on her back and neck but could not stop them. One of them pulled her hair to the side and a sharp stab split her skin. She would have shrieked, but couldn't draw a swallow of air. Another stab followed the first and then the pain went away.

Night settled over her like a warm cloud and she drifted into the darkness. "Sleep princess," the one said. "Tomorrow you become queen."

She didn't know how, but she understood his words.

Moktoh shook her awake, his face close and his breath warm on her face.

"Mir'ah sleep bad," he said, shaking her harder. "Ekan sleep bad, there."

Mir'ah opened her eyes and struggled to focus on the face of her wakat. She reached up to rub the back of her head and felt a bump. "Mir'ah night walking," she said.

"Mirah fall and sleep?" he asked.

She sat up and looked around. Her pouch and edge were across the zo'mar and the light from Sister Tarah was bright

6

in the sky.

"Ekan sleep bad," Moktoh said. "No wake little."

She looked over at the crumpled pile of Ekan's body and stared at him for several seconds. She knew him and she knew he was important, but couldn't remember why. Pushing herself up to a standing position, she stumbled over to her pouch and slipped the edge back inside. She stood there for a long while picking the lights of the New Star out of the glare of the bright moonlight.

The wakat stood up, walked over to her, grabbed her hand, and pulled on it. "Mir'ah, Ekan no wake little. Sleep bad?" he pleaded.

She turned her head to look at Ekan again and the feeling of something missing washed over her again. She stepped over to him and looked down, nudging him with a toe. He moaned but didn't wake. She bumped him again, this time much harder and he groaned.

Ekan won't understand. She heard the strange words of the Marat akUt'ar in her head like he was standing behind her. She spun, sending Moktoh back in surprise and nearly up into the trees.

He will stop you Tuula Ut'ar.

She swallowed a deep gulp of air and jerked her head up and down. "Ekan will not follow Mir'ah," she said, looking down at the wakat and baring her teeth. It chittered and grabbed a low hanging vine.

"Mir'ah angry at Moktoh?"

"No," she said, remembering her face might scare the wakat if she … *smilea.* "Moktoh first love. Moktoh follow me anywhere. Yes?"

"Yes," he said, turning loose of the vine. "Moktoh love Mir'ah forever."

"Good," she said. She bent over to pick up the largest of

the zo'mar utel, turned back to Ekan, and knelt down beside him.

"You wouldn't understand," she said in the words of the Marat akUt'ar. She brought the heavy stone down repeatedly on his face until he swallowed no more air.

She didn't notice that her companion wakat had disappeared up the tree in screaming terror.

From this time on, she controlled the stars. Those that would not follow her would serve.

She would be the Tuula Ut'ar.

Queen of all the tribes of the world.

CHAPTER TWO

Captain Ethan Walker sat alone in a dining alcove on the main concourse of Armstrong Station staring out the window and trying to pick the insignificant speck of the Tacra Un out of the darkness. It was only a hundred kilometers across and almost ten-thousand klick away. And it was dark gray.

But it gave him something to stare at while he was trying to do nothing.

He'd already sent two servobots away, so was ready to scream at the next one as it walked up and stopped near the table. He glanced at it and realized it wasn't another of the treaded carts with a brain.

This one walked on two legs and bore a striking resemblance to a person by comparison. It had a vaguely female form and stood just over a meter and a half tall. It stared at him with glowing blue optic eyes above a display faceplate that presented a human looking digital face.

After several seconds the face changed expression and smiled. "I am sorry for staring, Captain Walker. I am just getting used to my new body and the input channels are extremely sensitive for binocular vision."

"Marti?" he asked as he recognized the voice. The *Olympus Dawn*'s AA system had apparently decided it needed yet another automech body.

"Yes, Captain," it said, smiling even more realistically.

Its mouth moved when it spoke in a flawless reproduction of natural human facial movements. The more

Ethan studied it the more it looked like a woman inside an EVA suit with the visor open. He wanted to move his head from side to side and see if it was a three dimensional representation, or a trick of optical presentation. Though he felt like it would be rude to stare.

"I decided to acquire a new body while we were here at Armstrong Station," Marti said. "After our unexpected windfall profit from the last run, I felt it was time to try Humanform Dynamics' latest model. Because this is where their development lab is located, I was able to get several upgrades included in the negotiated price." It pirouetted as gracefully as a dancer with its arms extended.

"I have to say that's impressive," he said. "A bit short, but nice."

"I chose this height so that the body would be more efficient and useful for maintenance work in confined spaces."

"Of course," Ethan said. "Logic rules."

"This hardware is an order of magnitude more sophisticated than the Gendyne 6000 unit I have aboard the ship. I studied the specifications before I made the acquisition, but the bandwidth transfer rate is exceptionally high. It also has advanced sensing capability that is a somewhat novel experience for me. The sensitivity and range of detection is impressive. When I am utilizing this automech, I have a sense of smell and touch at least equivalent to human capability."

"I'm sure you'll regret that if we ever blow a recycler line," he said.

The face frowned. "I will have to learn to understand what you consider an unpleasant aroma," it said. "At this time, it would be something I experienced with no relational value."

"There are times I think that would be nice," he said.

"Would it be appropriate for me to sit?" Marti asked.

Ethan nodded.

"One major drawback to this smaller automech is that it has limited power capacity. Whenever possible it would be useful to conserve by curtailing lower body operations," it said, bouncing as it jumped into the seat across the table from him. "I assume this is why humans sit?"

"Close enough," he said. "How long will your batteries last without recharge?

"Eighteen to twenty-four hours under normal use loads," it said.

"That's not too bad," he said. "Roughly the equivalent of a human duty cycle."

"I purchased an external power pack for extended range and it will provide an additional twelve hours if needed. It is just awkward to carry in some environments, as it mounts to my back with a separable rack."

"Sounds like standard hiking gear," Ethan said, nodding.

"I am detecting an odor I cannot identify." Marti turned its head to look around the room.

"Is this it?" The captain picked up his coffee mug and handed it over.

"Yes," it said. "Is this what coffee smells like?" It raised an eyebrow as it looked down into the cup. It was easy to forget that the eyes were the glowing optics above the image of the face.

"It varies, but that is one kind of coffee," he said.

"May I taste it?"

"Excuse me?"

"It would be a chemical analysis of the organic compounds, but the way this body processes and stores information, it would provide a holistic integrated reactive data set across the spectrum of chemicals involved." A small tube slid out of an aperture below the faceplate and extended toward the cup. "I will only require a microgram for a taste."

"Help yourself," Ethan said, watching in amusement as Marti took its first sip of coffee.

Its eyes opened wide and it smiled again. "I am not sure how I am supposed to react to this flavor. Do you consider it pleasurable?"

"I do," he said. "That variety is Colorado Special Reserve. It is rather exceptional."

"Then I will log this sensation as pleasurable," it said, handing the cup back. "From the conversations around the breakfast table on the ship, I am eager to experience the sensation of bacon. It must be extraordinary."

"It is," Ammo said, walking up and landing in the chair beside the automech. "I assume, unless the boss has taken up cyber-sex with cute robot girls, this must be Marti in a new body?"

"Well if it isn't the often absent, Tiamorra Rayce," Ethan said, staring at his load broker with a fair amount of frustration. She'd been working her contacts since they arrived at Armstrong, and after two days he hadn't seen her aboard the ship once. He wasn't sure if she was working or partying, or maybe both, but he would have appreciated a progress report. Or an invitation.

"Sorry boss it takes time to dredge up boring work," she said. "The challenging ones I can lay hand to almost instantly."

"Boring is good," he said. The entire crew had threatened to go on strike unless they took an easy run this time. Facing down Captain Jetaar had given them all their fill of risk for a while, even if they had made an obscenely huge pile of profit for their trouble.

"So do we have anything?" He drained the rest of his coffee and set the cup on the table between them.

She nodded. "It's a short single-leg out, about forty parsec, with a dead head return."

"Nothing deadly, or bent on killing things?" He grinned. "Or worth enough that people who enjoy killing things, might be looking to take it away from us?"

"Nope. Just some medical gear and food type necessities for a sociology mission on a sib-civ," she said.

"A sibling civilization? Don't they restrict access to those unless they're on a par with us?"

She nodded. "I didn't catch the name of the planet but it's a primitive tribal world. We'll be delivering to an observation platform under the management of the Coalition Science Wing.

"A government job sounds boring enough. That should keep the rest of the crew happy," he said. "Being a Coalition job, I'm surprised they aren't going through the big contractors."

"This one is so small it isn't worth paying the commissions to Cochrane Space Logistics," she said. "We'll load up a single container of mixed goods, a civilian observer, and two or three scientists. Everything will be at the same transfer depot in Proxima so it will be a fast grab and go. Once we snag it we scoot back across to our part of the galaxy."

Proxima was humanity's largest extrasolar colony and only a little over a parsec from Earth, so even though it was in the Centaurus Sector it wasn't far out of their usual area of operation.

"That sounds perfect." he said. "The Doctor wants us to stay in Cygnus as much as possible. Assuming she comes back from the Institute. She's still pretty pissed at me."

"Kaycee's fine," she said, looking around the concourse for a servobot. "She'll be touchy for a while but she gets over things. Eventually. She knows you did the right thing even if she won't admit it yet."

"I can call a servobot for you," Marti offered, turning its head in her direction. After almost a second it made a funny expression that wasn't quite curiosity. "May I ask you a question?"

She glanced at the captain and shrugged. The expressions would take some time for everybody to get used to. "Sure. Go ahead."

"Is the smell I am currently detecting, human female pheromones?"

The captain slapped a hand over his mouth to keep from laughing out loud.

Ammo blinked. Several times.

"Marti's got a nose now," Ethan reminded her.

"And needs to figure out how to keep it where it belongs," she added.

"I did not mean to offend," it said, lines appearing between the image-eyes as it tried to emulate an expression of consternation. "I am trying to catalog the various odors I encounter, and without some input from humans it is difficult to determine the source of the scent. It is a very imperfect sensory system."

"It might be pheromones," Ammo said, looking down.

She almost looked like she was embarrassed, and Ethan decided it was best if he looked out the window again in the hopes of avoiding a conversation on feminine hygiene.

"I have detected similar smells as I traversed the concourse, although none as powerful as the one I am detecting now," Marti said. "Yours seems to be substantially more potent."

Ammo cleared her throat struggling for what to say. Finally she nodded. "Probably is. Suddenly I feel like I need a shower."

"Marti, just don't ask to taste it," Ethan said, glancing over and instantly regretting his words as Ammo shot him dead with a glare.

The automech's face turned toward him and leveled a matching expression in his direction. Obviously understanding emotional response was a matter of emulation, but it was decidedly odd being glared at by a machine. Even a sentient one. "Captain, I understand human physiology well enough to know that to taste the source of the pheromone emanation would require a less public location."

"Thank god!" Ammo gasped. "What the frak brought that thought out of your mouth?"

"Lack of restraint," he said, shrugging. "But along with smell, Marti now has a sense of taste. She sampled my coffee already, so it was logical—"

"No it isn't," Ammo said. "At least not here. Although, for the interests of scientific curiosity …"

Now it was Ethan's turn to blink, and Ammo winked at him as she pushed up from her seat. "I guess I need to find the servobot myself."

"I summoned one for you," Marti said. "It is approaching. ETA forty-five seconds."

"I hope it's carrying something stronger than coffee," she said.

CHAPTER THREE

The mid-deck of the *Olympus Dawn* was where everyone lived. Because the ship could haul forty passengers in addition to ten crew, most of the time the mid-deck was an empty room. Tables and chairs for more than fifty spread out across a room that resembled a comfortable dining lounge on a small cruise liner.

The ship felt almost luxurious, but it was a workhorse at heart. Since the crew was small, most days they sat together to eat firstmeal but otherwise spread out and read or watched tri-vid on the main view screen to pass the time. Passengers gravitated to the panoramic windows on either side to stare off into space. Especially the ones with limited experience in space travel.

Maybe that was what caught the doctor's eye as she sat watching the four new guests they picked up at Proxima. Keira Caldwell was an observer of the universe by nature and from the frown on her face, it appeared she thought something didn't swing like she expected.

Ethan and Nuko had just finished standing the ship up on cruise, and he'd left the pilot on the ConDeck while he came down to get a snack and introduce himself to the passengers. "What's got you thinking?" he asked as he walked by Kaycee's table. She glanced up at him, her expression saying he still had less than a fifty-fifty chance of her engaging in actual words with him.

She sighed and tossed her head in the direction of the passengers. "One of these things is not like the others," she said, apparently thinking whatever it was might be worthy of stepping over the wall she held between them.

Three of their guests stood staring out the window at the distorted view of space, while the other sat focused on his hands where he had them sitting on the table.

"Maybe he doesn't like space travel," the captain suggested.

"He also doesn't like food, or conversation, or even smiling," she said. "They've all been having a wonderful time watching the pretty lights out the window, and he's not even looked up except when one of them asks him something."

"Maybe he's the observer?" he suggested. "Ammo said one of them is some kind of overseer and not part of the team."

"I hope not," she said. "The only thing I've seen him observe is his knuckles."

He shrugged. "It's not our problem. They'll be aboard for about six days and as long as he doesn't go psychopath on us, we don't need him to join the debate team," he said. "You're not worried about that happening are you?"

"I'll get back to you on that," she said, her eyes telling him she was almost serious.

"Have you introduced yourself?" Ethan asked. "Maybe he only seems strange from across the room."

She shook her head. "Not my job. I just thought it was a good idea to point it out to the captain, since it is a bit odd," she said, stepping back over the wall to her side.

"I was going to introduce myself anyway," he said. "I'll let you know if he's strange after I talk to him."

She nodded but said nothing more. Ethan noted the irony of her complaining about someone refusing to engage as he walked toward the galley.

"Morning, Cap'n," Quinn said, jumping up from where

he sat cross-legged in the middle of the galley floor with Marti. The human form automech stood in front of him and its head turned 180 degrees to face Ethan as he came through the door. Its taste sample tube retracted as it smiled at him.

"Quintan Primm is attempting to educate me on the various flavors of breakfast," it said. "The chemical interactions and their interdependence are very subtle."

"I'm sure they are," he said, looking up at the handler and winking. He towered over Marti's body, but he towered over everyone.

"I'm still trying to teach her to call me Quinn," he said.

"I think it's part of *her* core code to not use casual names. Or contractions," he said. *I guess it is easier to think of Marti as female now that it has a face to match its voice.*

"I am perfectly capable of contracted colloquial speech," Marti said. "However I feel it invites a lack of precision in thought, so I avoid it by choice."

"Yah, us humans is sloppy that way," Quinn said. "We're just a gooey mess of imprecision, ya know."

"Exactly," Marti said as its projection face delivered a perfect human eye roll.

Ethan laughed. "It's going to take some time to get used to you being so … expressive."

"There are a range of facial sub-routines included in the new automech system," Marti said. "I detected sarcasm in Quinn's comment, and the local processor offered several appropriate expressive choices. I have always had an awareness of human emotional response, but was unable to manifest this additional channel of communication until I acquired this body. It is adept at providing accurate interpretive value to the human interactive methodology."

"So you've always had a heart in there, but had no way to

let it show," Quinn said.

The face tilted to the side and it twisted its mouth as it thought. Finally it nodded. "That is an adequate metaphoric representation."

Ethan shrugged. "Marti 2.0"

"Marti 12.9.0 would be more accurate."

"Why?" Quinn asked.

"I am a twelfth generation quantum hybrid AA. This body is my ninth automech variant and it is the base level of this particular model. Thus, 12.9.0," Marti said.

"You have nine bodies you keep stored in a locker somewhere?" the handler asked.

"Actually they are stored at various locations throughout the ship," it said.

"Maybe we should give you a room of your own," Ethan suggested. "We've still got three empty crew positions so it might be worth it to have all your bodies in one place."

"I had contemplated asking for a room, but it is a low priority since it would also require modifications for installation of support hardware," Marti said.

"We've got a no-stress, six-day leg to Cygnus 344," he suggested. "Why don't you and Rene get your heads together on it and get it set up."

"It is not necessary for us to place our heads in proximity to figure it out," it said. "We are capable of working on this from a more convenient position." It stood there for several seconds with a deadpan expression before it *winked*.

"Thank you, Captain. I will get right on it," *she* said as she turned and angled toward the door.

"Strange how much difference a face makes in understanding," Quinn said.

"I'm almost embarrassed to admit that I always thought sarcasm was over Marti's head," he said as he stared after her.

"Now it's easy to think of it as a person."

"So, Cap'n I assume you're standing around in my galley for a reason?"

Quintan's official job aboard ship might be security and cargo handling, but he loved cooking, so they'd all taken to letting him manage the galley. It was also convenient to just ask and have food delivered to a table without having to run the synthesizers.

"Yah, sorry. I missed breakfast. Is there any chance I can get one of those yeastcake-egg-things you made the other day? And a cup of coffee?" he asked.

"A megamuffin sammich?" Quinn offered. "Ham or bacon?"

"Surprise me," Ethan said.

"Cando, Cap'n," he said, grinning. "Five minutes."

"Good, I'll go introduce myself to the guests and you'll give me an excuse to get away before I get sucked into a long conversation."

"Understood," the handler said as Ethan spun and headed out the door.

Angling across the lounge toward their guests, he caught Kaycee watching him. She appeared to want to see how his interaction with Mr. Strange played out. As he approached, he decided maybe she wasn't too far off target with her assessment.

The man eyed him warily until he got to within a couple meters, and then he jumped up, almost knocking the table over in front of him. He was shorter up close than he looked from across the room but his shoulders and neck seemed almost as wide as he was tall. Ethan recognized the clumsiness as something he'd seen many times before.

He's not in his native gravity.

"You are the captain?" the man asked. His voice rumbled

from deep inside a barrel chest.

"I am. Ethan Walker," he said, offering his hand.

The man stared at his hand for almost a second before he said, "I am Marcus ... Elarah." He had a strange slurred accent with a noticeable clicking sound in the middle of his words. It wasn't enough to be overwhelming, but it was an odd speech pattern.

After several more seconds, Ethan dropped his hand and smiled instead. Marcus' eyes widened for an instant and then he looked down at the table in front of him.

"Where are you from Marcus?" he asked, trying not to invest too deeply in his obvious strangeness, but he wasn't making it easy to ignore.

"I am the observer from Quantum Science," he said, without looking up. "In Proxima."

Marcus said the name of the planet like it was two words. *Prock-zhima?*

"Of course," Ethan said. "I'm pleased to meet you. I hope you enjoy your trip."

"Yes, Captain Ethan," he said, sitting back down and placing his hands back on the table so he could stare at them.

Glancing over his shoulder at Kaycee, he nodded. She was right about him. He was more than a little out of spec.

"Captain Walker?" one of the other passengers said, coming over and smiling as she snatched his hand and pumped it vigorously. "I'm Tashina Daniels. I'm totally honored to meet you."

"Really?" he asked. Her enthusiasm seemed the polar opposite to Marcus' detachment. It set his instincts on high alert, though he couldn't figure out why.

"Oh yes," she said, reaching out and grabbing his elbow with her other hand. "You're the captain responsible for rescuing those children on Starlight aren't you?"

"I was there, but it wasn't much of a rescue," he said, looking down at the deck and shrugging. It still stung to think about it. "It cost me two of my crew."

"I'm sorry, I didn't know," she said, looking embarrassed but still clinging to his arm and hand. "They never said anything about that on the newswaves."

He shook his head. "Cochrane Space thought it would be bad for business to mention that part."

She looked at him sidewise for a couple seconds and then her smile erupted over her face again. "Saving kids still makes you a hero in my mind. Please, let me introduce you to my traveling companions. I know they're eager to meet you, too. Like I said you're famous, and well, that makes you exciting."

She towed him over to the window by his arm. "Captain Walker, I'd like you to meet Dr. Morgan Blake and his senior assistant, Alessandria Chang," she said. "Doctor Blake is the lead cultural anthropologist on the Watchtower project."

The Doctor nodded, studying Ethan in a way that made him feel a little like a sample in a lab.

Chang stepped forward and grinned. She looked down at where Tashina was still clutching his arm. Ethan pulled it free with some effort. "Apparently she thinks I'm famous or something," he said as he shook her hand.

"But you are, Captain Walker. Quite famous in fact," Dr. Blake said. "Sandi and Tash were just intimately discussing the desirability of your company in fact."

Ethan's mouth fell open while both women blushed furiously. "Morgan you need to be nice," Alessandria said.

"I am teasing," he said. "I figure that it's always best from a sociological perspective to put everyone on an equally awkward footing from the outset. Then we can build from there."

"Strange way to say hello, but I can live with it," the captain said, recovering his composure enough to smile.

Tashina looked like she wanted to melt through the deck. "Sorry he's an ass to everybody," she whispered, leaning in close and hanging on his arm again.

"It's alright," Ethan said. "I just wanted to come over and introduce myself and let you know that if you have anything you need on the way out, please don't hesitate to let me know."

"How long is the trip going to take?" the doctor asked.

"Five and a half days, threshold to threshold," the captain said. "Then about twelve hours at sub-light to planetfall."

"There's no way we can get there any sooner?"

"Not really," Ethan said. "The laws of physics make hauling freight a boring business. We have a full exercise room, but other than staring out the window and watching tri-vids there isn't much to do."

"Morgan gets homesick when he's away for one of these oversight meetings," Sandi said. "Unfortunately our work is at a critical point and the Regents of the University of Proxima want to keep a close eye on us."

"I'm sure having an observer hanging over you doesn't help matters much," he said.

"Observer?" Tash asked. "What makes—"

"Yes Captain. That is the purpose of an observer," Dr. Blake interrupted, glaring her into instant silence. "They are an unfortunate reality of academic life."

"Cap'n your breakfast is ready," Quinn hollered from across the room.

Good timing! These three are almost as strange as Mister Personality, he thought, glancing over at Marcus, who was still studying his hands, oblivious to the world around him.

"If you'll excuse me, I need to eat and then get back on duty," he said. "We do serve a sit-down style breakfast at 0700 every morning, and the rest of the time Quinn is usually on duty and can fix up a meal for you on short notice. He is quite the extraordinary cook."

"You have galley staff on a freighter?" Dr. Blake asked.

"He's one of our security and cargo handlers, so his skills in the galley are a bonus," he said, gently removing Tashina's hand from his forearm. "If you make it up here before breakfast is over, I'm sure you'll agree we're lucky to have him."

"I am sure you are," Dr. Blake said. "I have not had traditionally cooked food in quite a while."

"Good, then I'll make sure Quinn knows to set four extra plates for you."

"Oh, I doubt that Mister, uhm, Elarah will be joining us," he said, glancing over at the man where he sat. "I believe I overheard him say he had some digestive issues and he was on a special diet of some sort. But we will be there in the morning, thank you."

Without further comment or explanation, he turned and walked over to join Marcus at his table with Sandi following a half step behind.

Ethan watched them for several seconds before he shrugged and winked at Tashina. "If you'll excuse me my breakfast is getting cold," he said.

A strange cloud settled over her face as she nodded and turned toward the window without saying anything else.

Kaycee was right, but it wasn't just Marcus who was odd. *These are all some seriously strange passengers.*

CHAPTER FOUR

Cygnus 344 was a nondescript midrange K-class star, a little dimmer and a billion years older than the Earth's sun. Their destination was a small observation platform above the fourth planet in the system.

The planet's official designation was Dawn on the navigational charts and was what most people called a super-earth. It was close to 30,000 kilometers in diameter and had just over twice standard surface gravity. It was a warm wet world, covered with dense jungles and open grasslands in equal measure, with a massive single ocean that spanned most of the southern hemisphere.

Other than its raw beauty, what made this world unique was that it was home to one of the first sibling civilizations discovered by the Coalition. Within a few years of discovering the inhabitants, scientists confirmed they carried a genetic combination that later became known as the Progenitor String. The natives of Dawn were undeniably from seeds planted by the original Shan Takhu.

They were also one of the least known of the sibling civilizations, because their world made contact difficult. Their primitive tribal culture was not equipped for visitors that required extensive support suits simply to walk around and keep their blood moving in the correct direction.

Cygnus 344-IV was therefore restricted space, and only scientists, and an occasional freighter crew, ever visited.

Ethan stood behind his seat on the ConDeck and stared out the window at the cloud tops and the lush landscape that peeked through below. He had nothing to do but stand there while Nuko Takata sat beside him and frowned. She'd been forced to make a manual approach to the upper docking arm of the platform because the automated system was offline. Watchtower Station was an older observation outpost, but as far as she was concerned, there was no reason for it not to have a working approach controller.

The captain tried to ignore her grumbling, but the only other distraction on the ConDeck was Kaycee sitting behind him on one of the jump seats. For the last six days she'd been beating the same one-trick-wonder to death. He knew he shouldn't complain, since at least she was back to talking to him. For the most part.

"I'll admit he's not an ordinary passenger," he said, turning to face the doctor and shrugging. "The only thing I can say is he'll be getting off here, and if he goes psychotic, it won't be our problem."

"He's not human," she said. "He can't be. Nothing about him works right."

"You've said that before," he said.

"Did you know he hasn't eaten a bite of food from the galley in the whole time he's been aboard?"

"Dr. Blake said he has some kind of dietary issue," he said, shrugging.

"I know," she said. "He does eat every five hours, without exception. At least I think that's what he's doing in the cargo container when he goes in there."

"Every five hours?" the captain asked. He didn't see the idea that someone had brought their own meals along as enough evidence to be an issue.

"Regularly," she said. "You could set a chrono by it. He never sleeps through a meal time either."

"So? Some people have strange eating habits," he said.

"He's not human," she repeated.

"I get that you think so but, unless you scanned him, that's just a wild-ass assumption," Ethan said. "You didn't scan him, did you?"

"No, I couldn't get a chance," she admitted. "At least one of the others was with him every time I got close enough."

"You tried?" he asked.

"Damn sure I did," she said.

"You do know that doing a bioscan without consent is–"

"Yah I do, but you've got no room to lecture me on ethics and law," she snapped. "I know there's something going on. Even you have to admit he's not normal."

"But 'not normal' is still not a reason for violating his rights," he said.

"If he's not human, it might be questionable if he has rights at all," she said.

Nuko shot him a disapproving side eye but didn't speak up. She was in the process of flipping the ship to line the cargo container up on the docking arm, so couldn't spare any time arguing with Kaycee.

"Alright I'll ignore the legal side of this because you said you didn't get the scan, but you have to have a reason to say he's not human. That's a hell of a claim to make with no evidence other than his strange feeding habits."

"Most of the sibling civilizations are humanoid to some degree. The one down there is one that could pass outwardly as human," she said, waving her arm in the planet's direction. "In fact, when I looked it up, it was one of the closest to a perfect match to us that we've discovered."

"You think he's from Dawn?"

"I don't know, because I couldn't scan him," she said.

"They are a preindustrial civilization," Nuko said, without turning to look at the doctor. "We're supposed to have no contact at all with them."

"Exactly my point," Kaycee said. "If he is from Dawn, then he shouldn't have been taken off world at all. The bigger crime would be that he has been, and not that I tried to violate his rights by snooping."

"I'll give you that, but it takes more than oddness to prove something like that," he said "And honestly in another ten minutes it doesn't matter."

A slight vibration in the deck plates told Ethan that they'd made hard dock to the station. "As soon as Marcus Elarah walks through the lock, it's over in my mind. We'll be out of here and on our way home in an hour and you can quit worrying about it. You are starting to sound more than a little paranoid you know."

She glared down at the floor and shook her head. "Paranoid doesn't make me wrong though." Standing up and shooting him an expression that said she wasn't done with this, she disappeared through the door.

"Marti, let the passengers know that as soon as we're equalized, they're free to disembark," he said, sitting down and sighing.

"She's got to get a hobby or something," Nuko said.

"She's a high-credit medical professional running cargo in the middle of nowhere," he said. "That's a tough reality for her. Anybody with that kind of mental horsepower will create imaginary demons a lot of the time. Conspiracy theories are the luxury of a bored mind."

"I wonder if there's a medication for that," she said.

"I don't know, but the sooner we get disconnected from this load and out of here the sooner she can start digging up something else to chew on," he said.

"Captain, on that subject, the Watchtower Station Logistics officer is holding on the comm," Marti said. "He wants to know when we will offload the cargo."

"Offload?" he growled. "I'm going to have to have words with Ammo. As far as a broker goes, she seems to have a habit of not telling me about details like this."

"It is in the contract, Captain," Marti said.

"I guess I'll have to start reading them, and not relying on her, or you, to tell me what's going on," he said, sighing. "Put him on."

"His name is Axel Romanov," Marti said as the comm went live.

"Mr. Romanov, this is Captain Walker," he said.

"Captain Walker, I understand you didn't know that this would be a hand stack offload," Romanov said.

"Apparently it was in the contract but I didn't see it," he said. "I thought we were doing a drop and run."

"Unfortunately, Watchtower is a small station and we don't have the ability to leave a cargo module attached to an airlock," he said.

Ethan sighed. "It's not a big load but I've only got two handlers. I would have brought a couple more with us if I'd been paying better attention, but my AA does have several automech we can put into the effort. We'll get started on unloading as soon as the passengers have processed off the ship."

"We've got plenty of labor, but our docking arm is small and we need to distribute things as they come off. I'd say, from looking over the manifest, it will take a few days to get you completely unloaded and cleared."

Ethan scratched his head. "Alright. I'll try to figure out how to keep my people out of the way while you take care of the muscle work. Fortunately we're not on a tight schedule on the other end of this, so we can hold over as long as it takes."

"The Operations Manager has offered to give you and your crew access to the station and our recreation areas. I know this is a small station, but we have an extensive media center and there are two cafes and a fairly serious tavern on deck four. You might be surprised at the active social life we've got here."

"I'm sure it is a wonderful place," Ethan said, glancing over at Nuko and winking.

"We figured out a long time ago that when you're locked inside a bubble like we are, it's important to keep morale high. Good food and a lot of alcohol help."

"I'm sure that's true," the captain said, laughing. "I'll pass the word to my crew. Thank you."

"You're welcome, Captain," he said, cutting off the comm from his end.

He dropped his head forward and stared at the deck.

"It won't be that bad," Nuko said. "It'll be like a mini vacation. Treat it like a chance to learn something about the natives down there. Like a visit to a museum."

He rolled his eyes to the side and looked at her. "Yah, and another three days for Kaycee to chase her conspiracy demons."

CHAPTER FIVE

Watchtower Station was over forty years old. By no means was it as old as some original parts of Armstrong or Galileo, but it felt on the graying edge of obsolescence. Kaycee almost didn't notice the patina of wear, until she stepped out into the sharp contrast of the Medical Services Center. What had felt familiar and expected as the age of a well-worn deck, jarred against the top tier ... everything?

An automated receptionist greeted her as she came through the double biolock doors. "Please state the nature of your medical concerns," it said. A smiling face appeared on a holographic screen.

"I'm looking to check in with the Director of Medical Services," she said.

"He is unavailable at the moment. If your need is urgent, may I assist you?"

"No, it's not urgent," she said. "I was seeking some information regarding someone that recently arrived."

"Patient records are confidential and that information is restricted to credentialed medical personnel only, and only as relevant."

"I understand that," she said setting her thumb on the biometric scanner and waiting while it extracted whatever data it needed. It was a sophisticated interface, but she knew that behind the pretty moving picture, it would still be no more than a generation three AA system.

Several milliseconds later the screen blinked green. *Confirmed: Smythe-Caldwell, Keira A., MD. PhD. STIF.*

Nice. What kind of system are you?" she asked. "That's a fast scan you're swinging."

"I am a Cyberquan-Twelve AA system. My biometric scanner is a gas genetic spectrograph with redundant tomographic quantification," it said. "I have notified Dr. Forrester and he will be with you immediately."

How does an armpit station like this rate a first order AA? she thought as she walked over to the side of the waiting area and stared into an aquarium projection. It was, like everything else in the medical center, an absolute work of art. Exotic and unidentifiable fish swam in circles, in a perfectly synched display.

She was about to turn away and take a seat when something odd caught her eye. A dead fish lay half eaten in the back corner of the tank. *Why would they do that in a projection?* she wondered. *Nobody wants to see dead fish.*

"Unless," she whispered, reaching up and tapping a fingernail on the plasglass screen. One of the larger fish, a black monstrosity with a huge mouth full of rows of sharp teeth, launched itself toward her fingertip, smashing its face into the transparent wall with a resounding thud.

She jerked her hand away. "Those are real fish?"

"Yes, they are, Dr. Smythe-Caldwell," a man said behind her. She spun to face him embarrassed at her reaction to the fish attack.

"I don't recognize any of them," she said. "I prefer to use just Caldwell, or even Kaycee," she said, smiling and unleashing her assault level charm. She needed something from him and so she pulled out all the tools in her kit. "And you must be Dr. Forrester?"

"I am," he said, smiling.

She could see him start to thaw as he looked her over.

"The arm is a dead giveaway," she said. He was wearing a

medical augmentation arm and she recognized the tool end for neurological surgery as it dangled above his shoulder in standby mode. She added a wink for effect.

"Sorry, I just completed some work and haven't had a chance to unplug," he said, almost looking embarrassed. "What can I do for you?"

"I don't know if you can help me, but I'm looking for information on one of our passengers," she said. "I'm hoping I can tap your database since I assume his records would have traveled with him."

"That might be somewhat irregular," he said.

"You're a neurosurgeon?" she asked, ignoring his feeble protest and leaning in close to look at his arm. She lingered close enough to let him get a full dose of her pheromones. He seemed like a friendly enough sort for a small-station doctor, but she knew she had to work his libido against his mind. She just hoped playing his ego, would push him into bending the rules. "I always thought that was the highest level of surgical skill in medicine."

Of course, it was strange that a doctor on a station this size would casually be doing neurosurgery. Nothing seemed to stack up straight.

He nodded and glanced around nervously. "Since you've got credentials, I think we can give you a peak." He turned to head over to the console behind the receptionist and began log in. "What's this person's name?"

"Marcus Elarah," she said.

He froze in the middle of tapping in his access code, spinning back in her direction. His augment arm almost poked her in the face. "Was Marcus a problem in some way?"

"Do you know him?" she asked, jumping back and trying to read his expression. She felt a sudden need to be out of his arm's reach.

Since Marcus was an observer, and not someone who was regular staff or crew on the station, the fact that he knew him by name didn't make sense.

He paused, blinking several times. His face ratcheted down to a blank expression in increments. "No," he said.

"He presented with some abnormal behavioral patterns and I was wondering if he has some kind of underlying condition," she said, pressing forward against what had become a wall of resistance.

"He behaved incorrectly?" he asked. His eyes looked like he was struggling to say more but he couldn't form the words. His augment arm twitched behind his head.

Nervously?

"His behavior was odd, yes," she said. She felt a wave of frustration as she watched an emotional a curtain draw around him. It bore an uncanny resemblance to the one that shrouded Marcus.

"I do not have any information I can share on the patient," he said. The arm twitched again.

Patient? Either he knows him or he doesn't. To call someone a patient before he was one, was a degree of professional familiarity that didn't fit.

"Do you routinely do a baseline screening on new arrivals?" she asked, stepping back another half pace.

"No," he said. This time his arm snapped up and down rapidly. Almost like it was nodding.

"Not under any circumstances?" she asked. "Aren't you concerned about environmental contamination?"

The arm froze motionless as he thought about an answer. "We require them for personnel who will return to the surface after being away. Or for new arrivals on their first deployment."

"Will Marcus be returning to the surface?" she asked.

"Unlikely," he said, clearing his throat and shooting her with a glare that looked like he was in pain. "He, *will* ... has ... not ... *be, returning* ... been, *to*... down there." The arm twitched back and forth and his eyes glazed over. "I do not know if he will be deployed. He is an operational observer from Proxima."

"I understand," she said, raising an eyebrow as she tried to decipher what was going on. *He's acting less normal than Marcus.*

"If you do an exam on him before I leave, I would like to be present," she said.

"That will not be possible," he said. The arm jerked up and down again. "You are not a staff member here."

"I understand, but I have some expertise in abnormal psychology," she said.

"I appreciate your offer Doctor Smythe-Caldwell," he said. "However his psychology is not abnormal. As I said, it will not be possible. The medical condition of any of the people under my care must remain ... *hidden* ... confidential." His voice cracked strangely as he spoke, like he was fighting for control of his own words.

"Of course," she said, backing away. "I'll be on my way then."

"Thank you. I have noted your concerns and will enter them into my log." His head and arm both bobbed up and down in unison. "Please return to your ship now. And do be careful."

She didn't turn until she reached the door and she slipped out sidewise, never breaking eye contact with the strange and possibly psychotic Dr. Forrester.

Be careful? The feeling that she'd just been on the receiving end of a serious threat clung to her until she made it all the way to the main lift-shaft. It took a concerted effort to shake it off and not just run straight to her quarters on the *Olympus Dawn*. Leaning her head against the wall panel and punching the call icon for the lift cage, she struggled to breathe normally.

There's something else going on here.

She needed to figure out how to convince Ethan that this was more than her overactive imagination.

CHAPTER SIX

Axel Romanov had been right. The station was small, but it had a surprising level of social potential. Ethan had discovered that at any given time less than a quarter of the Watchtower scientific staff was on observation field trips and the rest were either studying and writing reports or enjoying several too many drinks in the station's bar.

Although the place probably had a real name, everyone called it the Slosh Pit or just The Pit, and it was where Ethan and Nuko found the gravity strongest, socially speaking. They'd spent several hours anchored to chairs watching the young, and over-educated, crowd drink themselves happily toward brain damage.

They were about to give up on the local entertainment, when two men, not in the same age bracket as the rest of the crowd, strolled up to introduce themselves. Ethan stood as they approached.

"Captain Walker? I'm sorry I wasn't available to welcome you to Watchtower. I'm Yahto Ansari. Most days I'm in charge of the science mission here," the taller of the two said. He had long straight dark hair and angular features that framed the intensity of his piercing blue eyes. He held his left hand up, fingers spread, and extended his arm forward like he was making a significant gesture.

Ansari smiled when the captain looked at him blankly. "This is the Ut'aran greeting. Like a handshake. It also shows social status depending on which hand is used. In this case, I'm granting you dominant social position."

"Ut'aran?" Ethan asked.

He nodded. "Humans named this planet Dawn before we discovered the native name for it. Most of us here on the station use the local name."

"Alright, so how would I respond?"

"If you accept my offer of submission, you would extend your right hand and press your palm to mine. If you consider us equals, you'd use your left hand and do the same," he said.

Shrugging, Ethan extended his left hand and they bumped palms.

"When it gets interesting, is if you extend your right hand to assume dominance, and I respond with my right hand," the other man said. "Then we fight for your wife and children."

"Really? I don't have a wife anymore and I don't think there are any children either, so you're welcome to take both of my exes," he said, "but I think I'll stick to a hand shake with you."

"Bradley Parker, OpsSec Chief," Ansari said, introducing the other man. "May we join you?"

"Of course." Ethan sat back down. "This is Nuko Takata my pilot and all around right hand. Unless that has some significance?" he added with a wink.

"Not at all," Parker said, swinging a chair around from another table and dropping into it.

"Brad is my right hand," Ansari said. "Or maybe I should say I'm his left hand? He's been here longer than any of us. Almost twenty years now."

"That's a long run in a single posting," Nuko said.

"It's not too bad," he said. "Doc Ansari's pretty casual and I don't go down to the surface unless I have to. The natives don't make me as crazy because I don't have to figure them out."

He looked around the bar and nodded toward three people who sat at a single table but had their backs toward each other and seemed to be talking to the surrounding walls. "Like that."

"That's how the Ut'arans debate without confrontation," Dr. Ansari explained. "It's another of their social rituals."

"No matter how many times I see it, you'll never convince me it's not insane to argue with your back turned on the one you're trying to piss off," Parker said with a sarcastic smirk.

"It shows trust and respect," the doctor said.

"I can see that," Nuko agreed.

"Would you like to?" the Mission Director said. "I mean, go down, and see Ut'ar firsthand?"

"That's a fascinating offer, but I thought the planet was off limits," Ethan said raising an eyebrow.

"We've taken guests down there before," Parker said. "Any time we have to keep a ship here to offload, we try to make it up to the crew. It's bending the rules a little but we've got plenty of people down there to keep an eye on you, so it isn't that much of a risk. I'm sure you'd enjoy it."

"I'm ready," Nuko said. Her eyes lit up like a kid looking at her first scoot-runner. "I so need to suck down some real air and walk outside under a real sun."

"It's a heavy world," the captain said. "I think you could get air into your lungs at two-g, but walking would get old fast."

Her face fell and Dr. Ansari laughed. "Captain you don't have to be a mean old man. We'll provide you with Pressure Support Exosuits. They help with muscle and circulatory augmentation. They're quite comfortable."

"We also have a well-outfitted basecamp where you could

stay between excursions," Parker said. "It would be like an old fashioned big-game safari. If you know the term?"

"Without the killing," Nuko offered. "They called those photo-safaris if I remember rightly."

"True. No killing," the doctor said, nodding. "I can guarantee it would be quite the experience."

"Boss, if you say no, I'll make you walk home," she said. Her words sounded like she was kidding, but her expression made him think she might be serious.

Dr. Ansari was right though, it would be a once in a lifetime opportunity, and anything would beat sitting around and drinking himself into a stupor while they unloaded the cargo.

"If I say yes, you've got to be the one willing to tell the rest of the crew we left them here and went on a safari," Ethan said. "I'm thinking the mutiny might be quick and we'll both be walking back."

"There's plenty of space in the camp for all your people if they want to go," the doctor said.

"I guess I'm out of reasons to say no," the captain said, winking. "Except—"

Nuko slapped a hand over his mouth and shook her head while she waggled her other finger in his face. "Except nothing! Or the rebellion starts now, Captain Walker."

She held her hand over his mouth until he nodded.

Parker snorted. "We can see who swings the right hand on your ship can't we?"

"Apparently so," he said, grinning. "So when would this happen?"

"We've got a staff cycle tonight," Dr. Ansari said, glancing across the room and squinting to read the chrono. "About three hours if you and your crew can be ready."

"Alright, go let everybody know and …"

She launched herself toward the exit before he finished.

"She doesn't seem too enthusiastic does she?" the doctor said, glancing at the OpsSec chief and shaking his head.

"I think she became a pilot because she couldn't afford to be a tourist," Ethan said, watching her wind up toward a full run. She nearly trampled Kaycee as she headed through the door. Fortunately, the doctor danced to the side and avoided the crash. Barely. He could see her say something to Nuko before the pilot pointed toward where he was sitting and vanished out into the corridor.

"Captain, I was looking for you," Kaycee said as she walked up. She glanced at the two men sitting with him.

"Well you've found me," he said.

Her face said she was still chewing on something and didn't like how it was sitting. He already knew he didn't want to go there.

"This is my ship medic, Dr. Keira Caldwell," he said, watching as Dr. Ansari stood up to do the greeting ritual.

Kaycee looked at him for a second tilting her head then responded by bumping palms with her left hand. *Without waiting for him to explain the significance.*

"May I speak to you for a moment please, if you don't mind?" she asked, returning her focus to Ethan in an obvious indication that she meant … *alone.*

"I was just going to ask if you wanted to take a field trip down to the planet with us," he said. Maybe if he could distract her, she'd slow down on whatever she thought was such a crisis. "Dr. Ansari has offered us a chance to go on a little safari and observe the natives in person. I think it would be good for you to get some fresh air while they finish unloading up here."

"From what I overheard on the ship I didn't think Dr. Blake would risk anyone down there who wasn't a trained sociologist," she said, clearly taken by surprise by the offer. "Social contamination and all that."

"He tends to be over protective of the tribes," Parker said. "We're very careful."

"Bradley's right. We've had no incidents and we've gotten good at watching without being seen."

"I don't think I'm suited to a safari," Kaycee said, letting out a controlled breath through her clenched teeth and frowning. "Especially on a two-G world that's covered in jungle. I wilt in the heat and gravity."

Wilt in the heat? Ethan thought. *She lived on Starlight Colony, and that has to be the hottest place humanity has ever settled.*

"Dr. Caldwell, I'm sure you'd do fine down there," Dr. Ansari said. "We use Pressure Support Exosuits and they make it very easy to get around on the surface."

She shook her head. "I can't. I've had gravity sickness from a PSE before, so I have to be very careful."

Ethan stared at her. *She's pushing back way too hard.* Finally, he nodded. "You could stay and look after the ship I guess, but it seems like this is an opportunity that would be a shame to miss."

"I'm sure it is, but really I can't," she said.

"The other thing that might affect your decision, is that we'll be doing some maintenance on the station," Parker said. "It might be a lot less hospitable around here for a few days."

"Honestly, we were hoping to give you a vacation and keep you from having to wait it out in your ship," Dr. Ansari said.

"What kind of maintenance?" the captain asked.

"This is an old station and we're planning a recycler purge," he said. "It's urgently over due and we were waiting for parts that you just delivered."

Ethan's closed his eyes and grimaced. He'd had to purge recyclers, and as long as he could pay to have it done, it wasn't something he wanted to experience ever again.

"It's alright. I don't mind staying aboard the ship," Kaycee said.

"You'll want to do that, too," he said.

"Of course. How long will this safari take?" she asked.

Ethan looked at Dr. Ansari.

"In order to see much at all, two or three days but you'll have to stay for a four day landing cycle."

"I thought we would be unloaded in a day or two," Kaycee said. "Won't that hold us up on getting back?"

"That's true, but we're self-employed and unlike someone I'm looking at, I don't think this is an experience I could forgive myself for passing up."

He studied her face trying to read why she was resisting so hard. *Is it more of her paranoia?*

"The basecamp has a controlled gravity environment. Wouldn't that make it something you could enjoy too, Doctor?" Parker said.

"Isn't the point of a safari to get out and explore?" she asked.

"Obviously, there would be day trips out to various observation points," he said.

"But it would only be for a few hours at a time and it's only for those you'd need a PSE," Dr. Ansari added.

"Unless you're in exceptional condition," the OpsSec chief said. He tilted his head to the side like he was sizing her up in a far more intimate way.

"I'm not," she said, glaring back at him. "So I think I will have to pass, but I'm sure the others will be interested."

"Nuko went to ask them," Ethan said.

"When will you be leaving?" she asked.

"In a few hours," he said.

"We've got a team shift change at the Rockpile tonight," Parker explained.

"Rockpile?"

"That's what we call the basecamp. It's disguised to look like boulders so the natives don't realize we're there," Dr. Ansari said.

"That makes sense," she said. "What about indigenous biology? Do you have any medical procedures you need to follow to avoid bi-directional contamination? Maintaining barrier protection protocols must be a challenge."

"As long as everybody's up on their inocs, we only have a specific set of boosters," Parker said. "It's a quick process."

"It's two hours to local sundown and, since we only do our flights in and out after dark, we try to shuttle in as close to sundown as possible," Dr. Ansari said. "The local day is about thirty hours and it's winter in the northern hemisphere so the nights are longer. It's actually very comfortable planetside this time of year."

"The heat won't be that bad," the OpsSec Chief said. He smiled at Kaycee. "You really should go along."

She shook her head. "I have some medical research journals to catch up on. The rest of the crew will have a wonderful time without me I'm sure. I know I'll regret not going, but I think I have to stay aboard the ship and let you all have the fun for me."

"Fine since you're determined not to go have a good time, I guess I can leave the ship in your hands," the captain said. "Just try not to get into trouble while I'm gone and if you do, Marti can help you clean it up before I get back."

"I promise. I have no desire to be breathing recycler blowby."

CHAPTER SEVEN

"Why doesn't anyone else see this is wrong?" Kaycee muttered under her breath as she stood inside the inner hatch to the docking arm watching several teams from the station unloading the cargo container.

Why do they have a security guard on their own personnel?

A station security officer stood at the opposite end of the long airlock supervising the work from where he could see in both directions. He was unusually attentive and not the typical station guard that stood his post with only enough enthusiasm to stay a half-eyelid short of sleeping. This one watched every move anyone made as they loaded the crates onto small roll-alongs and shoved them off down the corridor.

She waited for him to wave her through the traffic and he smiled as she got within a few meters of his end of the lock. "Afternoon, Dr. Caldwell," he said, nodding as she walked by.

She nodded, glancing at him. *Very professional,* she thought. *Too professional.*

It was just another thing that tickled at her awareness as she stepped through the hatch and into the interior of the cargo box.

Generally, freight was unloaded through the outside walls of a container, but since they didn't have the facility here to do that, they worked from the interior and removed the deck plating to access the load in stages. A massive pile of deck panels stood off to the side. A catwalk ran the length of the container, and because they'd already stripped out the end of the box closest to the airlock, it left the walkway suspended in an open space, twenty meters from anything.

What would have been an amply wide catwalk, was covered with open wheeled carts and she had to thread her way with care through the clutter, and the small army of laborers, for over half the distance back to the main part of the ship. Fortunately, there was a safety railing or there would have been several times she might have tumbled over the edge.

"Welcome back," Quinn said as she broke through to the inner edge of the traffic nightmare. "Good thing you're a dancer."

"I am?" she asked almost disturbed by the handler's observation skills.

He turned on a sarcastic smirk and when he let it linger just long enough he winked. "I only look big and dumb. Momma taught me to always notice the details."

He leaned against the railing with his arms crossed in front of him, watching the process at least as attentively as the guard on the other end. His eyes darted back and forth as he tracked the unloading with a surprising intensity.

"Something wrong?" she asked, reading him for several seconds before she turned to see what had his attention.

"Maybe," he said. "I'm just watching things."

"What are we watching?" Ammo asked, appearing behind him and startling them both. She always moved like a cat. Silent and probably deadly if something motivated her in that direction.

"A lot of sweaty boys and girls unloading stuff," he said.

"As fun as that might be normally, I'm about to be off on a field trip," she said, slinging a small bag over her shoulder and stepping around Quinn to brave the chaos on the catwalk.

"Damn, I wish you weren't going," Kaycee said. "I've got this problem, I think, and I was hoping we'd have a chance to talk about it."

"What kind of problem?" she asked. "I've got a few minutes before I need to report to the MedBay to get my inocs upgraded."

"You haven't been to the medical center here yet have you?" she asked.

"No, why?"

"It's the shiniest set up I've seen this side of STI," Kaycee said.

"Nice. But why is that a problem?"

"They've got a Cyberquan-Twelve manning the front desk," she said. "The entire traffic control network in Zone One doesn't need that much AA power. What makes it strange is that it's not the diagnostic system, it's the frakking receptionist."

"That's odd, but why is that something that has you up in a twist?" she asked.

"Let's put it another way," Kaycee said. "That quantum AA cost more in real chit than the entire rest of this station. Why the holy frak do they need that kind of resource here?"

Ammo set her pack down and leaned back against the railing across from Quinn. "I think that's a reasonable question," she said. "I assume you had a reason for going there in the first place?"

"I wanted to see if I could slick-whistle my way into their medical records and see what Elarah's story was," she admitted.

"Doc, I didn't know you played that way," Quinn said. He still stared down the catwalk, watching the activities. "Hard to do that with an AA isn't it?"

"Yah, but I figured the Director of Medical Services might be susceptible to charm." She shrugged. "And he was, for about ten seconds, before he melted a chip and developed a multiple personality on me."

"What?" Ammo blinked several times.

"Nojo," she said, holding her hand up like she was making an oath. "Completely blew his brain circuitry and was even having convulsions of his augment arm. I literally was thinking that it was going to come right over his head and beat the frak out of me."

"Augment arm?" Quinn asked, glancing at her. "Like a medical tool?"

"He was wearing a Polymed Microsurgery Arm with the neurosurgery attachment when he came out to talk to me. The damn thing went insane and started having seizures," she said. "There were several times it felt like I was talking to two different people at once. And that they were fighting for dominance with each other."

"Neurosurgery? That doesn't sound like a common need in a station like this," Ammo said. "Have you told Ethan about it?"

"I tried," she said. "He was sitting with the head of station security and the director of the science mission, negotiating the terms of your field trip."

"This might be troubling," Quinn said, without looking at her. "I know I'm new here, but I think you should tell him."

"Once I know for sure what's going on, I will," she said. "He's shut me down for days over my 'paranoia' and until I have something concrete, I don't dare take it to him again."

Ammo stared at her, drumming her fingertips on the railing, her nails making faint tinkling sounds that were barely audible over the sound of the crews working in the box. "You have been sounding over the top about Mr. Flatline the brainless observer," she said. "But that doesn't mean you're wrong. I've got my own things that don't balance square, but none of them were enough to raise a flag."

"He left me in charge, and if he thinks I'm losing it he'll never trust me again," Kaycee said. "Unless we can prove any of this to him, he'll never see it."

"How do you propose to do that?" she asked.

"Once you all head out on your field trip, I'll do some snooping," she said. "I'll have to be careful since I won't have anyone to watch my back, but I am pretty good when I need to be."

"Frak. You'll owe me for this, but I can't go now," Ammo said, glaring.

"Me either, but you won't owe me anything unless you want to," Quinn said. "Nuko asked me to go, but I don't fit in a small-people-sized PSE, so I volunteered to stay and hold the door."

He looked down at the catwalk like he was embarrassed. "I told the cap'n I'd keep you out of trouble."

"I have also been admonished to prevent you from entering into a situation that would cause difficulties," Marti said, walking up in its Humanform automech. "You are not seeking to do such a thing are you?"

"Of course not," Kaycee said, feeling like a kid caught stealing cookies.

Marti's face raised an eyebrow but said, "I advised the captain that I did not think you would do that while we were gone."

"We?" Ammo asked.

"Yes. They have invited me to go along," it said. "This will be an excellent opportunity to field test my new body,

49

and to experience a range of sensory input that would not be available aboard the ship."

"You're running from the recycler purge aren't you," Kaycee said.

Marti looked to the side for almost a second before it shook its head. "There is no recycler purge scheduled on either the ship or the station."

"Maybe they haven't gotten it in the log yet," she said. "The Mission Director said we brought them parts and they needed to do it urgently."

"This is not true," it said. "There are no recycler components listed on the cargo manifest, and the station maintenance records show that a standard maintenance purge was done less than thirty days ago."

"I must have misunderstood," Kaycee said, glancing over at Ammo and making sure she was reading that bit of data the same way.

She nodded imperceptibly.

"So you're leaving us alone up here?" she asked, changing the subject.

"My cognitive processor will remain aboard the *Olympus Dawn* even as my body experiences the environment of the planet," Marti said. "My awareness is capable of being in multiple places simultaneously."

"That kind of multiple awareness must be interesting," Kaycee said.

"I focus my attention where it is needed and let the body operate alone when it is necessary. This automech has the ability to function autonomously and possesses a rudimentary consciousness. I am simply the dominant awareness when I am connected."

"You're saying we'd never know if you were here, or just your skinsuit on autopilot?" she asked.

"I am sure you would see a different personality when I am in control," Marti said.

"I understand," she said, her eyes lighting up as she nodded. "Enjoy the safari."

"Thank you, I will," it said, turning and heading off into the chaos on the catwalk.

As soon the automech was far enough away that she was sure it was out of hearing range, Kaycee turned back to Ammo. "Is there any chance I can look at the load manifest?"

"Sure. Why?"

"I noticed a lot of crates labeled medical gear being loaded out," she said as a grin exploded across her face. "I think I need to see just what kind of gear they've been ordering."

CHAPTER EIGHT

Angelique Wolfe was right at the upper edge of what could fit in a Pressure Support Exosuit and Ethan stood watching as Tashina and Sandi struggled to stretch the polymorphic liner far enough to cover all of the handler's body. The somewhat limited space inside the shuttle made the process even more interesting.

As part of their shipmaster license training, he and Nuko had both worn a PSE before, so they needed no help getting suited. Rene also knew how to put one on since sometimes an engineer needed to have a strength boost to do his job. But the process wasn't intuitive and Angel struggled with it.

And the two anthropologists struggled with Angel.

"It's a good thing Quinn didn't come down," Nuko whispered, turning away from the spectacle and grinning.

"I would have paid to watch that," Rene said.

"Would you quit giving them a hard time and just let them get you suited?" the captain said. He wasn't sure if he should be annoyed or amused.

"You know it's only two-G. I could walk from here to the door," she said. "Maybe they'll have a bigger suit inside?"

"This will fit," Tashina said. "You just have to stand still and let it adjust to your skin temperature."

"That would be a damned lot easier if I didn't feel like I was getting dressed for a sex party," Angel said, glaring down at her. "This has got to be the strangest rubber suit I've ever put on."

"I'm not sure that's a visual I needed to have," Ethan

said.

"Wait until it turns on," Rene added.

"It turns on? I'm already there for frak sake," she said.

Both of the women helping her froze. She stood almost a head taller than Sandi and close to a half meter above Tash, and in that instant, both of them realized that their reality might shift profoundly.

Fortunately, the liner activated and other than Angel's audible squeak and bulging eyes, they escaped the ordeal with at least part of their collective dignity intact.

"Just backup to the autovalet and let it put the exoshell on you. Then we can go," Sandi said, stepping back and almost falling over the seat behind her.

"I can't watch this," Ethan said. "Is it safe to go outside?"

"It should be," she said. "We run continuous scans when we've got a shuttle on the ground, and if there's anything out there, they'll let us know. Tash why don't you walk them over and show them how to get inside?"

"Yah, if she fights the shell like she fought the liner, you might need more room in here anyway," Tash said, visibly relieved to be getting a pass on helping with the rest of the process.

"It can't be any worse than this can it?" Angel asked, looking at the captain like she was about to rethink the whole idea of the field trip.

Ethan shook his head. Then changed his mind and nodded. "Back into the rack and the sensor will trigger the unit to assemble and fit your limbs together. Just don't move unless you want to find out what it feels like to have a leg shell shoved up your ass." He ducked through the door and out into the night air before she could respond.

Jumping down, his PSE cinched up on his body to help push the blood back to his brain and his head bobbed as he landed. He recognized the delay in response from the exoshell's neck- support actuators as he crossed the transition boundary between gravity levels.

It was profoundly dark outside and an arm popped up over the back of his head and swung an infrared lens in front of his eyes so he could see. Nuko and Rene stood a few steps ahead staring at the trees and stars above them.

"Space looks so different when you're looking up at it," she said as he stepped up beside her. "And the air smells incredible."

"We should keep moving," Tash said. "Unless you want to be lunch."

"I thought you said it was clear?" Ethan said.

"A boar korah can cover a kilometer in about twenty seconds if they catch our wind," she said.

"What's a korah?" Nuko asked.

"It's a six ton carnivore," she said. "It hunts at night and has a sense of smell that's unbelievably refined. If there's one within ten klick downwind of us, it knows we're here. It's the alpha predator anywhere on Ut'ar."

"I detect no large creatures within a kilometer," Marti said, stepping up behind them. "However it would be prudent to move quickly to shelter as there are a great number of other life forms in close proximity and differentiating their intent is difficult."

"We're holding up traffic since they won't send the off duty team out, until we're inside," Tash said. She glanced back at the shuttle and nodded. "Here they come, so let's make feet."

She trotted off toward a large rock outcropping with the rest following along in a single file line. She turned and angled up a narrow slit between two large boulders and stopped at the end of the tiny channel. In infrared, Ethan could see a faint difference in temperature on one of the stone walls.

Tash reached out and set her hand in the middle of the rock and it slid back and then to the side to reveal a standard looking airlock hatch. She keyed in an access code on the panel and it swung inward. The lights were off inside and it wasn't until they'd all squeezed inside and the door closed behind them that the lights came on.

"We're home," she said. "Watch your step going inside, we're back to standard gravity on the other side of the door. Your suit should react quickly enough, but if you're moving fast, it might send you hard down first."

Ethan nodded and followed her through the doorway. He felt his suit loosen its grip and he sighed in relief. It wasn't uncomfortable, but a generic PSE tended to bind in some intimate places if you moved wrong.

"The locker room is to the right," Tash said, nodding toward the appropriate door. "While you're here, you'll keep the same suit and you'll have your own autovalet to hold it for you. Find an open locker and then remember which one you used. It will save having to refit everything each time you need to get your kit on."

"After you've done that, the mission commander and medical officer will meet you in the Main Gallery and walk you through your orientation," Sandi said. "The unofficial uniform of the Rockpile crew is thinskin, but if you'd be more comfortable, we can get you jumpsuits."

The captain glanced at his crew and nobody seemed worried about running around in their underwear. "I think we're good," he said with a wink.

"Marti, you can come with us since you don't need to gear down," she said. "Sandi and I will be taking you out tomorrow and maybe the next day, so we'll see you in the morning." The two of them disappeared through a different door with the automech following behind.

A few minutes later, and with only a minimum of grumbling from Angel, they all assembled in the Main Gallery. Above a huge wallscreen that rose four meters up the side of the vaulted dome, a hand painted sign said:

Remember, you are a rock.

Marti sat along one side of a table, waiting. "This is Dr. Tobias Stocton, the mission 1345 commander," Marti said, nodding her projection face at the man who sat at the end of the table. "And this is Dr. Leela Singh, the mission medic."

Please, we are casual around here," the commander said. "Toby and Leela is fine."

"Understood," Ethan said. "I'm Ethan Walker, and this—"

"Oh yes, we know who you all are," Leela said. "Even if you weren't famous, we have to read over and approve any guests that come down."

"I'm not ... Nevermind," the captain said. "So first names it is for all of us then."

"Excellent," Toby said. "Let's get the formal business side out of the way and then we can get you bunked in for the night. We'll be hitting the ground early in the morning and you'll need to get a good night's sleep since it's almost a twenty klick round trip."

"Sounds good to me," he said.

"We have to do this for everybody on their first time down here," Leela said. "Even though you probably know a lot of this, it's a matter of safety."

"We do the same thing with passengers," Angel said. "Emergency exits and all that."

"Exactly," Toby said. "We've got two different potential situations you need to be aware of and ready to respond to.

First is a failure of the basecamp's gravity grid leaving you abruptly in the local gradient. This hasn't happened in the forty years we've had the Rockpile in place, but it did once in one of the other expedition encampments. It was a fairly bad situation because four of the team there were standing upright and ended up with broken bones as the result of forcefully eating floor. Fortunately, the engineer was off duty and in his bunk when it happened, so he was able to get the artificial gravity in the ceiling back online and we got the injured evacuated before any of them had lasting damage."

"So that's how you control the gravity here," Rene said, nodding. "Overhead plating is cheaper than reversible bias panels like in a ship."

The commander nodded. "It's actually a simpler system and takes less power."

"It also gives an extra benefit because the gravity gradient effect relaxes the vascular system toward the top of an upright body," Leela added.

"If we have a grid failure for any reason, it is imperative that if you aren't injured, you get to your PSE and into the polymorphic liner as quickly as possible. It won't protect your skeleton but it will keep your blood in the right place so you don't pass out. If there is still power to the autovalet units, then get the shell put on. You have to do this before you render aid to any of the injured."

"The most serious injury that happened when that expedition encampment went down was one of the uninjured collapsed from muscle fatigue and circulatory deficiency and landed on the person he was trying to help," she said. "The one on the bottom ended up with broken ribs and nearly suffocated before the other one managed to get rolled off."

"Always get your suit on before you go back to help,"

Toby said.

"That makes sense," Rene said. "Sometimes it isn't human nature to save your own skin first."

"Exactly," he said. "Now the other gravity problem you might face is a PSE failure. Although rare, these do happen. Especially when you're not paying attention to power reserves. A suit will operate for several days without a recharge depending on how hard you push it. If your suit fails like that, it goes off in stages. The exoshell shuts down an hour or more before the liner fails. This gives you plenty of warning but it's still possible you could be caught too far from basecamp to make it back."

"If your suit stops working for any reason, you can survive and function for a while, but it will get to be exhausting quickly," Leela said.

"Always pay attention to your power levels," he said.

"If you reach the point where your suit has quit, do not push," she said, making sure she made eye contact with each of them. "Prolonged exposure to the high gravity can cause irreversible circulatory problems in twelve hours. Even if your suit has not failed, the most important thing to remember is that if you get light headed, lie down flat. A person who remains upright in this gravity cuts their survival time by over half."

"Also it's important to remember that a working PSE compensates for most of the problems of heavy gravity, but the effects do build up. We rotate observation teams on a twelve day cycle because of the cumulative impact," Toby said. "None of you will be staying with us that long, but gravity related problems could affect any of you, at any time. We train for this, and we only allow people down here on teams that have proven they have a long-term tolerance."

"Don't feel bad if you have problems and need to tap

out," she said. "We've got plenty of recreation space here in the Rockpile and we'll only need to keep you confined inside for a maximum of four days before the next ride home."

"Why is it every four days?" Angel asked.

"The lunar cycles give us a deep dark every fourth day," he said. "The outer moon works out to be totally down every 120 hours, and the inner one is in a close orbital resonance that only drops out of phase one out of every thirty-six dark nights."

"What if there's a problem?" she asked.

"We deal with it until then," Leela said, shrugging. "The one most important thing we've got to adhere to is a lack of cultural contamination."

"Which brings us to the next thing," Toby said. "We don't fool around with the potential for exposure. Nothing gets dropped, and nothing gets left outside. Ever. We don't even take a piss on a tree. We cart everything back. No exceptions."

"The issue is that there is a widely diverse environment out there," she said. "If we find out that a microbe is attracted to some artifact of our biochemistry that we leave behind and it goes out of balance or mutates from exposure, then it can have unpredictable consequences to the indigenous ecosystem."

"That makes sense," Nuko said.

"The Viroxycin Immunoxate-112-E injection you all got, will keep you safe from anything microbial," she said. "It also suppresses certain features of our own internal biome temporarily to keep us from contaminating things here."

"That doesn't sound healthy," Rene said.

"None of you had a reaction to the injection?" Toby asked.

"Not yet," Ethan said.

"Normally you'd know already," Leela said. "It takes twelve to twenty-four hours for the injection to cause a problem. If that happens the effects wear off in a few days."

"We only got our shots a couple hours ago," the captain said.

Toby rolled a side eye at the medic and she shrugged. The reaction wasn't lost on the captain.

"It shouldn't be a problem," she said. "The shots are pretty much benign. I don't recall anyone having a severe reaction to the Immunoxate in several years. The most common symptoms of a problem are a rash and some muscle weakness. Since none of you have that, we're good."

They all shook their heads.

"As long as you don't take any risks, you'll be alright out there," he said. "Although it's important to remember that even though we can protect you from the microbes and viral contaminants, some things you might encounter are just simply poisonous. It's best not to go native and eat or drink anything indigenous. Fortunately, if you get into something messy, in most cases it's unlikely that it'll kill you."

"Though it might make you wish you were dead," she added.

"The river water is mostly safe, but here again there are several species of carnivorous fish too," Toby said. "The ones in the local waters are smaller, so they can't bite through your PSE. As long as you keep your hands and face out of the water you'll be fine."

"The PSE are waterproof?" Rene asked.

"Completely," he said.

"But no swimming?" Angel looked like she'd just had her favorite toy taken away.

Leela shook her head.

"And the one last thing we have to enforce is that

anytime you're outside, even between here and the landing zone you will have an escort or a guide with you," Toby said. "There will be absolutely no exceptions to that rule. If you forget and even open a door to the outside world accidentally, we'll lock you down until your ride gets here."

"Understood," Ethan said.

"When we take you out on a day trip, you are only to watch the natives, but you will never get close enough for the natives to see you," he said. "Your guide and the escort team will do whatever has to be done to make sure it never happens, and that shouldn't be a problem because of the tech gear we use."

"What if a situation becomes unavoidable?" Nuko asked.

"That hasn't happened ever. And it won't happen on my watch."

His expression left no doubt he meant it.

CHAPTER NINE

Sixty-three thousand cubic meters was a lot of space for cargo.

Normally Kaycee would have had Marti sort the manifest down to a usable list, but with its ability to be in two places at once, she didn't want to risk Ethan finding out she was still digging into her hunch. So she sat in her room where the AA's presence would only manifest by invitation and instead of doing it the easy way, she was drilling through the manifest on a thinpad, storage bay by storage bay. She read each item, trying to spot anything that might jump out as odd.

She couldn't tell Ammo with any degree of certainty what to look for, so she worked alone. Kaycee had to consider each piece of cargo for its implication against the bigger backdrop of her suspicions. The process was brain numbing, and more than once she reconsidered whether it was worth the effort at all.

"Still shooting blind?" Ammo asked, startling her as she sat a gojuice down on the end table in her room. She had her feet up on the sofa and was reclining on a big pillow with the door open to the corridor.

She set her thinpad down, stretching her neck back and forth luxuriating in the pain of moving the muscles at all.

"Quinn said they're done for the shift in the box, and he's doing some galley work if you're hungry."

"Sure that would be good," she said. "Make sure he locks the hatches down. I'm not comfortable with all the workers that have been back and forth out there."

"I already did, but you know Ethan's right. You do sound a bit paranoid."

"I know," she said. "That doesn't mean I'm giving up on this, but it makes me question everything I'm doing with a little more intensity."

"What do you expect to find in that?" She pointed at the thinpad.

"Something unusual."

"Expand on that a bit? Give me something else to suck me into your paranoid delusion."

"Something medical and unusual," she said.

Ammo pulled the corner of her mouth up in a sarcastic sneer.

"It would help if I knew for sure," she said.

"Fine, so give me your best guess."

"Something bio-neural. Maybe." Kaycee picked the thinpad up and looked at it again.

"You can organize the manifest to sort," Ammo suggested.

"Not without bringing attention to the problem," she said. "Marti is Ethan's friend, and I don't want to put her in the position of having to keep a secret from him."

Ammo looked at her hands for several seconds and nodded. "If you find something, we should bring both of them in on it."

"I know," she said. "The one thing I know about Ethan is that he will do the right thing once he sees it. Unfortunately, he also has a bad habit of resisting that path until he exhausts all the wrong choices first."

"Excuse me ladies, but dinner is served," Quinn said, rapping on the door jamb. He was carrying a tray in one hand and a large dark bottle in the other. "We can either eat here or downstairs."

"Here is good," Kaycee said, getting up and pulling her larger table out of the wall cabinet. It slid out and unfolded into the center of the room.

"I guessed you'd be wanting to stay close to your work," he said, grinning and handing the tray to Ammo. She pulled a small table cloth off and uncovered three plates and an array of serving and eating utensils. Spreading the cloth on the table, she set the plates out. There were several too many plates for the arrangement to make sense so she left the extra ones in a pile off to the side.

He spun his hand around in a strange gesture and three oddly shaped glasses appeared from nowhere. Winking, he handed the bottle to Kaycee as she stared and he shot out the door.

"He does love the presentation doesn't he?" Ammo whispered, grinning and taking a seat.

She nodded. "And he does sleight of hand conjuring too. He's just full of surprises, isn't he?"

He returned, pushing a small serving cart.

"What are we having?" Kaycee asked. She could smell something sharp and tangy and she raised an eyebrow suspiciously.

He lifted the lid off one of the serving platters and pulled three small bowls out. A slice of something pale yellow floated in the top of what appeared to be water. He set one bowl down on the table beside each plate. "For your fingers," he said.

The next platter he uncovered had several bright yellow bumpy cylinders. They were dripping some kind of juice and covered with green flecks of something. "Herb grilled corn on the cob," he explained.

"I've never seen corn that looked like this," Kaycee said.

"That's what corn looks like," he said, looking shocked.

"I thought it was little tough skinned pellets," she said.

"Oh, you can make this look like that, but it takes a knife to kill it that way. This is corn on the hoof," he explained.

"On the hoof?"

"Yah the way god intended it to look," he said. "Upright and walking."

"Corn doesn't walk," Ammo said. "It's a plant." She looked over at Kaycee and added, "At least on Earth it is."

Quinn laughed, grabbing the next set of bowls off the cart. Bumpy things suspended in red-brown gelatinous goo. "I hope those came from a plant too," Kaycee said.

"We're on a starship," he said. "It's all synthetic, but I try to get it as close as I can. In its real form, it's a plant. Those are molasses sweet baked beans. I promise they won't give you the winds though. Not too bad, anyway."

"The winds?"

Kaycee shook her head in a sharp snap. "Don't ask," she whispered. Talking about food with Quinn was always a lesson in things you didn't want to know.

"Methane turbulence?" he offered.

Ammo stared at him blankly for several seconds before she realized what he meant. "Oh. People really volunteer to eat these baked bean things?"

"Yah, it is worth the risk," he said, setting out a basket of yellow yeastcakes. "But maybe that's because people back home live outside. Might be a good thing to remember when we breathe recycled atmosphere. But it's only us tonight so it won't ruin the air recycler too much."

Ammo picked up one of the yeast cakes and sniffed it.

"Sour cream cornbread muffins," he said, landing a bowl of honey butter beside the basket. It was the first thing that Kaycee recognized and only because it was part of the usual breakfast line up.

Turning back to the cart he grabbed the last tray and set it in the center of the table. It landed with a heavy thud.

"You do know there are just three of us to feed?" Ammo asked, raising an eyebrow and glancing at Kaycee who shrugged.

"Yah, their loss." He sat down and dropped a stack of small heavy cloth sheets on the stack of spare plates. "I started it cooking this morning after breakfast and planned for all of us. But when they all decided to run off ... well it just means we have to work harder to get to the bottom of it."

"What is it?" Kaycee asked.

He picked the lid up off the tray and a wall of an indescribable aroma launched a full assault on her senses. It smelled slightly acidic combined with an undertone of something that had burned. Yesterday.

A massive pile of *something*, buried the platter. It looked like square meat blocks with rounded handles sticking out of the ends. Dark red ... something ... oozed down over the whole thing. It was sticky, thick, and almost horrifying to look at.

For some reason, her eyes and her mouth both started watering at the same time.

"That is food?" Ammo asked. "I mean I trust you, but what the hell is it?"

"Kansas City style barbecue ribs," he said, laughing at their reactions. "I know it looks a little like a farm machinery accident, but it's another one of momma's secret recipes, so I know you'll love it."

He reached over the table, grabbed the bottle, and poured their glasses full of amber liquid. "That, I recognize," Ammo said grinning as she watched the foam swell on the beer.

"It's real too," he said. "I've been brewing it for a while but never had the right meal for it."

"Where did you put together the gear to brew beer?"

"Rene helped me build a cold storage locker behind the galley and promised to keep it secret as long as I keep him supplied with bacon." He grinned and handed them each a glass.

Grabbing several hunks of the barbecue with his pinchers, which he also materialized out of nowhere visible, he filled both their plates while they sat staring at him.

"How do you eat this?" Ammo said.

"With your fingers." Picking up one piece by its knobby end, he took a chomp out of the side. "It'll be messy but that's what the napkins and finger bowls are for," he said around a mouthful.

Kaycee shrugged, gingerly grabbed one piece, and brought it to her face. The acidic smell made her eyes burn even more and she wrinkled her nose.

Ammo sat watching her, obviously not willing to take the risk until Kaycee survived the ordeal.

Steeling herself, the doctor took a bite and gasped as every taste bud in her mouth exploded in pure screaming ecstasy. Nothing she'd ever had in her whole life was even close. All she could do was moan.

"Tasty huh?" Quinn asked, grinning.

She nodded, wiping the corner of her eye with the back of her hand. The intensity was almost overwhelming.

"Are you alright?" Ammo asked, looking concerned.

She nodded again, taking another bigger bite.

"Is it good?"

"Better than sex," she said, groaning.

"I don't know if I'd go that far," he said, laughing. "But momma said never pass up a compliment when someone throws one your way."

"You've got to try it," Kaycee said, staring at Ammo. "Really. If you don't eat your share I will, and then I'll probably regret it for days."

Taking a deep breath, Ammo closed her eyes and grabbed one of the ribs off her plate. As soon as it made it to her mouth and she bit in her eyes shot open then rolled back as she groaned in pleasure.

"See, I told you," he said. "It just looks scary to you space people."

About half way through the meal Quinn pulled out a second bottle of beer and they plowed on in a valiant attempt to clear the platter, talking little as they did serious damage to the pile of food. They each had filled one of the extra plates with bones before they slowed down at all.

"Wait, I almost forgot, we've got dessert too," he said. "Save room for some peach cobbler."

Kaycee stopped and glared at him while she licked her fingers. She'd realized that manners were impossible with food like this. "What's peach cobbler?"

Wiping his hands on a napkin, he twisted around and pulled a deep tray out of the lower rack. When he slid the lid off, another wave of smell filled the room.

Ammo let out a whimper as she looked at it. "I don't know if I can stretch that far," she said.

"Nojo," Kaycee said.

"No problem," he said. "It'll stay warm and we can have it later. I just wanted to make sure you both ate. It's hard to work on an empty stomach."

"But it's hard to stay awake on a full one too," Ammo said.

"Maybe a good night zeroed out will help," he suggested. "New eyes in the morning are a lot sharper than red eyes at night."

"Where do you come up with all those sayings?" Kaycee asked, leaning back and stretching. "They can't all be your momma."

He shrugged. "Momma was pretty smart, but I've learned to pay attention to things around me. I watch people because it always teaches me things."

"That's a survival skill too," she said.

"It is," he said. "I notice things that jump out at me. Then when I need it, I can pick the patterns out."

"Like what kind of patterns?" she asked.

He leaned forward and eyed another rib but apparently decided against it. "I know you're looking for something odd in the load, so I watched for something they treated with special attention when they were packing stuff out."

"Did you catch anything," Ammo asked.

"Only thing that caught my eye was the security guy got very interested in a crate of medical gear they pulled out of G12," he said. "He'd been standing at the back door watching them work all shift but when they got to that box he came inside and physically took charge of it. They hand carried it out rather than loading it onto a roll-along."

"You're sure it was G12?"Ammo picked up Kaycee's thinpad and tried to scroll through the screens. It refused to move and she glared at it.

"Wipe the screen and rinse your finger in the bowl. Then try again," he said, grinning at her.

Fortunately, it fixed the problem and she fast-flipped down the manifest until she got to the right cargo section. She scrolled through the list for that bay. "Only one thing medical in that whole section," she said, turning the thinpad around and setting it on the table in front of Kaycee.

"Why the frak do they need 300 neural transducers?" she

asked.

"That would be a good question," Ammo said.

"Who is Alphatron Inbit?" She shook her head. "I've never heard of them."

"AIT?" Quinn asked.

"Yah, the supplier is Alphatron Inbit Technologies of Proxima," she said.

"Before I applied to the Handler's Union, I worked at a deep security rehabilitation center in upstate New York," he said. "AIT supplied the behavioral control implants they used on the hard case prisoners. Violent ones."

CHAPTER TEN

As the small party made its way through the jungle and up a gradually sloping ridge toward the observation point, Sandi and Tash played tour guide and kept up a continuous running commentary as they walked along. They explained everything from the geology, to the flora and fauna pressing in all around them. It was a little unnerving to know that while there was so much they did understand, by their own admission they had only learned a hundredth of a percent of all the diverse life around them.

The six humans and Marti stuck together in a single line and followed what might have been a trail made by animals. While their guides stayed close to Ethan and his crew, somewhere ahead, they had escorts making sure they didn't accidentally walk up on a native, or some other hungry carnivorous inhabitant of the trees. The four scouts that protected them were adept in the jungle and moved with a stealth that seemed unnatural.

"Where did they learn to do that?" Angel asked after trying to spot one of the escorts who had seemed to vanish as he climbed a tree silently and faded into the foliage.

"They're Windwalkers," Sandi said. "Most of them come from Earth and were members of one of the indigenous nations of North America. It is a heritage thing for them."

"Dr. Ansari is Sioux and Apache," Tash said. "He picked and trained the Windwalker teams."

"I'd love to move like that," she said. "But I think I'd need looser underwear."

They hiked for almost two hours toward the rock ledge that was their destination before the canopy of the jungle opened up to reveal the sky. Emerging from the undergrowth, they climbed up onto a rock slab that stuck out above the dense tree cover and waited for a signal from their forward scout that their observation position was clear.

Tash turned and lowered her voice as she explained, "We're still almost three klick from the Ter'can tribe's village but we'll be in sight of them if they happen to look up in our direction. The Ut'arans have extremely good ears and we have to be extra careful not to make any loud noises that might carry that far. As we move forward, you have to keep low until we drop into the observation shelter. Just make sure you don't do anything that would attract attention."

"I'll go first," Sandi said. "Do what I do and you'll be fine." Crouching down she edged forward. A dozen meters from where they stood, she dropped over a ledge and disappeared.

They each eased out into the open and followed her down into a hollow in the rocks. Tree branches and leaves covered the top of a narrow slit and formed a sheltered tunnel that snaked all the way to the cliff face. They'd built a stone wall on the edge of the precipice to provide cover, and a dozen small slit windows opened up to let in light and give them a view down into the valley beyond. It was crowded and the ceiling was low enough that no one except Marti could stand upright. Fortunately, there were rocks placed behind each of the observation windows so they could sit.

"The village down there is the home of the Ter'can tribe," Tash said once everyone had settled into place. "They're a typical example of one of the non-migratory social groups. There are about twelve hundred residents in this village, but it will be hard to pick them out of the jungle without help. All of their construction is from indigenous materials and blends in well."

She leaned close to Ethan and pointed out through the window in front of him. "If you look right there, you'll see the roof of one of the buildings in the village center."

He followed her finger and could just make out the edge of something round. It had what looked like a smooth slab of dirt over it. "I see it I think," he said.

"Your PSE has optical enhancements if you want to use them." She turned his hand over and opened a small panel on his forearm. She tapped a button and the arm that had provided the infrared lens the night before popped up behind his head with a small display that swung around in front of his forehead. "The only one that auto-selects is night vision. To pick what kind of enhancement you want, look at the display and blink your right eye. Blinking your left eye makes it reset."

Teleoptic was the first on the list. He blinked and a thin visor dropped in front of his face. This time when he looked back, he realized how big the building he'd seen truly was. There were several natives standing around in front of it and it dwarfed them to insignificance. At least he assumed those were the natives he was seeing. They looked like naked humans.

"Either those are little people or that's a huge building," he said.

"It's a teaching center and a meeting hall. At first we thought it might have been a religious temple, but we don't have a lot of indication that they have any form of organized religion," Sandi said.

"I want to see," Nuko said, pushing toward the window.

"You can link your heads-up displays together," Tash said. "It's useful for making team observations. Each window looks out on a different area of the village so everyone can observe something else and still share what you're seeing if something catches your eye."

"I'm surprised they look so human," she said as she connected her own display to Ethan's.

"Me too," he said. "I almost feel like I'm invading their privacy."

"You are," Angel said. She linked in to his visor's feed and smiled in a not entirely wholesome way. "It's just that we're doing it in the name of science."

"I guess that's probably true." Tash shrugged. "Outwardly the Ut'arans are almost indistinguishable from us. They're shorter with almost no examples we've seen over 1.75 meters tall. Of course, they've adapted to have much more dense muscles and bones. Their lack of clothing also tells us they have a good tolerance for heat and cold. We've observed villages in sub-freezing temperatures and in the equatorial summer where the daytime heat can reach over sixty, and we've never seen any of them wear more than those belt pouches or shoulder packs.

"Must be nice," Rene said. "It's almost too warm for me now."

"You're PSE has environmental controls," Sandi said.

"I know they do. It's not that bad, but they don't seem to be keeping up," he said.

"When we get back, we can check them out," she said.

He nodded. "So go on. Naked superhumans?"

"We think they have better vision than we do too," Tash said. "Unfortunately, we've never had any way to confirm that because we've only had one body to examine, and it belonged to an elderly female who died of blunt force trauma to the head. Her eyes weren't in any shape to examine."

"Then why do you think their vision is better than ours?"

Angel asked.

"We've never seen them use any form of light at night," Sandi said. "Not even a fire."

"Do they use fire to prepare food?" Marti asked.

"No, they cook using chemical reactions," she said. "One of the other buildings down there is a food storage and preparation center. It's like a communal galley, but they protect it like a fortress. We think they do it to keep the wakat out."

"Wakat?" Nuko asked.

"Do you see any small humanoid creatures down there with them? They are like a hairless monkey with a pronounced brow ridge and large pointed ears." Tash leaned forward and gazed out the window for several seconds. "There. Next to the dark haired female by the door to the school."

Ethan focused on his visor display and picked out the creature she was talking about. At first, he thought it was a child since it was about a third the size of an adult and was holding the female's hand. Only after he stared at it did he notice it had feet that looked more like hands and that it moved oddly. It had a strangely elongated head and ears like a dog. Once he knew what he was looking for, he realized that there were at least a dozen of them running around and playing in the edges of the trees. "I thought those were children," he said.

"As near as we can tell, they're a domesticated species that share their society," she said. "They treat them like pets, but it seems to be much more symbiotic than that in some ways. The wakat also seem to be at least as intelligent as a terrestrial chimpanzee."

"The wakat have their own verbal language and most Ut'arans can converse with them," Sandi said. "Early in our work here, we tried to study the wakat, but they're extraordinarily quick and can get aggressive when threatened. They don't appear to be specifically carnivorous, but they would be the alpha predator in the food chain because they're remarkably cunning and they work well in large groups."

Tash nodded. "We wanted to examine them, but they killed several of our people before we realized it was best to leave them alone. We also discovered they could talk to the natives, and we didn't want to risk them revealing that we were here and affecting the Ut'aran's social development."

"If they've domesticated the wakat, why do they have to protect their food supplies?" Marti asked.

"Some wakat are integrated into the Ut'aran community, but there is a larger wild population. They can be a nuisance," she said.

"You can tell domesticated ones because they always wear a carrying pouch," Sandi said. "The Ut'arans often use them to carry messages or other small things since they can cover more than a kilometer a minute in the treetops."

Angel whistled. "Speed seems to be a survival skill in the jungle."

"Don't whistle. Ever," Tash said. "That is a mating call of a specific wakat clan that lives in this area. Unless you want to find out if you can outrun one, you might want to be careful."

"Nojo?" Angel asked.

Tash and Sandi both wore expressions that said she wasn't kidding.

"Except during mating season, the feral wakat are shy and tend to pull back when they see our Windwalkers. We seldom run into them and we're careful never to corner one," Tash said. "If they scream for help, there are always dozens within a kilometer, and the results get ugly fast."

"Won't stunner rounds take them down?" Angel asked. Ethan could tell from her face she was feeling more than a little exposed.

"It takes two or three rounds to stop one," Sandi said. "You're looking at an animal with four fists, that also understands basic tools, and has natural strength based on this planet's gravity. You might stop one of them. Unfortunately, the ten reinforcements that come out of the trees within seconds make a mess of you and your stunner gun in short order."

"We've lost a few of our escorts to that over the years so we just don't risk it," Tash said.

"With that kind of guard dog living down there, how do you do more than study them from a distance?" Ethan asked.

"We use microdrones that resemble some of the local insects. We've managed to get them inside many of the buildings in the village and have installed permanent recording devices in some locations. Including the learning center," she said. "That's how we've learned their language."

"It is unusual for a primitive culture to have school facilities, is it not?" Marti asked.

"By our thinking it is," she said. "On Earth, tribal societies have little or no written form of communication until they've started building advanced city-states. Yet everyone here seems to read and write a common language."

"This tribe has a written language?" Nuko asked.

"Actually, all the tribes we've studied anywhere on Ut'ar have the exact same language."

"We're assuming that this might be because the three distinct types of tribes are all linked through trade," Sandi said.

"Three types?" Rene asked. He'd leaned far forward and

was staring out a window of his own while paying attention to the conversation.

"There are two geographically fixed types of tribe like the Ter'can," she said. "One type hunts for wild game, while the other farms and harvests edible vegetables and grains from the local flora. The third type is a nomadic trader-herder social group that inhabits the grasslands. The written common language may be the result of the nomads providing a transport mechanism for learning and knowledge."

"Although we don't understand the nuances of the process, we've seen it work on a global scale," Tash said. "One tribe, a few dozen klick to the east of here, is domesticating several plant forms for food stock. We've seen their hybridized seeds show up all over the continent with other farmer tribes, so the nomads are transporting the seed to various locations. In the process, they seem to be imparting knowledge of how to use the seeds they carry, and not just trading commodities."

"Another example of this global network transporting technology is one we think started here in the Ter'can village," Sandi said. "The hunter type tribes focus on building things. They're much more skilled at construction, and one development that started here was a specific type of arched roof support. In the last decade we've seen that design show up in buildings over a thousand klicks away."

"They travel that far?" Ethan asked.

"Some of the tribes migrate much farther over the course of many seasons," she said. "Since nomads live in tents, they have no use for that kind of rigid structural technology, but they carried the knowledge of how to build these arch designs to the other geo-fixed tribes strictly for its potential," she said. "This tells us they appear to consider information on a par with tangible goods."

"That's a very civilized concept," Nuko said

"The free exchange of information seems, according to some of our scientists, to keep them from fighting for either territory or accumulation of resources," Tash said. "When a nomadic tribe moves into an area close to one of the other tribes, they have a ritualistic festival where they spend as much as several months learning and sharing ideas, as well as food supplies and other goods."

"Because of this they've lived in a non-competitive balance with each other since well before we arrived and started documenting their society," Sandi said. "We've found no evidence of them ever having fought a war at least as far as we can see."

"Too bad humanity didn't develop this way," Ethan said. "We've wasted so much of our time on competition and are only now learning to cooperate."

"That's another thing that gets a lot of debate," she said. "What caused humanity to evolve its aggressive nature? Was it because of the advent of some kind of technology that knocked us out of balance, or because we didn't have a cohesive language and culture to keep us locked together?"

"Now that we're spreading further and further apart, I wonder if the fact that communication is getting harder might make it worse again," he said.

CHAPTER ELEVEN

Kaycee angled across the dining hall like she was on a mission. Dr. Forrester sat at a table staring at a thinpad as he poked at his food. It was only after she landed in the seat across from him that he even noticed her.

"Dr. Smythe-Caldwell?" He blinked several times as he tried to fit her sudden appearance into his reality.

"I understand our last meeting was awkward," she said, turning on her charm with a shy smile. It was pure affectation, designed to knock him off guard, and she caught his expression shift in response. "I wanted to apologize for putting you in an uncomfortable position. I've just been trying to settle my curiosity. You understand how that works I'm sure."

"Of course," he said. "Being a research associate with the Shan Takhu Institute it's probably your nature to chase answers to ground."

"I used to be with STI," she said. "Now I'm a medic on a freighter."

"I'm sure that's an interesting story," he said. "But I won't pry."

"It's no secret. I joined the crew of the *Olympus Dawn* because I felt like I owed it to Captain Walker," she said. "He lost two crew members trying to rescue me from a situation and since one of them was his medic, I offered to fill the position. It seemed like a good way to settle the debt."

He shrugged, obviously unconvinced but willing to accept her explanation at face value. "I should also apologize.

I'd just finished a rather complex surgery and was having trouble with my implant."

"Your implant?" she asked, her mind leaping in a direction she hadn't expected.

"Yes, for my augment arm," he said. His eyes flashed to the side for an instant before he refocused on her. "I don't know if you've ever used a neuro-transducer, but they are fiendishly hard to balance the buffers. Particularly with a microsurgery interface."

"I've done microsurgery but the tech we used at STI was experimental," she said.

"This one needs a lot of calibration yet, but when there's work to do, you put up with the problems." Again his eyes lurched sidewise but this time they lingered for almost a second. "Fortunately, the controls calm down when you focus on just the manipulation interface."

"I'm surprised you have that kind of technology here at all," she said, leaning back. "You have quite an impressive medical center."

He closed his eyes before he nodded. "The environment on Dawn is very hard on our teams. The gravity can cause all manner of injury if it takes someone by surprise. I treat a disproportionate number of spinal trauma patients since the gravity control in our basecamps down there is at least as old as the station here. In its infinite wisdom, the Science Wing of the Coalition decided that it was more cost effective to build one top tier MedBay, than to invest in new gravity hardware across the operation."

She nodded, smiling but not buying his explanation for an instant. Gravity hardware was cheap. His augment arm alone would cover the cost to replate the entire station's grid. "If I may ask, what kind of surgery was it yesterday?"

"A C-2 reconstruction with neuro-transceiver bridge," he

said.

"Then you know about biological transducer implants?" she asked.

"Enough to get through," he said. His eyes narrowed and he stared at her like he saw her agenda.

"Wasn't that risky to do with your own implant acting up?" she asked. "Don't you have a tech to help you adjust your interface sensitivity? If you don't mind me saying, you looked like you were having a complete buffer cascade."

He put his elbows on the table, crossed his arms, and glared in a way that made Kaycee wonder if he was going to come over the table at her. "Are you questioning my competence because I did a surgery under questionable conditions?"

"Not at all," she said, holding her hands up and trying to look shocked that he jumped in that direction. "I know that buffer-burn is a result of endurance issues in the implant. I'm sure when you started into a long and complex procedure you didn't have any sign of it. Once you're in, there isn't much you can do but get out the other end."

He looked down at the table and frowned, slowly bringing his eyes backup. The anger had evaporated and something else replaced it. Almost helplessness? "I had no choice," he mumbled. "I had to install the implant to establish control."

"What kind of implant did you use?"

"Are you a specialist in neuro-implant tech?" he asked. His face again hardening.

"No, not at all," she said. "I know you had some implants in the payload we brought, but I didn't think you had time to get them into your medical stock before we met. They were still barely unloading at that point."

"It was hardware we had here already," he said. He sat up

straight like he was preparing to leave. "I don't believe I ordered any implant technology that would be delivered in your cargo."

"Actually, you did," she said, pulling out her thinpad with the manifest. "We just delivered 300 Alphatron Inbit Transducers. They unloaded them yesterday." She thumbed down through the list to the right cargo section and offered it to him.

Ignoring the manifest in her hand, he shook his head. "I am certain I have no idea what you're talking about Dr. Smythe-Caldwell."

He turned his head to the side again and closed his eyes for several seconds, several micro expressions flashed over his features and Kaycee got the clear impression he was having an internal conversation. Finally, he looked back at her with an expression of frustration that seemed completely out of place. "I did not order any AIT 3650's. If these devices are on your ship, it is a mistake."

"Like I said, they were unloaded yesterday."

He stood up. "I will look into it, but I do not believe this to be true. Now if you will excuse me, I have to get back to work." He spun and headed toward the door, leaving his half eaten meal and his thinpad sitting on the table.

She looked down at the screen before it autolocked. He'd been reading a medical record for a patient. The first couple lines were all she caught before the screen went dark.

M-210-Marcus.

Procedure: *AIT 3650 Transducer Implant. C-2 bridge mode.*

Status: *Operational.*

She closed her eyes trying to hold the image of the screen in her mind but nothing else had been clear enough to see. "Damn it," she muttered.

"Damn what?" Ammo asked. She'd apparently followed her into the dining hall.

"He was looking at Marcus' file when I sat down," she said, pointing at the thinpad. "It autolocked when he walked away and all I saw was the headerfile."

"Let's talk about it when we get you back to the ship," Ammo said, looking pointedly toward the door. "I think you attracted some attention and it might be better to have this discussion elsewhere."

Kaycee followed her gaze to where three men stood with Bradley Parker. He was staring at her with intent. She nodded, standing up and looking around for another exit. The only one available was through the galley and there was no guarantee that wasn't a dead end.

Ammo tapped into her collarcomm. "Quinn, if we aren't back in five minutes come looking for us."

"Do you need help now?" he asked, his tone pure professional.

"Let's see if we can walk this out, but if we aren't back in five, do what you have to. If they don't want to talk, it might get physical," she said.

"Standing by. I'll tool up and be ready. Five minutes," he said.

As they headed toward the door, Parker angled to intercept. He put on a smile that looked like a viper trying to grin. "Dr. Caldwell, I'm surprised to see you in the staff dining hall," he said. "The food is much better in either of the two cafes."

"I was here to talk to Dr. Forrester," she said, smiling and trying not to look like she was concerned about him approaching them. "I had a question on a procedure and was after a medical opinion."

Over his shoulder she saw two of the men with him slide

toward the door, while the third one walked up behind Parker. He was short and wide and gave off the same feel as Marcus. Ammo caught it too and shifted her position to get a better view of him as he dropped into Parker's shadow.

"Someone with your credentials?" He shook his head and frowned. "I mean Morris is a good doctor, but I don't think he's likely to breathe air from the same deck as you."

Kaycee looked down at the floor. "Alright, the truth is, yesterday I checked in at the medical center to offer my services while we're here, and I noticed he was having problems with his surgical arm. I didn't want to make it an issue out of it, but that kind of problem can be a huge liability issue, and I am obligated to report it to the Coalition Board of Medical Licensing if I see it. I didn't want to do that and just wanted to make sure it wasn't anything serious."

"He hasn't mentioned problems that I know of," Parker said, glancing at Ammo who had taken another half step to the side and was sizing up the small man behind him. He didn't say anything but his eyes indicated she should step back into place. "I'll talk to him about that, but I wanted to make sure I escorted you both back to your ship."

"Are we in trouble," Ammo asked. She still hadn't moved from her position and had settled herself into a much more defensive posture. It was clear she expected problems.

"No. Not at all." *Unless you resist.* He didn't add it, but he meant it. "We're about to start that maintenance on the recyclers and I wanted to make sure you weren't out and about when that starts." He held his arm out toward the door and waited for them to head out before he dropped into step behind them.

"How long is this maintenance supposed to take?" Kaycee noticed the other two men had dropped into position and were walking a few meters in front of them.

"At least until the rest of your crew gets back," he said. "You need to stay on your ship until then."

"I know a recycler purge is unpleasant, but it seems extreme to keep us confined." Ammo turned and glanced over her shoulder at him as she spoke.

"It is for your own safety," he said.

"Safety?" She frowned.

"There will be a lot of open engineering systems on the station and it would be unfortunate for you to stumble into a dangerous area," he said. "I'm just trying to make sure you don't end up having a tragic experience."

There was no doubt about it now. *That was a threat.*

CHAPTER TWELVE

They'd left early and were almost four hours into the morning hike when Ethan smelled it.

Smoke.

Within a minute, one of the Windwalker escorts had swung down from a tree and had pulled Sandi aside to have a hushed conversation. He watched the two of them discussing something before she nodded and pointed forward on the trail they were following.

The scout frowned, apparently not agreeing with whatever instructions she'd given, but he disappeared backup into the trees without an argument.

"Problems?" Ethan asked when she came back over to join them.

"Probably not, but we've got something strange going on in the Ar'ah encampment we're approaching," she said.

"The smoke," Angel straightened up and scanned the jungle. "How close are we?"

"About a klick," Tash said.

"It looks like something happened and most of their tents have been destroyed by fire. I'd like to see if we can figure out what's going on, but it might be better if we take you back to the Rockpile first," Sandi said.

"It just happened," Ethan said, tapping the side of his nose. "It's four hours home and then almost that long for you to get back. That would make it sundown, so you'd need to put it off until tomorrow. If you want to find out what's going on we should at least get eyeballs on it while we're out here."

Angel and Nuko both nodded. Rene shrugged.

"Captain Walker's assessment is correct," Marti added. "If determining what may have occurred is time critical, I would suggest we proceed forward. Since I am equipped with a substantial sensor kit, I may be of assistance in making a determination."

Tash looked at Sandi and sighed. Undoubtedly, the two of them shared a deeper understanding of the significance of the situation because neither spoke, but Ethan could feel the communication between them. "It's your call, Boss," Tash said. "Blake will burn us both if we foob this."

"If it's any help, I'll take responsibility for my people and we'll tell them we refused to go back," he said.

Sandi glanced up at the trees. "There are witnesses up there who know better. If we go forward, it might be dangerous. We've got no clue what's happened."

"Let's not waste daylight then," he said. "If we get there and it looks ugly, we can change our mind and run back to our cave."

She waved her arm and pointed in the direction they were traveling to let their escorts know they were going on.

They'd covered little more than a half klick when they dropped into a ravine and she stopped abruptly. "Frak me," she whispered, tapping her earpiece. "Isaiah found an Ut'aran body. He says it's been dead a while."

"Why didn't the korah take it?" Tash looked stunned.

"It's inside a zo'mar utel," she said. "He says it looks like it's had its skull pounded in with a rock."

"What's a zomar whatever?" Nuko asked.

"It's a stone ring they set up when they have to be outside at night," she said. "It keeps the wild animals out."

"Magical stone rings?" Angel's tone showed skepticism.

"The zo'mar stones are slightly radioactive, and we think the infrared glow they emit scares the animals off," she said. "We don't know for sure why, but even the biggest predators in the jungle won't cross one. Not even to feed, as far as we know."

"Iz says the body has a zo'mar still embedded in its forehead," Sandi said.

"The only thing that will cross an utel is a wakat, or an Ut'aran," Tash offered. "That would limit the potential suspects."

"To get to the lookout blind we'll have to go past the body. It's right on the edge of the trail," she said. "None of you are squeamish?"

"It's not high on my list of fun things, but we need to figure out what's going on," Ethan said.

Around the next bend in the trail, they walked up on the utel and stopped. "If this is on the trail to the hideout, why didn't any of you see this before?" he asked standing back and letting the two anthropologists examine the scene in detail.

"We come in from a different direction," Tash explained. "The other trail is shorter but brings us down a cliff face. It's not for someone in a borrowed PSE."

Nuko and Rene stood well back under the trees and watched from a distance as they recorded everything. The corpse had enough of an odor that neither of them wanted to get downwind of it. Angel knelt on the edge of the stone ring staring at the body. She ran her fingers through the tall yellowish grass and shook her head. Marti stood beside her, motionless and absorbing all the data its sensors could take in.

After several minutes, Angel stood up. Getting the captain's attention, she tilted her head toward the trees.

"There's something fraking foobed here," she whispered as he joined her.

"Other than a murder scene in a world of happy people?" he asked.

She held out her hand and dropped several pieces of shiny ceramic into his palm. "Stunner pellet casings. The victim was stunned several times before his skull lost the fight with the rock. It looks like there are several more casings over on the other side of the ring but I don't want to attract attention to them by walking over and checking to be sure."

"You're saying that a human attacked this one and then beat his head in to cover it?"

"That is one possibility," Marti said, walking up and joining in. "Regardless of what transpired, this situation is now much more complex. It may now be impossible to know who is trustworthy."

Ethan stared at their two guides and shook his head. "I don't think either of them knew about it. They both look like they're about to lose containment of breakfast."

"And more from shock than the smell," Angel added.

"We should keep it to ourselves for now and play ignorant."

"Is that the encampment?" Nuko had walked a short distance down the trail and pointed toward the end of the canyon. She obviously wanted to get some distance from their grim discovery.

Smoke obscured the view, but several spots looked like they were still burning.

Tash looked up and nodded. "The blind is just over the next rise and to the right of the trail by a few hundred meters." Turning to Sandi she added, "We should get them into the shelter and then figure out what happened here later."

"I have a sub-millimeter three dimensional recording of the local environment I can download to the AI in the Rockpile when we return," Marti offered. "This event does not appear to be recent, but until we can assess what has happened in the encampment below, it may be dangerous to remain in the open any longer than necessary."

"Alright then, let's move," she said, bracing herself as she turned back toward the trail. "The Windwalkers say there's nothing moving this side of the Ar'ah encampment so we should be clear, but keep your eyes open, anyway. Fire makes wild animals act strangely, especially on a world where it's so damp that it's rare for anything to burn."

They made it the rest of the way to the blind without incident and once they'd all perched themselves on rock seats to look out at the burning village, Sandi paced the small floor of the shelter with measured strides. The forward wall of the blind was dirt and grass and the entire roof hung low with layers of huge leafy fronds from one of the jungle trees. Nowhere near as well constructed as the one above the Ter'can village, the scientists clearly threw this shelter together in a hurry when the Ar'ah had set up camp.

"What are we looking for?" Angel asked. She'd picked the seat closest to the door and was already staring out the window with her heads up in place. Once she'd realized that things were stinking strange, she'd gone from happy tourist to security handler instantly. She dropped the smile and it was all business.

"Anything unusual?" Tash said.

She rolled her eyes. "That helps a lot. Everything is unusual since we're new here."

"What are we supposed to be seeing?" Rene asked. He was almost as focused on his observation as Angel.

The Ar'ah are a larger migrating tribe with almost 500 members. They have substantial herds of domesticated livestock that they keep penned up while they are encamped. They set their camp up in rings around a large central pavilion that is maybe seventy-five meters across."

"What are the tents made of?" he asked.

"The outer covering is made of bleached and processed animal hides and they drape the interiors with textiles to divide them into rooms," Tash explained.

"How do they set up the pens?" Angel was craning her head out through her observation slot and scanning far to the sides.

"They are zo'mar utel. The animals stay inside those," she said. "And then the entire encampment will be set up with a ring around that too. For some reason that we've never figured out, they change the ring every day. They have a team that picks up yesterday's zo'mar and another one follows behind and drops new ones in their place."

"Do they use a cart to move the stones around?" the handler asked.

"Yes. One to pick up and one to place new ones. They are large, high sided—"

"Then the encampment was attacked," Angel announced.

"Attacked?"

"How do you know?" Ethan said.

"Because I'm looking at what's left of two carts flipped up on their sides and burning. Both of them look like they were carrying rocks," she said. "It looks like someone rolled them up on their sides intentionally."

"I concur, Captain," Marti said. Based on the burn patterns it appears there are at least four points where the fire started simultaneously. The fire spread around the perimeter edge of the encampment then toward the center. There also appears to be a clear trail visible in the grass that heads away to the north."

"I don't understand," Tash said. "We've never seen the tribes fight with each other. It just doesn't happen."

"Obviously that's not true," Angel said. "Do you know which tribes are to the north?"

"There are two harvester-gatherer tribes north of here. The Cha'nee are northeast a long day's hike and the Sha'tana are northwest about two days."

"Nothing says it was either of them." Sandi shook her head and stopped pacing. "They're both agrarian. I'd look at the Sho'can. They're game hunters and would have the tools for an attack."

"But they're almost 300 klicks south," Tash said.

"We're pissing blind," Sandi said. "I'm not seeing any signals from the surveillance transponders on my display, are you?"

Tash shook her head. "It's probably the heat from the fires."

"We can deploy new ones but that will be slow. I don't think either of us is carrying a control kit."

Sandi knelt down along the edge of the room and heaved one of the seating stones to the side. Under it was another flat rock and she pulled it up from the floor with her finger tips. She flipped a lid up on a storage box and brought out a container full of what looked like small winged insects.

"We can each fly one at a time," she said, handing a small pile of the bugs to Tash. "We'll need at least a dozen of them in place to get any kind of image resolution but maybe we'll get lucky and we can get some idea before we waste too much time."

"Are these standard RF controlled drones?" Marti asked, holding out a hand and waiting for one to look at.

"Yes," Tash said. "They work together with a collective AI algorithm but we can only control them individually with our PSE comm systems. We don't have the bandwidth to work them as a swarm."

"I have more than adequate comm capacity," Marti said. "With your permission I can deploy them en masse."

"As long as you're sure it won't overload your own control system," she said.

Marti's face glanced over at Ethan and rolled its eyes.

"I think we're safe on that," he said.

The entire swarm of robot bugs snapped to and launched into the air in a buzzing cloud of flashing wings as they funneled out the open window and toward the burning Ar'ah camp.

"The drones have limited visual acuity," Marti said. "Imaging anything through the smoke is difficult. Once I get closer to the camp, I will drop lower to the ground and make an approach."

"Can you describe what you're seeing?" Sandi asked.

A blurry image of what might have been grass and smoke appeared on Marti's faceplate. "I can feed the signal to your heads up display if you would prefer," it said. Everybody snapped their visor's into place and opened the feed.

"Once I am in position with the microdrones, I will stabilize their positions and integrate the image to provide better resolution."

"Wait," Tash gasped. "Is that a body?"

Marti stopped the drones and swung them back toward the object. "It does appear to be at least part of a body." The image cleared as all the drones took up a stationary position. There was no doubt that someone hacked parts of the corpse off in what looked to be a monumental fight, although that didn't appear to be the cause of death. There was a thin straight stick protruding from the upper left quadrant of the body. The end had four thin vanes spread around its circumference.

"That looks like an arrow," Nuko said.

"The Ut'arans don't have archery," Sandi whispered.

"Apparently they do now," Rene said. "And I'd say that's a damn finely manufactured arrow too."

"It would be plenty deadly I'm sure." Ethan stood up and set himself in Sandi's line of sight to make sure he had her undivided attention. She looked like she was on the verge of passing out. "I am seriously suggesting it's time for us to leave."

She nodded. "Yah. I'm thinking this is over my air supply."

CHAPTER THIRTEEN

Quinn stood guard inside the *Olympus Dawn*'s cargo access airlock watching the activity in the container on the internal optics. After the obvious warning that Parker dropped on them as he escorted them back, Kaycee had suggested that the handler tool up and keep watch on the door. They were short handed until the rest of the crew returned, but if they got lucky, it wasn't a situation that would escalate.

She wasn't of a mind to wager on luck as she and Ammo chewed over what might be going on. They sat alone in her quarters.

"All we've got is the strange behavior of a passenger and a doctor with multiple personalities," Ammo said. "That's really not much."

"That and some unusual neuro-transducers, but I know it's not much," Kaycee said. "Although when the OpsSec Chief gets heavy-handed on us that sets off my short hairs."

"Yah, mine too, but other than the fact that he smells funny, that isn't enough to get us into the shitpile."

"Smells funny?" Kaycee raised an eyebrow. She'd noticed that he had that strange pheromone effect that she recognized from some of the older genetically augmented staff members she'd met at the Shan Takhu Institute. As far as she knew the plusser funk wasn't common knowledge outside STI.

Ammo nodded and winked. "It's that reek that some people with power get. Arrogance in a bottle."

"Yah, he does have that doesn't he?" she agreed. "What I need to find is some kind of physical evidence that there's something going on. Something bigger than a station full of strange people."

"Hey doc, are you near a screen?" Quinn interrupted over the comm.

"Yah, what's swinging?" she said, thumbing her thinpad to activate her wallscreen.

"Thought this might interest you," he said as one of the optic feeds opened up. "First thing you need to notice here is they've put guards on both ends of the box. Technically, that puts them inside our territory and right outside the airlock I'm standing in."

"I don't like that," she said.

"Me either, but we can always power down the box and they'll have to leave," he said. "But what I wanted you to see is what they're doing in there. Just watch the workers for a minute."

They were replacing the deck plating that they'd removed to get to the cargo. Several workers were carrying panels into place while others reattached the retaining pins.

"What are we looking at?" Kaycee asked.

"I want you to keep in mind that each deck plate weighs at least 350 k-gram," he said.

Two workers dropped one panel near where a crew was putting them into place. One of the smaller female workers grabbed the plate and swung it up over her head to hold it in place while the other one pushed the pins home.

"I'd say that's not normal," he said. "I could carry one of those, *probably*. But I'm not a meter seventy and sixty-five k-gram. A few minutes ago I saw a single one of them carry two panels at the same time."

"Alright, that doesn't stack at all," Ammo said.

"I think it's obvious they're from the planet," Quinn said.

"That's what I was telling Ethan about Marcus," Kaycee said, grinning in spite of the glueball that represented. "They have to be Ut'aran."

"Or they're genetically engineered," she said.

"They'd have to be unregistered and that's almost as massive a nogo as bringing natives up to the station," the doctor said.

"Yah, but other than the video we've got no other proof," he said.

"I need to get a med scanner on one of them," Kaycee said, jumping up and bolting for the door. "I'm on my way."

"How close do you need to get?" he asked as the comm shifted to the shipwide system and followed her out into the corridor.

"A couple meters," she said.

"They won't let you do that." Ammo chased after her.

"One of the natives is standing right outside the inner airlock," Quinn said.

"I don't know if I can get much through the closed hatch, even if he was leaning against it," she said, sliding to a halt at the lift gate and waiting for Ammo to catch up.

"Maybe we can get the door open long enough to scan them before they shove us back in our box," he said. "How long will it take?"

"A minute at close range," she said.

"I think we can cover that." Ammo grinned. "Quinn, honey, you needed to go dancing tonight didn't you?"

"I'm not dressed for it," he said. "But if you're still on the crewdeck, my leathers are in my quarters."

"I'm on it," she said pushing the lift gate closed behind Kaycee. "I'll be there in two minutes. Be naked when I show up."

She spun and disappeared back down the corridor as the lift dropped to the mid-deck so she could grab her handheld scanner.

"I am aware of what you are attempting to do," Marti said. "I have not yet informed the captain, as I also understand your need for hard evidence before you bring it to him. Good luck. And do not get yourself in trouble."

"Thanks Marti," she said, jumping out of the lift and darting toward the MedBay. "How are things going down there?"

"Not as well as they are for you, in fact," it said. "We have encountered a situation that has adversely affected our desire to remain on the surface. Unfortunately it is another two days before the shuttle returns to bring us back."

"What's swinging?" She grabbed her handheld scanner out of the drawer and flipping it open, made sure it had a full charge.

"Without further analysis it is difficult to say with any certainty, but it appears that there have been severe cultural contaminations in the local tribal civilization," Marti said. "If you confirm the workers up there are members of the Ut'aran race, then we may be looking at opposite ends of the same issue."

She opened the program screen on the scanner to modify the settings but she paused. *How do I optimize it for an alien physiology that I know nothing about?*

"Do you have any access to medical information on the natives down there?" she asked.

"The information in the local AI system files is limited," it said. "Most of what they know about the Ut'aran physiology they keep in the station and I can no longer access the Watchtower Station network. It appears they have locked us out."

"Wait. Contamination?"

"There is direct evidence that at least one native was attacked using a stun weapon," Marti said. "Another individual was terminated by severe blunt force trauma. We do not know if the individuals in possession of the advanced technology conducted the murder, but the unavoidable conclusion is that there has been blatant interference in the social environment."

"I'll let you know what we find out," she said. "Right now I have to focus on making my best guess to get this scan done."

"Understood. We are currently traveling with maximum alacrity back to the basecamp. The tension level here is extreme. Especially for the scientists and our escorts."

"Be safe," she said.

"Always."

Shaking her head, she tweaked the settings to widen the range of diagnostic possibilities and closed the scanner.

"Are you still in MedBay?" Ammo hollered from the lounge area.

"Yah. Just tuning the tools," she answered, leaping through the door.

"Shake it fast. Quinn says they're almost done in the box and he doesn't know if the two at the door will hang once they're finished." Ammo had what looked to be a dead black animal hanging over her shoulders and was just finishing the lacings on a red corset she'd cinched up around her waist. Somehow, she'd changed into a flesh colored thinskin and for the most part, it failed to cover even the important bits of her anatomy.

Or maybe it's flesh colored flesh instead?

It didn't matter since her intent was to keep the guards attention off what Kaycee was doing, and whatever she was, or wasn't, wearing would certainly do the job. When they got to the inner airlock, Quinn was standing there even more naked than Ammo appeared to be.

Being a doctor, Kaycee was past shock at seeing skin, but it was the first time she'd seen the handler's physique in all its glory. It wasn't the skin that held her attention so much as the massive amount of perfectly carved anatomy it covered.

The airlock suddenly seemed far too small an area for that much flesh.

"I'll wager you didn't think to pick up some of my silkies, did you?" Quinn asked as he picked up the dead animal from over her shoulder.

"Sorry, you're just going to have to swing it commando there big boy," Ammo said, leaning back to either watch the show, or give him flailing room as he shimmied into the tight outfit. The leather creaked and groaned as he pulled it up over his legs and then bounced several times to settle his muscular buttocks into place.

"I think I should wait in the hall," Kaycee said, surprised at the visceral reaction she was having to watching him get dressed. Not only was the airlock too small, it was getting too warm.

"Coward," Ammo mouthed in her direction with a wink.

"I'm in fear of being trampled," she said, refusing to acknowledge any other aspect of her desire to step out of range.

Quinn rocked his shoulders back and snagged the upper part of his outfit, pulling it up and over his chest with a snarling grunt. "That's the least amount of fun I've ever had getting kitted up," he said.

Ammo grinned. "I'd offer to make it up to you—"

"That's alright," he said. "Everybody likes tattys, but they really aren't my thing. Unless I've had way too many beers. And then well, stranger things …"

"I think I'm over dressed for this party," Kaycee said, shaking her head and trying to get her mind back on their objective. "So what's the plan?"

"That's the easy part," Ammo said. "Quinn and I will stand in front and try to keep them from noticing you. You should be able to squeeze up behind us and get close enough to get a good scan while they're trying to figure out what to look at."

"The one you want to scan is on the left, so let me take that side, and you can shadow me," he said.

"When the hatch opens, we'll take a half step forward to make sure they can't close it on us and then we have to look surprised that there are guards out there," Ammo said. "If we can keep them thinking we're just going out for a night of play, they'll have to take time to explain why we can't go. Every second counts, so we just stall as long as we can, and if it looks like they'll get ugly, we give up and retreat. Slowly."

"Got it," he said. Grabbing both his stunners, he handed one to Kaycee. "You know how to use one of those, don't you?"

She flipped it over, snapped the charge chamber open to check the level. Spinning it back over, she popped the pellet cartridge out to confirm it was loaded and slapped it back in. She finished the inspection by jerking the loading armature back to chamber a round.

"Nope, never used one of these in my life," she said, winking at him as she shoved it down into the top of her thinskin.

It wasn't the best place to carry a pistol, but she didn't figure she'd have to be too quick, and she needed both hands on the scanner to make sure she got what she was looking for. Opening it up, she tapped the main screen and brought up the control interface.

"Then I guess it's time to dance," he said, keeping the other pistol in his hand and tucking it behind Ammo's back like he was putting his arm around her. He leaned in tight to conceal that he was hiding something behind her and reached out with his free hand to palm the hatch release. They both stepped forward and Kaycee squeezed in tight behind.

"Where do you think you're—" the guard on the right said, his voice faltering as he took in Quinn's giant leather clad frame, or as Ammo's proudly flying tattys leapt out to say hello. In any case, his brain obviously went offline.

"What's swinging? I heard there was a party on deck four?" Ammo said, adding a false giggle to her voice. "What's the name of the place Quinn?"

"I don't remember, it's supposed to be a bar." He shifted to the left so Kaycee could squeeze forward along the wall.

The scanner screen lit up and she held her hand over it to keep it from reflecting off anything.

"What's it called," Ammo said, shifting her shoulders. She was trying to keep the guard's attention on her.

"The Slosh Pit?" he said. The croak in his voice indicating her wiles were working.

"They must to stay on ship," the other one said. His accent had the same strange click and abrupt syntax as Marcus. His tone also said Ammo's charms were falling flat with him.

"That's the place," she said, shifting to the right. Kaycee pushed tighter into Quinn's shadow. "Where is it? On deck four, right?"

She uncovered the screen. *Forty-five percent complete.*

"Yah, but he's right," the first guard said. "None of you

are supposed to leave the ship."

"Pa, why you gotta be busting my bag?" Quinn said. "We're just looking to play slick. Bossman never lets us off the deck."

That was pretty convincing slango for a ground locked farm boy, she thought. She glanced over at the stunner where he held it behind Ammo and realized that he was flexing his hand. *Bad sign.*

"Doesn't matter," the guard said. "They're doing maintenance work on the station and only authorized crew gets a pass. You need to go back and party in your own bunks. Nothing I can do to help you on that."

She looked down at the screen again. *Sixty-five percent.*

"Eyeball me, pa. There's no room in my bunk," Quinn said. "It's way too squeezy to play."

"That's more than I needed to think on," the guard said, chuckling nervously. "Seriously, there's not a frakking thing I can do for you. You need to get back on the ship."

"Cut us a break," Ammo said, leaning forward and lowering her voice. "This is our only chance to tangle. Captain Tightpants has rules and he won't let us romp each other on the ship. His AA keeps an eye for him, so we gotta get out of here so we can have fun."

Eighty-three percent.

"Your skipper's rules are not my problem," he said. "Get back inside."

Kaycee heard what sounded like a sidearm slipping out of a holster and she felt Quinn's entire body tighten up in front of her. His hand twitched, but he didn't move.

"Go back on ship," the other one said.

"You don't have enough ugly to make that happen, tiny man," Ammo said, her tone dismissive. "What kind of maintenance would keep us in tonight?"

"The kind that will get your floater-toys all kinds of stunner fun," the first one said. "Unless you want to go down right where you stand, you need to turn your pretty parts around and get back in your ship."

Kaycee stole another check of the screen. *Ninety-six percent. Another few seconds.*

"I am not tiny," the one on the left said. "You do go now or it will be ugly."

Quinn set one of his legs back, bracing himself. Kaycee stepped to the side to make sure that if Quinn had to get physical she would not be under him when he launched.

Almost there.

"They are not alone," the tiny one said. "Someone is behind."

"You in back, what are you doing back there?" the first one said. "Step out here where I can see you."

"Your little buddy is hallucinating, but we'll go back inside. It's not worth it," Ammo said, leaning even further forward. She had to be almost touching the one in charge and she lowered her voice to a whisper. "I don't know what your problem is, but I was about to invite you to come party with us too."

Quinn eased back, his thumb snagging the back of her corset and making sure she retreated with him.

"Hold!" he said. "Who's with you?"

"Ah well, your loss," she said. "It would have been fun, too. My friend here likes little boys like you."

The handler slapped his hand on the door actuator and the hatch slammed closed. He locked out the override and just stood there for several seconds shaking his head. "I think I need to go shower. That has to be the sleaziest thing I've ever done in my life."

"You grew up on a farm, so I'm sure it's not," Ammo

said, winking. "But you did real well. By the way, where'd you learn slango?"

"My first boyfriend was from LEO-6 and he just loved to talk dirty. I sucked some of it up over time," he said.

Turning to the doctor, he nodded at the scanner in her hand. "So did you get what you needed?"

"I'll have to download it in MedBay, but you were right. He's definitely not human," she said.

"We need to tell the cap'n," Quinn said.

"As soon as I get it sorted out," she said, glancing at Ammo and raising an eyebrow. "This one also has a transducer implant."

CHAPTER FOURTEEN

Even with a PSE doing the work, jogging in two-G was not a pleasant experience. But the eighteen klick that had taken them four hours outbound, took them just over two to get back. They made a lot of noise, and had pushed their Windwalkers hard to keep them safe, but fear trumped everything else.

"My suits eating too much power," Rene said as they topped the last ridge about two klick from the Rockpile. "I've got to slow down."

"We're almost there," Tash said, coming up and turning him around so she could open the back of his suit to access the panel and check the power pack.

"I know, but I've been watching the system readouts." He was sweating and gulping air. "The actuators are hot and they're pulling too much current. I've got to stop a minute and let them cool off or I'm not going to make it."

"You've been complaining about that suit all along," Ethan said as he walked up and pulled a gojuice out of his beltpack to hand it to the engineer.

"We're only two klick from home," Sandi said. "We really need to push on."

"I'm down to three percent on the batteries and for the last twenty minutes I have been pulling almost three percent per klick."

"Do these things have spare batteries?" the captain asked.

"No. They have a backup power pack that will keep them operating for an hour but he's already into his," Tash said.

"His actuator cooling system is completely offline."

Rene nodded and leaned forward, putting his hands on his knees, while he stared at the ground. "Yah, it's hot in here," he managed, rolling his eyes up and looking at Ethan. "I've got to lie … down." Collapsing onto his hands and knees, he rolled over on his back and blew out several long hard breaths of air.

"How long will it take for his suit to cool enough that he can move?"

"I don't know, I've never seen one overheat like this," Sandi said, looking around at the trees and shaking her head. "We can wait a few minutes but we've got to keep moving."

"I understand that, but if that suit won't make it back when it's running that hot, we've got no choice but to wait here until he can move," Ethan said.

She nodded, stepping away and tapping her earpiece to comm with one of the Windwalkers.

There's something else going on here, he realized as he studied her body language while she talked in hushed tones. *She's terrified of something.*

He leaned over Rene. "You just keep breathing, I'll be right back."

The engineer nodded, closing his eyes and laying his head back on the mossy grass. He looked like he was broiling in his suit.

The rest of his crew stood back, watching. Making significant eye contact with Nuko he said, "Keep him company. I don't want him passing out. Talk to him or whatever, but if he passes out we'll have to get him out of that suit."

She nodded and went over to kneel beside the engineer.

"Angel, how's your suit charge doing?" He walked over to where she stood with Marti.

She flipped open her arm control panel. "Sixty percent. I can carry him if that's what you're thinking."

He nodded.

"Captain, I believe we have an additional problem," Marti said.

"I thought something else was stinking out here. What else?"

"I have maintained control over the microdrones and although they were not designed for long duration flight, several of them are still operational. I have been using them to enhance my situational awareness while we have traveled."

"And?"

"I believe we are being observed," Marti said.

"Where," he said, spinning and trying to pick anything out of the jungle.

"Several wakat have been pacing us for at least the last hour. They are keeping a distance of approximately 150 meters and remain high in the trees."

"Are they the feral ones?" Angel asked.

"I do not believe so," it said. "Although my optical resolution is severely degraded because of the attrition of the microdrone swarm, I can tell that at least one of them is wearing the carrying pouch that indicates domestication."

"Do Sandi and Tash know about them?"

"Yes," it said, looking down in almost an embarrassed expression. "I have also been eavesdropping on the radio communication between the Windwalkers and our guides. The escorts have been unable to run the wakat off and are concerned that there may be an Ut'aran hunting party tracking us."

"Frak, then we need to get Rene up and moving," Ethan said.

"We should dump all of his exoshell but the arms and

back panel so it will stretch his power supply," Angel said. "If he can hold on to my back and let his legs hang, it will make him easier to carry. I think I can jog the two klicks that way."

"Do it," he said. "Marti give her a hand."

As the two of them headed over to help unsuit Rene, he angled for Sandi. She was still talking on her comm.

"We'll be ready to move in a couple minutes," he said when she glanced at him. "But we need to have an understanding first."

"Excuse me?" she asked startled at the tone he had taken.

"Yes. You put me and my people in danger by not sharing that we've got wakats following us," he said.

"How do you know that?"

"We've got a walking, talking, sensor kit with us." He jerked his head toward where Marti and Angel were ripping pieces off Rene's suit and tossing them into a pile. "I also know those are domesticated wakat and your Windwalkers don't intimidate them, so you all think there's a hunting party out there tracking us."

Holding up a finger she tapped her earpiece. "Iz, can you come here a second, I think you need to talk to Walker with me." She nodded as he replied.

Above them, something chittered in the tree and Ethan glanced up. Fifty meters above him, a wakat flashed between two treetops and vanished off into the distance. Immediately behind it, he saw one of their escorts swinging down toward the ground.

"That bastard was right on top of you," he said, as he landed softly several meters away. "Fortunately, they don't like company."

"Walker knows about the wakats," she said. "And that they're not the feral ones."

"He does? Alright then," Iz said. "Care to tell me how

you figured that out?"

"Marti's still running the microdrones," he said. He chose not to mention that it had also been monitoring the comm.

"Never thought about that," he said, nodding slowly. "Smart robot. Wondered why you brought it along."

"Marti's a level twelve AA aboard my ship. This body's only an automech."

"So it's on an uplink," Iz said. "Nice tech."

"What I want to say here is that you should have informed us about what's going on," Ethan said. "By keeping it to yourselves you're risking my people's lives."

"Look, Walker, you don't know this environment. That means anything you might try to do to help, might be harder to undo than if you did nothing," he said. "Nothing personal, but you're not qualified to help make decisions, so there's no real upside to us telling you frakking shit."

"I'm not sure it's worth wasting time arguing with you, but if you'd told us we were being followed we wouldn't have wasted time deciding to unsuit and carry Rene, we'd already be moving again. Right there is one reason that proves your thinking is foobed."

The Windwalker sucked his lips tight against his teeth and nodded.

"Now you want to tell me what else you know?"

"Not much," he said. "There are six or eight Wakat following us—"

"There are eleven of them," Marti said. "Six males and five females. All of them are carrying pouches and three of the larger males also have packs."

"We haven't seen any with packs," Iz said, glancing at Sandi.

"That's not good," she said quietly.

"And that's why we should be sharing intel," Ethan said.

"We're ready to go," Angel said as she swung Rene up onto her back. She settled him into position and headed off along the trail toward the Rockpile, gaining speed until she reached a steady loping gallop.

"Wait! We can't leave the pieces of his exoshell out here," Sandi said. "If the Ut'arans find them, the contamination will be catastrophic."

Tash was scooping up the pieces and handing them to Marti.

"If you want to carry them back that's fine, but I think it's a little late to be worrying about that," the captain said as he reached into his beltpack and pulled out a piece of stunner pellet casing.

"What's this?" she asked.

"Something we found next to the body back there," he said, dropping the fragment into her hand. "It's a ceramic piece from a stunner pellet shell. Unless the natives have learned to build stun-guns, I think you have a lot bigger problem than a pile of PSE pieces."

Her mouth fell open as she looked at the shard.

Iz took it from her and nodded. He obviously recognized it. He also didn't look surprised. "If he died before he woke up, there's no contamination. This is bad, but it doesn't mean they've been exposed yet."

"Except that there was another person there when they were attacked," Ethan said. "There were several more pellet casings on the opposite side of the ring. Whoever that one was, walked away."

"Captain, we need to be moving," Marti said. "There are several larger creatures approaching along the trail behind us. I do not have adequate resolution in the remaining microdrones to determine exactly what they are, but they appear to be upright, bipedal creatures at least twice the size

Eric Michael Craig

of the wakat."

"How far off are they?" Ethan asked.

"Just over four kilometers," it said. "ETA under seven minutes."

"Let's go," Sandi said, leaping over to help Tash gather what she could of Rene's exoshell. "Grab what we can carry and leave the rest. We'll try to come back for it later."

"You can't leave anything out here," Iz said, looking shocked she'd even consider it.

"Then you pick it up," she snapped. "I'm with the captain here. I think letting them catch us would be worse than leaving scraps behind."

CHAPTER FIFTEEN

"They're done in the cargo container and they moved the two guards outside the airlock to the station end of the box," Quinn said, bringing in a small tray of food and setting it down on the counter in the MedBay. "They've got four standing watch out there now, and two of them are probably from the planet."

"So they're determined not to let us out," Ammo said as she appeared at the door. She'd lost the corset but still looked almost naked in her flesh colored thinskin.

"Hopefully, I've got enough data to figure this out," Kaycee said.

"Well you know that Tiny isn't human," she said. "What else do we need to know?" She took a seat on the edge of the diagnostic bed and grabbed a grilled yeastcake off the tray. It had bacon and slices of bright red and green vegetables stuffed inside it.

"It would be good to figure out what they're physical capacities are, in case things get ugly," Quinn said. "All we know is that they're strong as a horse with an eating disorder."

"What?" Ammo asked, raising an eyebrow at his metaphor.

He grinned. "We rescued a Haflinger on the farm when I was a little, and that horse would push over fences, and walls, and even beat down the barn door, to get to the hay bales. When he was hungry, there was no power on Earth that would hold him back," he said. "Vet said it was an eating disorder, but all I know is when something was between him and dinner, he was the strongest animal I'd ever seen."

"I've seen pictures of horses," she said, shrugging.

"I don't think the Ut'aran is that strong, but he has at least four times the bone and muscle density of a human, and a spinal column that looks like it is designed for heavy work," she said. "They've also got a circulatory system that's at least double ours."

"It's a good thing that we didn't dance then," Ammo said.

"His spine has only twenty seven vertebral bones, so we have an advantage in flexibility, but he'd be a lot to handle if you couldn't get away from him."

"That's useful to know," Quinn said. He held out a sandwich to Kaycee and she smiled as she took a bite.

"His lungs look like they have at least twenty five percent more capacity too, so he has a lot better endurance than you'd expect."

"You're saying it wouldn't be a fair fight," Ammo said.

"Leverage and maneuverability," the handler said.

She nodded. "I also think his eyes are a lot better than ours. The scan wasn't deep enough to know for sure, but there is an extra lens inside the eyeball that might be a light gathering structure. I'd have to get one on a table to do more than venture a guess, but I bet he can see in near total dark too."

"You're saying they look like us but they aren't even close," he said.

"If he's typical, then they're only cosmetically similar." She leaned back and stretched. "Even a basic bioscan would catch most of this, but at a cellular level it's much more obvious."

"That brings us to the next question," Ammo said.

"Why are they on the station if they're a protected sibling culture?"

"That too maybe," Ammo said, "but I was thinking about the implant."

"I don't know," Kaycee said. "There are several pieces to it, but the biggest one is on the back of his skull. Then there is another one in a position on his spine near what would be the human equivalent of the C-2 vertebra. Without having the specifications on the implant hardware it would be almost impossible to guess."

"They used to use implants for comm before there was all that backlash after the Odysseus Coup," she suggested. "Maybe that's what it's for?"

"If it's an Alphatron Inbit 3650, with the right modules they could use it for all kinds of things," Quinn said. "They were part of the rehabilitation training process at Upstate Supermax."

"Training?"

"They can be used to upload knowledge and skills directly to the brain," he said.

"That's pretty old tech too," Ammo said.

"That's probably true, but they also were experimenting with ways to overwrite violent personality disorders and replace it with a more socially acceptable personality."

"I thought that was against the law," she said.

"They had all kinds of legal armor around the project, and they told us that the prisoners in the program were all volunteers," he said. "I don't know if that was true, since some of them didn't seem too willing to participate. They only implanted the worst hard cases, but that's part of why I got out of there once my contract was up."

"Some of the prisoners were forced against their will?" Kaycee asked.

"I know a lot of them fought it," he said. "They might have volunteered and then gotten chicken legs."

"Can a determined patient overpower one of these implants?" The edge of an idea was forming in her brain but it wasn't clear enough to be sure she liked where it was going.

"There were some that tried at first. Eventually they learned to cooperate," he said, his eyes going empty as he thought back over the memories. It was a scary look on his face. He set his sandwich back down on the tray. "An AIT can inflict a lot of pain through the nervous system. If it's cranked up to an extreme level it will burn through the nerves and paralyze."

"Is that permanent?" Ammo asked.

"Surgery could fix it," he said. "But it depended on where on the spine the implant was. If it interrupted above a certain point, it shut off control of the diaphragm and the prisoner suffocated unless they got them into a MedBay and on life support immediately. Sometimes it caused brain damage too."

"Holy frak," she whispered. "They're still using this technology?"

"As of five or six years ago the program was still ongoing," he said. "I didn't think it was something momma would have approved of, and that's why I moved on as soon as I could."

"You said they could overwrite a person's personality?" Kaycee asked. "Was that a permanent change?"

"Not unless they did a BES before they did the implant," he said. "I don't know exactly what it did, but it basically erased the mind and then when they overwrote things, they could fill in the blanks. Without the BES they had a lot of trouble getting the prisoners to stay fixed."

"A BES is a Brain Engram Scan," she said for Ammo's benefit. "What happened if they didn't do a BES?"

"Depends on how hard they pushed back," he said. "The pain induction tended to make the prisoner want to behave, but even without it the implant could keep reloading new core behaviors or skill patterns and they went a bit... spastic, maybe."

"What do you mean?"

"Like they were arguing with themselves all the time. Unpredictably." He shrugged. "When you dealt with one that hadn't had the BES wipe first, it was like you never knew if you were talking to the hardcase or the implant."

"Really?" she asked, suddenly understanding what she was looking for. "I assume the implant had a preprogrammed behavior for the patient?"

"Not at all," he said. "They were comm enabled and the main AA could update it any time it needed to."

Kaycee slapped her palm down on the counter beside her and grinned. "Dr. Forrester has an implant."

"Why would he have one?" Ammo shook her head. "He's the one putting them into the natives."

"And who did it to him?" "Quinn asked.

"Those are all good questions," she said. "Maybe we should ask him."

"How do you propose we do that?" he asked. "They've got us locked down and sure as frak won't let us talk to him."

"And won't his transducer just override him as soon as you ask about it?" Ammo said.

"We get Dr. Forrester to come in here instead," Kaycee said.

"That still doesn't keep his transducer from cutting him off," she said.

The handler grinned. "Leave that to me."

"I understand the need for discretion given your findings, but should I relay this information to the captain?" Marti said.

Quinn and Ammo both nodded.

"Can you do it without being overheard?" she asked. "Until we interrogate the doctor, we don't know who's in on this."

"There is an RF shielded utility area in the basecamp where I have been recharging. With the door closed there would be no potential for them to intercept or overhear. I would be disconnected from my automech but I could download a report and preprogram my body to deliver it to him once we were alone."

"That's a good idea," she said. "I'd like to get what we can from Forrester first, but it might be best to give him a preliminary assessment of what we know so far."

"We have just arrived at the basecamp," it said. "The situation is unstable at the moment. It may take upward of an hour to get an opportunity."

"That gives us a chance to work out a plan to get the doctor to make a house call," Quinn said.

"A what?"

CHAPTER SIXTEEN

Ethan stood beside Dr. Stocton in the main gallery of the Rockpile and watched the massive display screen. Doc Leela was checking over Rene, but he seemed to be mostly tired and sweaty, and not much worse. "This stinks like a blown recycler and you know it."

"It's a little bit of a problem," Toby said, nodding. "It's not the first time we've had hunters camping so close, but given how soon they arrived after you got back, it's worrisome."

"Toby, they were hunting us," Sandi said. "They were attempting to run us down."

"That would be an assumption, and you'd better hope it's not true," he said, holding up his hands in reaction to her obvious indignation. "If they were hunting you down, then it means they saw you. That makes you at the very least partially responsible."

"How dare you…" she said, sputtering to a halt.

"You can take that up with your boss when you get back to Watchtower," he said. "It wasn't my call, but Dr. Blake wants you and Tash on the next shuttle back."

"We're supposed to be on the rotation," she said. "That's not fair."

"Maybe not, but I'm far more concerned with why this hunting party isn't behaving normally." He waved in the direction of the screen.

"I think that's obvious," she said. "There's been a contamination incident."

"I think that's a far bigger assumption than that they were hunting you," he said, turning away to stare up at the image on the wallscreen. "And you better hope that's not true or there will be careers cashing out."

"Someone had to shoot at least one of the natives," she said. "That is a fact and not an assumption." She held out the pellet fragment and waited for him to take it.

He stared at her hand in disbelief but didn't move. "I thought you gave the fragment to Isaiah?"

"I gave her another one," Ethan said. "There were plenty of them out there."

"I will need all the pieces you collected for forensic evidence," he said, looking at the captain and frowning. "I was monitoring your Windwalker's comm channel, so I heard what you found. Unfortunately, you didn't gather the evidence in a way that preserved its scientific integrity, and as a result there's no way of knowing if it is indeed something that's connected to the body, or just a matter of coincidence."

"Coincidence?" It shocked him that the mission commander could so easily dismiss it.

"Most of our personnel carry stunners," he said. "Sometimes they have to use them on animals. No one reports those kinds of incidents unless it results in an injury. There's no way to know if one of our earlier expeditions got tangled up with something at that location and then this dead Ut'aran coincidentally set up his zo'mar utel in the same place but at a later time."

"What about all the other irregularities?" Sandi asked as Nuko and Angel came in and sat at the table behind them.

Toby sat and drew in a slow breath. "No matter how I say this it will sound dismissive, but I swear that's not my intent. I know you all just lived through an unbelievably tough day. Any of you would have to admit that the things you witnessed could be coloring your perception. I just don't see any real scientific evidence to connect it together."

"How many coincidences does it take, to make it not one?" Nuko said.

Toby turned in his chair and glared at her like he was about to tell her to butt out, but he bit down on his response.

"When you run a starship, you learn not to be caught behind the data curve," Ethan said. "I know you're going to tell me that science depends on factual data only, but survival has to be more flexible than that."

"Captain, I appreciate your concern but we're far from a survival situation here. We've locked the Rockpile down tight and there's virtually no way they can get inside," he said. "We're perfectly safe in here and we can wait them out. I think it's best if we remain focused on what we can learn from this situation and not pursue wild conjecture."

"Of course… Doctor," Ethan said, clenching his teeth and taking a deep breath. "I have a crewman to check on, and I don't want to be in your way while you analyze yourself into a happy complacency. So if you will excuse me, I think I'll see how he's doing."

Nodding at Angel, he pivoted to walk away. "After I'm done, I'll be in my bunk."

"I'm sorry, Captain Walker. I didn't mean for that to come out sounding like I am not concerned," Toby said. "It's possible you may be right about the complacent nature of science, and that might imply that it's wrong for me to exclude things that are extremely unsettling to contemplate. I just don't know what good conjecture is, when we don't have enough information to form an accurate through line in our thinking."

Ethan turned back and leaned forward putting both hands on the table as he looked at Nuko. She raised an eyebrow and shrugged. Angel shook her head. Both of them knew him well enough to know he was thinking about telling Toby to frag himself. Finally, he sighed.

"In command school they teach a decision tree for assessing problems," he said sitting down in the nearest chair. "You start with what you know for sure. If that doesn't give you a complete answer, you start gluing the pieces together with what you might know."

"And if you don't get an answer with that, you throw the widest possible net that encircles all the things you know and can guess at," Nuko said. She'd taken the same classes he had.

"Then at least you are ready for anything that might be inside your reality," he finished.

"So how does that apply here?" Toby asked, staring up at the optic images on the wallscreen.

"For sure, you have a long dead native that had his head bashed in. You also have a massacred tribe from last night or this morning. And now you have wakats and Ut'arans camped out on top of us."

"And they are using weapons we've never seen them use before," Sandi added.

"There has to be a lot more to it than that," Ethan said. "I'm sure I don't have the expertise to contribute meaningfully, but I know how to piss people off enough to keep things stirred up. Eventually, that will get the creativity flowing."

"Maybe we should get everybody in here and break this up into pieces," Toby said. "More eyes on it might make it easier."

"I think that's an excellent idea," he said, wondering just

what he'd volunteered to do. *Me and my stupid mouth.*

He looked over at Nuko who was clearly thinking the same thing. *You and your stupid mouth.*

"Captain Walker, I need to recharge," Marti said. "I have completed downloading the information I recorded during today's expedition, and would like to shut down my automech for internal maintenance."

"That's fine," Ethan said, glancing at the mission commander to confirm he didn't need Marti's input.

"If I may have your assistance for a moment," it said, raising both eyebrows on its projected face and looking toward the door without moving. "Please?"

Assistance? As far as he knew, unless something was broken, Marti took care of itself without help. "Do you need me to get Rene?"

"Negative, Captain. Your assistance will be adequate," it said.

"Adequate? I think I've been insulted," he said, standing backup and heading toward the power locker Marti had conscripted to use as a charging station. "I'll be right back. Let me know what I miss." He made sure that Nuko caught the idea that he suspected the AA was trying to get him out of the room.

She nodded and glanced over at the automech. *Message received.*

Marti spun and walked over to the shielded electrical closet and pulled the heavy metal door open. It stood to the side so that Ethan could go in first and followed him in, pulling the door closed to seal them in.

Offline, flashed on its faceplate.

"This is an automated report delivery from Marti aboard the *Olympus Dawn* to Captain Walker in the basecamp," it said in a strangely different voice. "I programmed my body in advance to make sure you were isolated from being overheard, or from this communication being monitored. The AA in the automech is capable of operating the body, but while we are in the shielded locker, there is no way for you to respond to me in real time regarding the information that I am about to deliver. When the message is complete, you will be given an opportunity to record a confirmation and provide instructions that can be delivered securely back to me once you open the door."

"I understand," he said.

The automech walked past him in the narrow space and hooked up its connections to the power feed lines. *Acknowledged and logged*, flashed on the faceplate.

"Message follows: Captain Walker, Dr. Caldwell has confirmed her suspicions that there are Ut'aran natives living and working in various capacities throughout Watchtower Station. She has completed a clandestine biomedical scan of one native who was serving security duty outside the airlock of the *Olympus Dawn*. This particular Ut'aran native has a surgically installed neuro-transducer implant capable of modifying and controlling its behavior. The reason these individuals are not still on the planet is unknown, but as they are present in large numbers and intermingled with the human residents, there must be widespread knowledge of the situation. Dr. Caldwell further suspects that the passenger, Marcus Elarah is also an Ut'aran native as he exhibits a marked physiological similarity to the subject of her bioscan. If this is true, his removal from the planet and transport to Proxima would constitute a major criminal act.

"The situation in the station has become extremely volatile, and until she can come up with more answers, she advises you to interact with staff in the basecamp with caution as this scale of operation will undoubtedly also involve personnel on the surface. Anyone involved in illegally removing the indigenous Ut'aran people from their home world, and subjecting them to surgical implant procedures, must be assumed to be dangerous.

"I have analyzed the doctor's data and concur with her findings.

"End Message. Standing by to record reply."

Ethan leaned back against the wall and took several deep breaths. Holy frak. *There's no way of knowing who I can trust.*

"Begin recording," he said, rubbing his forehead as he struggled to fit this new bit of information into his thinking. "Kaycee, first thing I need to say is I'm sorry I doubted you. Right now, we're trapped inside the Rockpile, so we're safe as long as we don't stick our noses into places they don't belong. We won't be going anywhere, and with any luck that will keep us out of trouble, but that goes both ways. You also need to make sure you don't get into anything up there to get yourself into a stink.

"We've got two days before the shuttle returns to pick us up. We'll figure out our exit strategy, when we get back aboard.

"Marti, I assume you will also listen to this message once I open the door, so you need to make sure that everything we've recorded down here for the last two days is also available to Kaycee. I know her well enough to know she won't turn loose of this, but she needs to do whatever she has to in order to keep the ship safe. That has to be her first priority. We will keep our heads down, but you all must do the same.

"Walker out."

He thumped his balled up fist against his forehead and growled.

This was supposed to be a gravy run, and a once in a lifetime vacation. How the frak did it go this far sidewise?

"Are you ready to transmit?" he asked.

"Yes, Captain Walker," the automech said. "As soon as the door opens, I will reestablish communications with the Marti awareness. Is there anything else I can do for you, sir?"

"Remind me never to doubt one of Kaycee's hunches again."

"As you wish, sir," it said. The face reappeared the instant he pushed the door open.

When he walked out of the closet and looked around, the main gallery had filled with staff members. There were no open seats around the table but Ethan realized the less they interacted, the safer they'd be. Several groups of anthropologists were arguing with each other about what might be happening, and Angel and Nuko had moved out of the line of fire and were standing near the back wall.

The captain caught the handler's eye and jerked his head toward the door to the dorm rooms and the MedBay.

Angel nodded, tapping Nuko on the arm to make sure she followed as they slid toward the door. Fortunately, no one saw them sneak out.

CHAPTER SEVENTEEN

"Operations control," the face of a middle-aged man appeared on the screen in the MedBay. Ammo had swung the screen so he could see that she was in a diagnostic chamber but nothing else in the room.

"We've got a medical emergency on the *Olympus Dawn*. We need help. It's our doctor." She stared at him like she was studying him for dissection, even as her voice carried a tone of almost abject terror.

"What kind of medical emergency? Don't you have your own medic?" he asked, apparently unperturbed by her plea.

"It's our doctor who's injured. She's having seizures," she said.

"What happened to her?" he asked.

"She was exercising and one of the machines slammed her. She's got a serious head wound, and the seizures just started. We got her into our MedBay but they're getting worse."

"You don't have anyone else aboard with medical training?"

"Quinn's got basic emergency triage only," she said, glancing off screen like she was watching something. "This looks like a brain injury, but without a doctor we can't tell."

"Bring her to our medical center, I'll have doctor Forrester meet you there," he said.

"Problem with that. Last time we tried to leave the ship they chased us back inside with guns. Your OpsSec Chief ordered us not to leave the ship under any circumstances."

"Stand by, let me check that."

"Frakking hurry. She looks like she's dying," she said.

"Copy," he said as the comm went blank. Ammo winked at Kaycee who stood out of optic range outside the door to the MedBay watching her performance.

After several seconds, the screen lit up as the controller came back. "Mr. Parker said you can bring her to the medical center. He'll send a team to the airlock to escort you, and you will not be allowed access anywhere except—"

"Did you miss the part where I said she was having seizures?" she challenged. "She's got a head and neck injury and she's flopping around like a slug on a hot recycler manifold. We have her strapped down to a diagnostic bed. We can't transport her. Send the frakking doctor you dimflatch."

"I work for a living, bitch," he said. "You got a problem with my boss, that's you and him."

She rolled her eyes and looked like she was going to jump through the screen at him. "What I've got is a problem with somebody who doesn't understand how liability works. Our doctor is Keira Smythe-Caldwell. Does any part of that name register on your feeble scanners?"

"Not really," he said.

"You ever hear of Smythe Biomedical?" She paused while he connected the data points in his brain. "Yah, she's part of that family. Do you know how many frikking lawyers they will have ripping you and your lousy station to space dust if you let her die because you got your shorthairs twisted?"

He started tapping something into the console in front of him. Probably checking their identity records to confirm who their doctor was. "Stand by. I'll explain your situation to the boss."

"Just hurry the frak up," she said as the screen went off

again.

When it lit backup, it was Bradley Parker. "The doctor will be there in a couple minutes. I don't want any problems. Is that clear?"

"That will depend on you," she said. "Just hurry." She slapped her hand down on the panel and disconnected the comm.

Kaycee was grinning and trying not to laugh out loud. "You really do have steel eggs. You know that?"

"Nah, I just read the shift-boss's face. He wasn't going to fall our way unless I spanked him, so I grabbed the closest paddle."

"Why'd you think that would work?" she asked, stepping back into the MedBay and taking a seat on the stool by the bed.

"Looking at him I could tell he's a low-mid-grade administrator in the upper-middle of his career," she said. "He's comfortable when people above his paygrade push, or he'd have risen farther up the stack by now. I borrowed your family name to make sure he knew I was breathing better air than him."

"I'm ready with the collar," Quinn said. He'd been working on modifying a cervical support brace at one of the lab benches in the back of the MedBay. Marti had printed several components and they'd cobbled them onto the collar.

"What will that do?" Kaycee asked.

"One of the prisoners in the program at Upstate had been a doctor before he grew an unhealthy fascination with cutting people into little pieces without anesthetic. He was a smart guy though, so he figured out a way to jam the comm to his implant. It was almost a week before we realized he'd done it and it got a lot messy before we figured it out."

"It doesn't block the communications channel," Marti

corrected. "When activated, it will generate a moderate level electrical impulse that should scramble the internal signal pathways in the implant."

"You built one of these? In a half hour?"

"It's not that complex. I just ripped the guts out of a contact stun wand, and dialed down the power so that it won't knock him out," he said. "It'll sting enough that it won't be a pleasant experience for him, but it'll work."

"Dr. Forrester and Operations Director Parker are entering the far airlock on the cargo module," Marti said.

"Parker's with him?" Kaycee asked. "I don't trust him a short millimeter."

"Affirmative. They are cycling through the outer lock now." Marti brought up an optic from the cargo container so they could watch the two men approach. "Mr. Parker is carrying a stun pistol in a back pouch. They left four extra security officers outside the container."

"Frak, let's go see if we can get the doctor inside on his own," Ammo said, biting on her lip.

"If Parker pushes to come along, then what?" Kaycee asked.

"Then I pound him for ruining my night out." Quinn grinned. "I can make sure he gets no farther than the inside door if I have to."

"Let me see if I can sweet talk him first," Ammo jumped up and headed out the door with Quinn close on her heels.

"I'll keep an eye on things from here," Kaycee hollered after them, spinning the screen around where she could see it as she set up her scanner equipment. This would be their only chance to get the info they needed, and if they missed something important, it might be bad.

Maybe not as bad as it would be if Quinn had to get physical with Parker, but still, this had the potential to go foobed quick.

Marti split the viewscreen to show an internal optic from the ship's airlock along with the one that showed Dr. Forrester and Parker outside the hatch.

"You stay here and try to look worried," Ammo said.

He laughed. "That's easy enough. We're about to do some top tier stupid shit you know."

"I know, but not worried like that," she said. "Worried like the doctor is injured and we're in a rush to get back to her."

"I never thought I'd need acting classes to be a security handler."

She winked at him and palmed the door open. She stepped out onto the catwalk and they both took a step back as she intentionally crowded them to put them off balance. "Nothing personal, but just the doctor."

Parker shook his head and swung his arm toward where he had the stunner concealed.

Quinn widened his stance in the airlock and also reached behind his back. In the optic, Kaycee could see him lock his hand around his own pistol.

"Why?" Dr. Forrester asked.

She shrugged never looking away from the OpsSec Chief. She was talking only to Parker. "Seems to me you had your security people pointing guns at us to keep us from breathing recycler stink. That's more like the question you need to answer first."

"I'd told you to stay in your ship—"

"Let's go back and re-emphasize the *guns* part of what I just said." She shook her head. "You're welcome to keep your guards and guns outside our cargo container until the captain gets back, but in the meantime the doctor needs to follow me."

Parker shook his head. "Then we're done." He turned to leave.

Dr. Forrester didn't move. "If their doctor is critically injured, I need to help."

"No doctor. I can't let you go in there alone." He reached out to grab the doctor by the arm.

"Bradley, if I may have a word with you," he said, backing up along the catwalk far enough to not be heard.

"Can we still pick them up?" Kaycee asked, as the optic tracked them. Marti turned up the gain on the audio.

"I don't want you in there alone," Parker whispered.

Forrester shrugged. "I'm not big with it either, but you're worried about what they were doing when they tried to get past your guards. Maybe I can find out. If there was someone else in the airlock and it wasn't your people getting over excited, then we need to figure out what they were up to."

He shook his head again. "There are at least three of them in there, and you'd be alone."

"Dr. Caldwell is down. There are only two others on the crew that aren't planetside," he said.

"But have you seen the size of their handler? He's a freak of nature." Parker glanced back at Quinn. "He counts for three by himself."

Kaycee grinned despite the tension of the situation.

"I'll be alright. They won't give me trouble while I'm working on her," he said. "If she needs more than what I can do in their MedBay, I'll have to bring her out."

"That would put her in a position where we'd have more control over the situation," Parker said. "You can make sure that happens. Can't you?"

"Probably so," Forrester said. "I'll have to do an assessment of her condition, and I'm sure if she's convulsing she'll need a standard of care that they can't provide on a freighter."

Parker sighed, nodding. "I don't like it but maybe it's worth the risk."

"I'll maintain constant communication through my link anyway," Forrester said, reaching up and rubbing the side of his neck.

Finally, Parker turned back toward where Ammo stood waiting.

"I've agreed to let the doctor assess the situation," he said. "He can get your doctor stabilized, and if he determines that she needs treatment, he'll make arrangements to transport her to our medical center."

"Thank you," she said.

"You need to understand that I know you tried to pull something when you flashed your boobs at my men," he said.

"Disappointed you missed the show?" Quinn asked.

"Hardly," he said, waving his hand dismissively. "I also know that Dr. Caldwell has been sticking her nose into things she should be leaving alone. I don't trust any of you, so if we don't see him back here in thirty minutes, we will board your ship. Even if we have to cut through the hull to do it."

CHAPTER EIGHTEEN

"I don't feel safe talking about this in the open, but there's a problem and we need to be ready for a stink," Ethan said as he sat on the edge of his bunk and leaned forward. The rest of his crew, with the exception of Marti sat in a close circle on the floor in front of him.

"What kind of stink?" Angel asked, she sat forward and her eyes narrowed as she switched back into her security handler personality.

He shrugged. "I don't know, but it turns out that Kaycee was right and there was something more than personality deficit disorder wrong with Marcus Elarah. She says she thinks he's Ut'aran and that there are others working on the station."

"Working on the station?" Nuko asked, shaking her head but more in bewilderment than disbelief. "They're all freaked out over making sure nothing gets left outside, and they've taken natives up there?"

"That makes sense though, if you think about how they look," Angel said. "Short. Wide. And over-muscled. Just like him."

Ethan nodded. "His last name is also the same as the Ut'aran word for the grasslands."

"I wonder if he was from the Ar'ah tribe?"

"No telling," Rene said. He sat back against the side of Ethan's bunk and shook his head too. "But where he came from is less important than how he ended up on Proxima."

"And why," the captain added. "I think we—"

The air pressure changed and Ethan's ears popped. It was subtle, but years of working in space tuned them all in to the early warnings of an atmosphere fluctuation. They didn't have a pumping airlock in the Rockpile, but double doors kept things stabilized. The air pressure inside wasn't much different from outside, but moving winds made the effect enough that there was no doubt.

"We've got a breach," Angel whispered as she leapt to her feet. The sound of a slamming door thumped in the distance. Nuko and Ethan bounced up almost as fast as the handler, but Rene was exhausted from his outing and rolled over to push himself up using the bed.

The captain slipped over to the door and pulled it open a crack. The corridor was empty but there were strange sounds in the distance. He listened for several seconds before he leaned back and shook his head. It sounded like people fighting. "We need to get to the locker room and suit up."

"What's going on?"

It sounds like there's a war in the main gallery right now.

"You think they gave up on talking it out?" Rene asked.

"No, I think they're killing each other," he said. "It sounds like screaming and crashing things."

"If the Ut'arans got inside, we don't have time to talk it over," Angel said, stepping past him to check the hall.

She waved the rest of them out and Ethan took off at a dead run down the corridor to the back entrance to the locker room. He pulled the door open slowly to make sure the room was empty, then shot across to the exit on the opposite side. He could hear voices on the other side. Undeniably not human voices.

Kicking a bench loose from the floor he jerked on it several times before it came apart enough he could get it wedged under the manual door handle. It wouldn't hold much, but if it slowed them down enough that they could get into their PSE then at least they could give the natives a fair fight. Once it was as secure as he could make it, he turned around and helped Angel wedge the opposite door.

Nuko and Rene were backed into the autovalet and suiting up. "What if the others want to get suited," Nuko asked while the arms swung pieces of her exoshell into place.

"Staff all keep their suits in their rooms and not here," Angel reminded her.

"If they can get there," Ethan whispered. "There are extra suits here in case any of them run in this direction."

"If they run in this direction, they're being chased," she said. "Opening the door to an Ut'aran would be nogo."

He nodded, looking at Rene who stumbled forward out of his alcove and was looking decidedly unhappy to be back in his suit. "See if you can connect to Marti," he said. "Nuko, come listen at the door while Angel and I get our kit on."

He jumped over to his locker as she slid into his place at the door. Slamming his back against the sensor, he triggered the polymorphic liner to unfurl and watched as Rene shook his head and took up a position at the other door.

"I can't reach Marti," the engineer said.

"Did they take out the automech?" Ethan asked.

"I don't know," he said. "I don't know how tough that body is, but I think it's more likely that the power locker got shut, and the body's AA hasn't figured out what to do to reestablish a link."

"Will our suit comm reach the ship?" he asked. The actuator arms on the autovalet started assembling the exoshell around him and he struggled to ignore it while he tried to work their situation over in his mind.

There have to be options.

"I don't think so," Rene said. "The PSE comm are pretty low power. Ordinarily they'd link with repeaters to a major transmitter, but I don't know if they'd risk deploying something like that outside. The Windwalkers carry special comm gear but we're probably limited to a thousand meters."

"What are our options?" Angel asked, stepping forward and swinging her arms around to settle the exosuit onto her shoulders. "We can't fight them in here. The PSE limiters are overriding us and so we're lightly armored but nowhere near as strong as the Ut'arans."

"Good point," he said as his autovalet turned loose and he stumbled out of the unit.

"I am sure there's an override," Rene said, waving Ethan over so he could try to figure it out. Leaning his back against the door, he spun the captain around and opened a side panel on his power pack. He poked around for several seconds and then Ethan shot up off the floor nearly smashing his head into the ceiling.

"Be careful. It'll burn power and heat up quick if you push it too hard," the engineer said.

"Angel, trade me places," Ethan said. Bouncing across the room in a single step and crashing into the wall beside the door. "Holy shit, it's like being back on Mars, but fast."

"It'll give us an edge in strength, if we can keep from killing ourselves," she said, nodding as he set his shoulder against the door.

Nuko walked over and watched as he adjusted the power levels on Angel's suit and she launched the same way. She had curled her arms over her head to keep from driving her skull through the ceiling. As a result, she bounced twice, once up and then again as her arms shot her back to the floor.

"Shuffle," Ethan said. "Like you were on an asteroid."

"It's the accelerometers," Rene said. "I don't think I can adjust those without tools."

"We'll learn to adapt," Angel said. Apparently taking the captain's advice, she shuffled over and leaned against the door.

"Next," he said, looking at Nuko.

"You first," she said.

He shook his head. "I don't think my suit will handle it." He spun her around and started making the adjustments. We didn't do any repairs to it since it didn't look like we were going back outside. The overheating is bad enough that it would flat line and bake me alive before I could be useful."

"Then what the hell are you going to do?" she asked.

"Depend on you three to keep me alive," he said as she rocketed off the floor and curled to let the back of her suit take the hit.

"Voices," Ethan said, pressing his ear against the door. "Human, I think."

"We need to let them in," Nuko said, hopping across the floor to stand beside him.

The door actuator motor hummed but the bench they'd wedged under it held. The handle rattled and then someone started beating on it. Several people from the sounds of it.

"For the love of frak open the damn door," someone roared like distant thunder. It sounded like Toby if he had his eggs in a vice.

Another voice screamed. "Let us in." That one was Tash. There were others out there with them, but he couldn't pick them out.

Ethan nodded at Nuko and she kicked the bottom of the bench out of the way as he settled his shoulder against the door and pulled it open slightly. Hands shot through the opening and started grabbing at him and he opened the door the rest of the way. Toby, Sandi, and Tash all shot in but the two others behind them stood for a moment staring back down the hall.

Ethan hesitated for an instant and in that moment an arrow, almost the size of a spear, whistled through the air and drove through the ribs of the mission medic, driving her out of reach, and pinning her against the wall at the end of the corridor. Leela blinked in surprise and opened her mouth like she wanted to scream but no sound came out. Instead she made small gurgling noises and spatters of red splashed out all over the other person who had turned to see what had happened.

The captain reached out and grabbed the back of his thinskin. Remembering the power setting of his PSE, he stopped before he broke the man's neck. It didn't matter because a wakat was on him a second later, grabbing him by the arm, and twisting him around. The sound of breaking bones preceded his scream of agony by only an instant.

Without thinking Ethan leapt forward, grabbing the creature by its head and with a twist, flung it away. It smashed into the opposite wall with a howl and crumpled in a heap of red and brown, its body thrashing uncontrollably. Realizing he was outside the room, he spun, stealing a glance down the hall. Three Ut'arans charged in his direction with several more wakat chasing behind them.

"Frak, he growled, shoving off the wall and scooping the injured man off the floor as he dove back into the locker room. He hit the floor and rolled to a stop half way across to where Angel stood. Nuko slammed the door behind him and shoved the bench back into place with one hand.

"What the fuck happened?" Ethan roared.

"I don't know," Toby whispered as he crawled across the

floor to the man that Ethan rescued. His arm was twisted almost all the way around behind his body and he was rocking back and forth in silent sobs.

"I think they got in through the overhead exit," Sandi said. She sat with her back against one wall, and was gulping air as she stared at the one on the floor.

"Do we have a medkit in here?" Angel asked. Tash nodded to a cabinet by the door to the entry room.

"Angel, you tend to him," he said. "Nuko, you watch her door. And you three get suited."

When Toby refused to leave the man on the floor, Ethan jerked him up by the back of his thinskin. "What the hell is your problem. Get suited," he shouted as the door behind him started rattling.

"That's his boyfriend," Tash said. She'd already backed into an autovalet and a liner was wrapping itself around her.

Shit. He felt like an ass for almost a full second before the door handle twisted and the sound of metal stretching snapped him back into the reality of their situation. *I can feel bad for him later.*

"That's not going to hold," he growled. "Rene, is there anything in here we can use as a weapon?"

The engineer shook his head.

Another sound started up outside the door, but this time it came from beside it. *Wall panels being shredded.* "Shit, they're determined aren't they?"

The lights flickered and then a loud shriek and a sizzling noise before total darkness fell on them. A sudden surge of gravity slammed Toby onto the ground with a heavy thud.

"Main power is out," Rene said, reporting the obvious.

The night vision visor swung over Ethan's eyes and he could see the glow from where something had grabbed one of the wires in the wall and fried itself. It hadn't gotten hot enough to burn, but the sparks from the short circuit were visible through the wall in infrared.

"Remember, they can see in the dark," Sandi hissed. Ethan turned to face her.

"So can we," he said.

"I can't" she said. "My suit didn't power up all the way." She was struggling to pull herself out of the now dead autovalet. Her liner glowed as its power supply heated the surface. She had both arms and her body backpanel on, but her legs pieces hung loaded into the assembly arms waiting to be attached.

"Obviously your liner did," he said, spinning in the opposite direction. Tash was almost completely suited although it looked like none of the augment parts were even close to the right size. She threw herself forward and twisted to get her body pried loose.

Taking inventory of their situation, he turned toward where Angel was working on Toby's boyfriend. She rocked back on her heels and looked up at him, shaking her head. Glancing at the mission commander who couldn't see her in the dark, she slid a finger across her throat. *He's not going to make it.*

"I think we're all losing this one," he muttered.

He turned and looked back toward the door to the hallway and squared his shoulders, determined not to go out without taking a pound of alien ass with him. Angel stood up and stepped up beside him while Nuko took the other side.

"This is going to get ugly," he said, glancing at both of them.

"But it's been a good ride," Angel whispered.

"Too soon," Nuko said.

To the side he heard Rene grunting and straining to get

Sandi out of the autovalet. Tash was helping and the two of them were prying furiously at it.

The door rattled several times before four hands broke through the wall on one side of the frame. With a guttural roar it exploded outward taking shards of frame and metal with it. Two male Ut'arans bounced through the opening and stopped, lowering their arrow throwers and staring wide-eyed at the three of them in the middle of the room.

A female with long flowing hair stepped through behind them. Both of the males took a step to the side and she walked into the room with a wakat behind her. "Marat akUt'ar?" one said, offering his left hand to her, palm forward but with his fingers down. "Oo'aka at'ah echa pra'keet."

"Mo'oh ke'esha." She reached out and turned his hand over so that it faced up and bumped it with her right palm.

"She's in charge," the captain whispered, remembering what Dr. Ansari had explained.

Her head snapped in his direction. "Ta'raht shee Marat akUt'ar?"

Behind him, from where he still knelt on the floor Toby translated, "Of tribe is shiny man?"

Tribe of the shiny man? Ethan thought. Glancing around he understood. The heat from their PSE made them glow in his night vision, and the Ut'arans see in the dark. In infrared.

She's seen people in exosuits before.

"We are of the shiny man tribe," he said. "Marat akUt'ar?"

Looking down at the floor, she held out her left hand, palm forward.

Now what?

CHAPTER NINETEEN

Kaycee watched the internal security optics as Dr. Forrester followed Ammo through the interconnect corridor with Quinn following behind. They stopped at the entrance to the main lounge of the mid-deck and Ammo turned to face him. "I'm sorry Doc, but Quinn says this might be unpleasant."

"What's going on—" His eyes bulged as the handler twisted both arms behind his back and held them with one hand while he slapped the modified cervical collar around his neck with the other. He cinched the latch closed and tapped the button.

Forrester collapsed to his knees and made a strange gurgling sound as the stun wand circuitry jolted him with what was probably more charge that it took to scramble his implant.

"I thought you said it would sting, not liquefy him," Kaycee said from where she stood out of sight in the MedBay door.

"Yah, oops," he said, shrugging. "It might be a little high."

Ammo dropped in front of him to see if he was still alert enough to register her presence. His eyes rolled in her direction. "Do you know where you are Dr. Forrester?" she asked.

His head snapped up and down several times as he gasped for air. He obviously couldn't talk.

"Can you turn it down?" She looked up at Quinn, almost pleading on the doctor's behalf.

"I'd have to shut it off for a couple seconds to do it," he said. "Whoever's on the other end of his implant might grab control."

"We've got to be able to talk to him," Kaycee said.

The handler knelt behind him and knocked Forrester flat down on his face with a gentle nudge. Tapping the button on the collar, he set his knee in the middle of his back to hold him pinned to the floor. He slid his finger up under the unit and fumbled around for a couple seconds before he hit the switch again.

This time when the unit powered up the doctor only gasped. He struggled to pull his hands under him and push himself backup onto his knees. Reaching up, he tried to grab at the collar but Quinn swatted his hand away.

"Leave it alone," Ammo said. "We're trying to help."

"Marti, can you tell if it interrupted the signal?" Kaycee said.

Forrester turned in her direction but Ammo reached up to grab his chin to hold his head in place. She jerked her hand back. "Eyes on me," she whispered.

"I am unable to detect RF from his implant," it reported, "However that does not mean the device is not broadcasting in some unknown manner."

"We'll have to risk it," Kaycee said, walking out to join them on the deck. "Dr. Forrester, are you alright?"

He shook his head. "What the hell are you doing to me?"

"We wanted to cut you off from your implant," she said. "I need to talk to you and I don't want our conversation being overheard."

"Implant?" he asked, looking confused. He reached up toward the collar and Quinn smacked his hand down again. "That's a commlink." He tried to glare at the handler but it came out looking weak and helpless.

"I'm afraid it might be much more than that," she said. "I'd like to get you in a diagnostic bed, so we can take a look at it and get you to answer some questions for us."

She reached out to help him up.

"Careful he bites," Ammo warned.

Quinn bent over, grabbing him around the waist and set him on his feet. "Only if you grab him gently. A hard contact keeps it from sparking you."

"We need to hurry," Kaycee said, spinning to head back to the MedBay.

"I thought you were injured," Forrester said as the handler led him by his arm after her.

"We had to get you here," she said, stepping to the side as Quinn picked the doctor up and strapped him down onto the diagnostic bed. "I need to know what's going on with the Ut'arans."

"Nothing is going on with them," he said.

She swung the diagnostic imager over his head and pulled the screen in front of her. The unit powered up and she watched as the data began to coalesce into an image.

"I know that's not true," she said. "I came to your office to ask you about Marcus Elarah."

He looked confused. "When?"

"The day we got here," she said.

He shook his head like he genuinely didn't remember.

"It doesn't matter," she said. "Marcus is Ut'aran, isn't he?"

"Of course not," he said.

"Then explain this." She grabbed a thinpad that contained the scan of the guard and held it up where he could see the display.

"Marcus let you take a scan of him?"

She shook her head. "That's a native isn't it?"

He looked at the screen for several seconds before he clamped his eyes and his mouth closed.

"He's also got an implant doesn't he?" she challenged.

Again, she got no response.

"You use those implants to control their behavior don't you?" Quinn asked.

"That's an Alphatron Inbit 3650, isn't it," she said. "You just received 300 of them."

"We've used implants to track migration patterns of the natives," he said, opening his eyes again. "It's a little controversial, but it helps develop a better understanding ..." his voice trailed off as he apparently realized she wasn't buying it.

"We know what you can do with an AIT implant," she said. "You might use them as tracking devices, but you can also use them to implant knowledge and control behavior."

"It's just a tracking device," he said.

"Then why have you implanted them in natives working here on the station?" Ammo asked.

"There are no Ut'arans on the station," he insisted.

"Really?" Kaycee leaned over him and glared. "Then explain where I got that scan?"

"It's not Marcus?" he asked, his voice sounding strange, almost like he was pleading for something.

"It was one of the security people stationed outside our airlock several hours ago," she said, tossing the thinpad to Ammo. "But thank you for confirming that Marcus is a native too."

"I think I need to just quit talking and let you draw your own conclusions," Forrester said, staring up at the bottom of the scanner head.

"I'm trying to give you a chance to explain what's going on here," she said. "The conclusion I'm leaning toward is most definitely not one you want to be a party to."

"And that is?" He didn't look at her.

"Let's talk about something else first," she said, pulling the scanner back and swinging it out of the way. "When did you get your implant?"

"I've had it for a long time," he said. "Almost as long as I've had my surgical arm controller implant."

"How long?"

"A long time." His eyes flashed in a moment of confused agony and he blinked several times. "Why?"

"Before you took your posting here?" she prodded.

He closed his eyes and nodded. "It's just a sub-vocal commlink."

She shook her head. "No it's more than that." She turned the screen so he could see it. "If I'm not mistaken that's an AIT 3650 isn't it?"

The color drained from his face and he nodded.

"Who did it?"

"I don't remember. It was before I got here ... I think." He'd started sweating and closed his eyes.

"Doesn't that strike you as funny that you can't remember?" she asked.

"Some patients have ... post surgical ... memory lapse?" He struggled to find a logical reason. Obviously, there wasn't one he liked within his limited number of potential options.

"Or the memory was overwritten," she offered. "With an AIT 3650, new memories can be uploaded."

"That's preposterous," he said, weakly.

"I've seen it done," Quinn said from the doorway. "They did that as part of a prisoner rehab program on Earth."

"I don't know how it works, but I assume it's like a localized BES scan, but backwards," Kaycee said. "Your implant has three modules. One on the C-2, one on the C-3, and another one carved into a hollow in the occipital bone. There's also an array of nanowires inserted along your spinal column and into your brain. Does this sound at all familiar?"

"Yes. It's the same design as the ones I've implanted," he said.

"Now we're getting to the truth," she said, glancing over at Ammo who was watching the chrono over the bed. "So let's revisit why you have natives with implants working as labor here in the station."

He let out a slow breath. "As far as I know they're all accidents of culture contamination."

"Culture contamination?" Quinn asked.

"We've been here more than forty years," he said. "In that much time, we've had more than a few instances where a native Ut'aran ended up exposed to something that would have affected their culture."

"When that happens you bring them up here and implant them," Kaycee offered.

He nodded.

"Do you also wipe out their memories of home?" Quinn asked.

"I didn't like the idea either, but it's better than just killing them," he said.

"So you overwrite their memories?" she asked.

"We give them new skills. That might replace some of their previous knowledge," he said. "It wasn't my idea to do this. I've only been here for ten years. It's been happening a lot longer than that, and before … it was a lot less … surgical."

"But why do you have an implant?" Kaycee asked, glancing up at the screen again.

"I didn't know I did until you showed me," he said. "I thought my comm implant was getting old and causing me pain sometimes. There's nobody else here with the skillset to check it over, so I just put up with it. Most days I don't have a problem."

"Until a nosy ship doctor shows up and asks questions," Kaycee said. She would have felt sorry for him but she couldn't absolve him of responsibility.

"How many Ut'arans have you implanted?" Ammo asked.

"I don't know. I only remember a few," he said.

"There were at least fifty doing hard labor in the container by my count," Quinn said.

"If what you say is true, I don't know if I can trust my memory," he said, looking up at the screen and shrugging.

"Who's behind this program?" Quinn asked.

"The only one I know who is aware of it is Brad Parker," he said. "He's been here longer than anyone else."

"It's easy enough to spot a native so there have to be others who know," Kaycee said. "For frak sake, everyone who's seen a native Ut'aran should be able to pick them out. We've been here two-and-a-half days and can spot them."

He shook his head. "You may be right, but I can't think beyond what they might have overwritten. I just don't know."

"Do you know if there's any way to override an implant?" she asked.

"You intend to cut them loose?" he gasped. "Even a few of them might be unstoppable."

"I don't know what we intend to do, but I have to explore the options," she said. "Can it be done?"

"Not easily," he said. "The brainstem tie in would take hours. The commlink is in the C-3 module, the upload data buffer is in the occipital unit, and the C-2 is the ... the failsafe."

"He means the kill switch," Quinn said.

"You've only got fifteen minutes before he has to get back out there, or they'll be sending a squad of mini-brutes in," Ammo said.

"You can sever the connections to my failsafe in a couple minutes," Forrester said. "If you disable it, I can fight back. It has no independent transceiver and won't work alone. At least then I have a chance."

"How do you know you can fight it?" Kaycee asked.

"We've had a couple patients successfully resist," he said. "Without the pain side of the implant, it's hard to condition the responses and the patient becomes uncontrollable."

"Won't someone just hook you backup?" she offered.

"I'm the only qualified neuro-surgeon on the station," he said. "Other than you."

She made her decision even though she wasn't sure she could explain why. "Quinn, untie him and flip him over."

"You're sure you want to do that?" he asked. "What about his memories of what he's seen in here?"

"If I don't give them a reason to suspect anything funny happened in here, they won't probe me," he said.

"Eventually, it will happen." Ammo shook her head but stepped up to help roll him over, anyway.

"You all should be gone before it comes to that," he said. "I don't like where this whole program might be going, and I swear I will do everything in my power to help you shut it down."

"Why should we believe you?" the handler asked as he uncinched the restraints.

"C-2," he said. "They've got a knife to my spine literally. Knowing what we've done here, there's no way they'll ever let me walk away. My only hope is to take them down first."

"Who are they?" Ammo asked.

"I don't know. It's got to be well above Parker's air supply," he said. "But at this point I'm the only one who can find that out."

Twelve minutes later, they'd given Dr. Forrester a dose of a mild psychotropic to confuse him, and Kaycee lay on the table with a surgical seal around her head. Hopefully, it would give him enough of a mnemonic image to cue a false recollection to cling to if his implant tried to dig.

Quinn and Ammo held the doctor by both arms as he wobbled on his feet. "Thank you for your help," he whispered. "I'm ready."

Quinn jerked the collar off his neck and flung it on the counter where it would be out of sight.

"Thank you, Doctor. You've saved her life," Ammo said, driving the false memory deeper into his mind. It wouldn't be much of a shield, but it was the best they could do in the short time they had.

"If you'll follow me, we need to get you back before Parker comes looking for you," the handler said.

"Of course you're right," he said, turning to follow Quinn out the door. Ammo fell in behind them, shutting the lights off in the MedBay so that Kaycee could open her eyes and get the surgical hardware off.

She swung the screen around to watch them escort Forrester back while she peeled the skullcap and sensor lines off her head.

"I did not want to interrupt while you were involved in your procedure doctor," Marti said, "but there is a problem on the planet."

"What?" she said.

"I have lost contact with my automech body," it said.

"That's an engineering issue isn't it?" she asked, watching

as the optic feed showed Parker and Dr. Ansari trotting across the catwalk in the cargo container. A group of security guards followed them.

"Perhaps, but I do not believe so," Marti said.

"Stand by," she said, sliding her finger along the edge of the screen to bring the sound up. "Quinn you've got a wall of trouble coming across the container."

"Copy, now be quiet," he said, glancing up at the optic behind him in the airlock. He palmed the door mechanism open just as the party arrived.

"Where's the patient?" Parker asked, looking shocked that they didn't have her with them.

"I got her stabilized, so there's no need to transport her," Forrester said.

"And we weren't too fuzzy with having her off the ship where we couldn't visit her," Ammo added, glaring at the OpsSec Director.

"There's been an incident on the surface," Ansari said, pulling a thinpad out of his pocket and handing it to her.

"What kind of incident?" Quinn asked as Ammo opened a file on the screen.

"We've had a major contamination incident," he said.

"What he means to say is that the Rockpile was attacked by a native hunting party, and it looks like either everyone was killed or captured," Parker said.

"What?" Ammo gasped and leaned against the doorjamb with one hand while she watched the file play out. Marti had linked into the thinpad and was displaying the image as it ran.

"We think your crewmates are among the ones taken prisoner," he said. "Unfortunately, until we go down there and look around, we don't know anything."

"You're putting together a rescue mission," Quinn said.

"I'll get my gear and—"

"You will not be going with us," Parker said.

"There's already been enough contamination without having another inexperienced person on the ground," Dr. Ansari said. "We will be leaving as soon as it's safe to do so. In the meantime you need to tend to your injured crewmember and let us do our jobs."

CHAPTER TWENTY

Ethan sat and watched their captors doing things he didn't understand. Even a little. When they stopped for what he assumed was a mid-day meal, it was the first time he'd seen all of them at once. As they traveled, they remained scattered out along the trail and he'd guessed there were twenty-five, but when they all gathered together, there was double that number. There were at least twice that many wakats.

This was the first break they'd taken since they left the basecamp. They'd been walking since just after sunrise and he guessed it was around noon.

While they were walking, they kept the humans tied together with a rope loop that wound around their necks and then back around their ankles. Once they settled into a clearing to rest, the Ut'arans untied their prisoners and forced them to sit on the grass with the rope that had bound them, laid in a ring around them like a border. Obviously, their captors expected the prisoners to remain inside the ring, because otherwise they seemed to pay them little attention.

The wakats reclining just on the other side of the boundary line like guard dogs, made sure trying to escape was not something they'd care to risk. Up close, a wakat had more than enough teeth and speed to terrify anyone.

Several of the natives stood at a distance staring off into the trees like sentinels, but most sat and talked while they ate. The warrior princess perched on a rock and stared at the prisoners, never smiling and barely moving. She listened while several members of the party took turns talking to her. Each time they repeated the greeting ritual, always with a left hand, and often with the fingers down.

As close as Ethan could tell, her name was Tuula Mir'ah since that was always the first phrase any of them said when they approached her. "Do you understand what she's saying?" he asked, looking at Sandi and Tash.

They both shook their heads.

"I know some words, but not enough to follow the conversations," Tash said.

"Some," Toby said. He rolled his eyes open. He lay flat on the ground almost unconscious and gasping as he struggled to gulp down enough air to think. The mission commander wasn't going to make it much further. He was the only prisoner that wore no part of a PSE. For the last several klick, Ethan and Angel had literally carried him along. Even though it meant he didn't have to support his own weight, his blood was clearly not moving in the right direction.

"She's the one in charge," the captain said.

He nodded. "Tuula means leader or queen."

"She's too young to be ascended," Sandi said. She'd been staggering for the last kilometer but at least she was wearing a suit liner that kept her blood from pooling in her legs. For her, it was the fatigue of trying to walk upright and carry a body that weighed over twice her normal weight. Nuko had been propping her up since they first went outside the Rockpile.

"It sounds like they're all asking forgiveness for not being with truth," he said. "Whatever that means? I'm having trouble concentrating, so I'm not sure…" He gasped again and his eyes glazed over for several seconds.

"One of them is unhappy we move too slowly," he said.

"I think."

"Might be prudent to move as slow as we can then," Angel said. She was working on Toby's legs trying to help his heart push the blood back to the top of his body. She looked like she knew it was a lost cause, but she wasn't giving up on him.

Mir'ah looked at Angel and stood up, pushing the Ut'aran in front of her to the side. Lowering her eyes, she walked across the clearing and stopped just outside the edge of the rope ring. "Echa et'ah marat akUt'ar. We'ir sharrah kan'doh nee."

She's asking your permission to leave me behind," Toby said. "I think."

"I look to know your mind," she said, looking only at Ethan. "He is to we'ir Sharrah Ut'ar. We give him to … all trees and korah."

"You speak our language?" Sandi gasped.

The captain glanced at Nuko and she nodded. *If there are natives on the station, why would she be surprised?*

"A small amount I know. Yes," she said, still refusing to look away from him. "You are Marat akUt'ar, but words of your brother lead Mir'ah."

She looked down at Toby and touched her forehead with the back of her right hand. "Slow is not good. Mor'et pra' korah," she looked off to the side. "Weak one is slow. Will kill all Cha'nee to be slow. Must we'ir Sharrah. We live and make nature good. Yes?"

"She is saying it's time to leave me to the jungle," Toby said. "The we'ir sharrah is the ritual of giving the weak or old ones to the korah."

"No frakking way," Angel said, launching herself up and almost a meter into the air. Their suits were still running at full boost. "I didn't carry his ass all this way only to leave him here to be eaten."

Before she hit the ground, every wakat was on its feet and most of the hunting party had their arrow slings ready to let fly. "Stand down," Ethan growled, grabbing her arm to force her back to a seated position. "This is not the time for it."

"We can't let her—"

"Korah feed at night," he said. "Watchtower has to know what happened. There will be a shuttle before then."

"But what else—"

"The captain is right," Toby said. "Predators only feed in the dark. I can lay here and rest until help finds me."

"I'll stay with you," Sandi said. "We'ir sharrah … me too." She slapped her hand against the breast plate of her partial PSE.

"You will not," he said, swinging his eyes toward her and then to Tash. "Let them leave me here and you two stay with Walker. He is the shiny man, and they will not cross him lightly."

Ethan had no clue why Mir'ah had reached that conclusion. All of them in PSE would be shining to them.

Tash looked down at her hands in her lap and nodded. After several seconds, she stood up and grabbed Sandi by the hand, leading her to the far side of the ring, away from Tuula Mir'ah.

"You all need to step away from me," Toby whispered. "Don't cross the rope but give them room to do this."

The captain started to stand but leaned down over him first. "You're sure you want to do this? We can keep carrying you."

"No. I don't want to do this, but I really cannot go on," he whispered. "I don't need you to burn your power trying to postpone the inevitable. Parker's probably already sent a rescue party, and I've only got to hang out until they find me."

Something in his eyes told Ethan that he'd lost something important enough that he didn't care if they found him or not.

He thought about refusing, but couldn't find a reason other than it felt like he was abandoning a piece of hope if they left him behind. He stood up and stepped over to join the others.

With a grunt, Toby forced his body over, face down and dragged his arms straight out to the side. Sucking in a face full of dirt and grass he coughed once and then closed his eyes. "We'ir sharrah," he whispered.

One of the other Ut'arans stepped forward and Mir'ah and the other one bent low, picking the rope loop up. They moved it over his body to enclose a smaller circle around the prisoners and leave Toby on the outside.

Two others joined them and they all dropped to their knees. They said something between them so quietly that Ethan couldn't hear it, and then each grabbed one of Toby's limbs. Standing up, they carried him to the edge of the clearing and placed him face down at the base of a tree.

Tuula Mir'ah pulled out a thin edged blade from her pouch and with the skill of a surgeon, slit his jumpsuit up the back side of both his legs and the center of his back to his collar. Carefully she split only the fabric and the thinskin beneath it and peeled it back. She rolled him out of his clothes and returned him to his face down position entirely naked.

"I've never seen it done for someone in clothes," Tash whispered, her fascination at the anthropological aspects of what she was seeing outweighing everything else in her mind.

If she can cling to that, it will probably keep her alive, Ethan thought. For him it was hard enough, but when he looked at Sandi, she was sobbing into Angel's chest. He already knew that she wasn't going to make it if she couldn't pull it back together.

Turning back to watch, Mir'ah was standing with a leg on each side of Toby, and had balanced her knife on the back of his head. She was facing away from them and she was saying something again. She bent down suddenly and snagged her knife, raising it high above her head she shouted, "We'ir sharrah. Mor'et wakat ak al'mor korah. Toh'bee ak Marat akU'tar. Ut'ar sharrah. We'ir."

"We'ir sharrah!" the others said in unison.

She plunged the knife into the ground beside his head and turned to walk back to the prisoners.

"He will … Ut'ar Sharrah al'mor under sister Tarah," she said. She studied each of their faces, lingering for several seconds on each. When she got to Ethan, she lowered her eyes.

"Travel now more fast?"

He nodded. *Now we'll travel faster.*

She looked at him sidewise and then her eyes lit up as she understood what he was doing. Imitating his nod, she jerked her head up and down.

But not so fast that they won't find us, he thought. *I hope.*

CHAPTER TWENTY-ONE

Kaycee, Ammo, and Quinn spent hours re-watching the security file and trying not to think about the idea that they still hadn't heard anything from the Watchtower bosses. Instead, they focused on sucking any detail out of the optic records in an effort to find any hope to hold on to. They'd pulled the table up in front of the wallscreen in the mid-deck and stared at the images.

When the surveillance feed cut out, the captain and the others had managed to get into their exosuits. There wasn't much else to give them a reason to be optimistic.

"I am uncertain how the Ut'arans managed to get the entire power grid of the basecamp to fail," Marti said. "This record shows their only access to the electrical system occurred when they contacted the wiring in the controls for the door to the locker room facility. It is unlikely that the door circuit would not have a breaker and would have sufficient short potential to draw down the entire facility. Therefore, we can assume this is an incomplete security file."

"I don't know as it matters," Quinn said. He was drumming his fingers on the table where the meal he'd thrown together for them sat uneaten. "The power went down, and that's the last thing we see. Based on this Parker has to be making an assumption that they were taken prisoner."

"Or they know more than they're sharing," Kaycee said.

"Correct," Marti said. "I believe that my automech body is in the main power distribution room. To shut the grid down would require them to access the breakers in that room."

"And you'd know if they'd done that because the door being opened would have given you access to your body," Ammo said.

"That is also correct," it said. "Even making an assumption that they somehow damaged the body to the point where I cannot reestablish a link, there would have been an interval between the door opening, and it being incapacitated that would have indicated such an event was occurring."

"At least that means your body is probably alright," Kaycee said.

"That implies there's got to be another point of attack we haven't seen. Where else could they have accessed the whole grid?" Quinn asked. "I'm not an engineer, but wouldn't a power plant be a distance from the facility?"

"Such a design characteristic is to allow for thermal management," Marti said. "However, as the Ut'arans see in infrared, typical techniques for radiation of excess heat would be visible to them."

"You know, that's all fascinating as shit, but we've got no legs here," Ammo said. "We've figured out they haven't shared everything with us, and beyond that we're pissing blind. Maybe it's time for us to take this backup the stack and see what they'll say if we push."

"I agree," the handler said. "We're no closer to knowing anything."

Kaycee leaned back and wrapped her fingers behind her head. She nodded and looked at Ammo. "You up to chewing some butt? If they see me up and around too fast they're going to look sidewise at Forrester."

"When have I ever passed up a fine feast of ass?" she

asked, tilting her head to indicate that the doctor should get out of sight of the optic.

As soon as she was out of view, Marti opened the channel.

It took almost ten minutes for Ammo to shred her way to the top of the Watchtower food chain, and when she got there, she'd worked herself up to a fine edge of frustration. Dr. Ansari and Bradley Parker were sitting together in an office when the last bureaucratic wall crumbled and she finally got the ones she wanted on the comm.

"Gentlemen, since you're both there, I expect I can get all the answers I'm looking for at once," she said. "What the frak is the hold up?"

"Mounting a rescue mission is a complex endeavor," Dr. Ansari said.

"No, it's not," she said. "You get some people with guns in a shuttle, and you go down there and get them back. That's not quantum physics."

"I understand your concerns, Miss Rayce," he said. "But—"

"I don't think you do, Doctor," she snapped. "You've got people supposedly being held prisoner by a tribe of overexposed savages. There's none of this 'contamination' shit to consider. This band of natives has been all over the inside of your very modern basecamp. They are as exposed as they're going to get."

"Yes, but landing a shuttle is a very visible endeavor. There would be witnesses for hundreds of kilometers in every direction," he said. "There may be a handful of the Ut'arans exposed thus far, but there are thousands and thousands that would be damaged by witnessing a spacecraft coming down from the sky."

"I'm more concerned about my crewmates than your

precious non-interference rules," she said.

"Actually those are laws," Parker said. "The Science Wing of the Coalition got the non-intervention policy codified several decades ago. Right after the first landing parties here discovered the indigenous culture."

"I know the laws, but they don't apply in this case," she said.

"In fact they do," he said. "Director Ansari is vested with both ambassadorial title and governor status. As such, if he says nobody ever goes down to rescue them, that carries the weight of law."

"He's not saying that's my intent," Ansari said, "but Brad is right. I can do that."

"As it stands we plan to launch a mission tomorrow evening local time. At that point, we'll do what we can to extract your crewmembers," Parker said. "We only have a landing window every four days, and unless we want our rescue team to spend four days down there, we need to make sure they can get in and out in less than the seventeen hours of darkness."

Ammo shook her head. "That's a load of recycler biscuits and you know it. We have to get our people out of there."

"We're developing a plan to give us the best chances," Ansari said.

"Care to share what you're thinking?"

"No," Parker said. "To be blunt, you have no expertise of relevance in the environment, so time wasted in explaining the situational topography would only delay the process."

"I'm not buying that. It would take us an hour to do it ourselves." She jerked her head at Quinn. "Maybe you should let us."

"I absolutely forbid it," the Director said. "Even if I were to consider it, you don't have the experience in the environment to try, and you cannot survive in that environment without a PSE."

"So give us the gear we need," Quinn said, shrugging.

"No," he said. "The contamination to the civilization down there would be profound and unrecoverable. We don't know how far that's gone. But I guarantee it will make it worse if we launch an ill conceived rescue mission."

"And even if we were to let you throw your lives into jeopardy by trying, you still cannot leave until tomorrow night local time," Parker said. "That means we have to wait thirty-six hours. Then we will go get them."

"In the meantime, we have much to plan, so if you will excuse me I have to get back to it," Ansari said, cutting the comm without giving her a chance to reply.

"The odds of them remaining alive after another thirty-six hours, is extremely small," Marti said. "Their PSE power supplies are limited and likely will not last that long."

"How long have they got?" Kaycee asked, walking back to the table and sitting down.

"That will depend on their activity level," it said. "If they can conserve and not move vigorously, they may be able to continue until late afternoon tomorrow. I would anticipate none of them would last beyond thirty hours."

"What happens then?" Quinn asked.

"If they can lie down flat and stay that way, they're all in good enough shape to be alright," she said. "On the other hand, if they're forced to be active, then it will tear up their circulatory system. Blood will descend into their legs and their brain will get less and less oxygen as that happens. Over the course of a day or so they'll get progressively worse."

"Is it permanent?" he asked.

"Vaso-regulator drugs will restore circulatory pressure, but brain damage from oxygen deprivation could be irreversible. Fortunately, that's one of the later stages."

"How long would they have?"

"There'd be some damage within a few hours, but they might fight it off for a day or more. Especially Angel. She's in the best shape of all of them."

"Then I don't think we have a choice but to try ourselves," he said, glancing at Ammo who shrugged then nodded.

"With hand scanners and stunners we should be able to get them back with a minimum amount of interference in the planet's culture," he said.

"We don't have exosuits," Kaycee said.

"I'm sure Parker won't loan us any either," Ammo added. "So we'll have to go naked."

"Naked?" Quinn grinned. "I enjoy feeling wind on the skin, so I'm good with that."

"I didn't mean it that way," she said. "Quinn and I can handle a two-g endurance workout I'm sure. I used to train in a gravity tank when I played slamball in college."

"That was years ago, and it's not easy to get back that kind of condition without some hard work," Kaycee said. The glare that launched in her direction would have vaporized her if she hadn't been expecting it.

"Can you amp us up on those vaso-regulators? Preemptively?" Quinn asked ignoring their eye lock.

"They're not intended for prophylactic use," she said, leaning back and scratching her head while she thought it through. "I don't have any in stock and it'll take me several hours to synthesize enough."

She stood up and walked in a slow circle around the table. "I should give you a supply to carry with you, so you don't have problems, and I can load you up with four auto-syringe doses in case you can't find them until after they're having problems."

She stopped and stared at them both. "You need to understand that you will have a maximum safe endurance of no more than thirty hours, and you're going to feel all kinds of foobed for a few days when you get back. The longer you take down there, the worse it will be on your bodies. They don't intend this class of drug for extended use."

"But will it work?" he asked.

Kaycee nodded. "They'll work to get you hotwired short term and through it ... hopefully, with no lasting damage."

He shrugged. "How long will it take to synthesize that much juice?"

"A minimum of eight hours," she said, shaking her head. "I also need to see if I can come up with the specifications for the local inoculation compound that they give everybody. No point in sending you down there, only to let the local micro-flora incapacitate you."

"Viroxycin Immunoxate 112-E," Marti said. "I have already sent the specifications to the pharma-synthesizer."

"Excellent," she said, turning toward the MedBay to get started.

"That still puts us down there a day ahead of them," Ammo said.

"That only leaves having to figure out how to make that part happen," Quinn said. "Even an old base like this has to have a defense grid."

"That's easy," Ammo said. "We push out and coast with the power off until we get far enough away to do a freefall entry. After that we can make a low level swoop back through the grass to the basecamp."

"If you say so." Quinn raised a very skeptical eyebrow in her direction. "You do know how to fly a shuttle don't you?"

CHAPTER TWENTY-TWO

Ethan sprawled flat on his back on the soft mossy grass, staring up at the heavens and watching the bright moons drift across the almost luminous vault of the sky. He'd cut off the power to all but the essential parts of his PSE, so the surrounding darkness was shot through with bright moonlight and deep shadows, and not the artificial green vision of his suit visor. It put him at a disadvantage against the Ut'arans, but it conserved what battery life he had left.

He and Angel had spent half the day packing Toby and so they both had to have burned more of their suit's energy than the others, but he didn't know. He'd asked Angel to take an assessment of their collective status so he could figure out what to do when the next suit failed, and they had to drag another doomed body through the jungle. It was futile and he knew it, but he refused to accept that they should just give up and accept their fate.

Fuck their we'ir sharrah.

Beside him, he heard footsteps in the dark. Shuffling and heavy. Probably one of the humans. A section of the stars eclipsed and he recognized Angel's silhouette.

"They should have gotten here by now," she whispered as she crashed down on the grass beside him. She landed heavily, making it obvious that her suit was on minimum power mode as well.

"Maybe they got to him," he said.

"Hopefully," she said, her voice showing she didn't expect that to be the truth.

"Where do we stand," he asked.

She let out a slow hiss and flopped the rest of the way down onto her back beside him. "Nuko and Tash are alright," she said. "Smaller suits pull less power. Nuko's got almost fifty percent and Tash has forty-seven."

He nodded, then realized she probably couldn't see him. "They will make all day tomorrow then."

"The rest of us probably not," she said. "Sandi is clear dead. Even her liner is out of juice. If she can stand up at all in the morning, I'll be surprised. I think she walked in on muscle."

"She's only wearing the top half of a suit, why'd she burn so much?"

"A PSE liner has a small emergency battery. The real power supply is in the exoshell. She was still suiting up when the Rockpile went dark, and her main pack hadn't connected yet. She's been running the arms and neck portions of the shell on the reserve battery all day."

"They're not needed to walk, so why didn't she cut them off?"

"She said she didn't know you could," she said. "Honestly, I think she's just given up."

It's hard not to, he thought, but he held his tongue. The silence hung for several seconds, broken only by the sound of something moving in the trees beyond their glowing rock ring.

"Rene is going to be in trouble though," she said, rolling to face him with a low grunt. "He's got less than ten percent because of that damn problem with his actuator micro-motors. He's even powered down his liner tonight, and he'll conserve everything he can, but he's not got three hours left, best odds."

"What if he's only running the liner?

"And we carry him? Then we're all dead by mid afternoon,"

"Not all of us," he said. "What about you?"

"I'm at thirty-eight," she said. "I've been cutting my exoshell off and muscling it until I can't walk, then I power it up until I recover. It kicked my ass today, but I think I might make it the whole day."

"I should try that tomorrow," he said.

"How are you doing?"

"Just under thirty." He lied. He was just under twenty, but with Angel's idea of gravity sprinting, he might make most of the day before he was dead.

"Company," Angel whispered, tapping his arm and pushing his face to the side to make sure he was looking in the direction she was pointing. Another silhouette broke the arc of the sky. Female, with a wakat close behind.

"Tuula Mir'ah?" he guessed before he activated his night vision and confirmed her identity. Powering up his suit, he sat up.

"Moktoh, nerada cha'toh nee."

"Mir'ah cha'da nee, ak-tok click-tick, tap-tap clickak tic, click!" The wakat language sounded completely different, but even Ethan could tell it was unhappy with the Tuula.

She growled, snapping her tongue in a series of slapping sounds. The wakat hissed and swayed its body back and forth.

Grunting, she swept the wakat away with a gesture. It made another series of rapid fire sputtering sounds as it danced back and sulked off to sit in the distance.

"Moktoh not good on Marat akUt'ar," she said as she knelt just outside the rope ring that pretended to be their prison cell.

"Moktoh is your wakat?"

"Moktoh is big love wakat boy," she said. "Mir'ah need knowing of Marat. I speak not big words. I know small but look to your mind."

"You want to know something?"

She jerked her head up and down.

Nodding is obviously not a universal gesture.

"Kep'tan Woh'kah is not tribe of Marat akUtar?" she asked.

"Careful," Angel whispered. She rolled up into a sitting position behind him.

"We are Marat akUt'ar," he said. "Not the same tribe as the other Shiny Man."

She sat in silence for several seconds. Mir'ah akCha'nee. Ekan akAr'ah. All AkUt'ar?"

"Yes. All akUt'ar. Marat ak … Earth," he said.

"Er'tah?" She wobbled her body back and forth. "Kep'tan Woh'kah akEr'tah. Marat akEr'tah? Yes?"

"Yes." He nodded.

She jerked her head up and down. "Mir'ah not good to be in utel akEr'tah." She looked down at the ground and swayed back and forth.

"Utel?"

She put a hand on the ground beside her left knee, and then she put it on the ground beside her right knee. Moving it half way back to where it was originally, she thumped the ground. "Utel!"

"Guessing games with an alien." He sighed.

"It's not good to be in the middle," Nuko supplied. She'd crawled up with her suit off and was on her hands and knees beside him.

"Shiny man tribes in big fight. Yes?" she asked. "Mir'ah no good utel … middle?"

"She learns language fast," Tash said, from where she lay

apparently trying to conserve power since her suit was dark and she was struggling to get enough air into her lungs.

"She thinks we're at war with the other shiny man, and she doesn't want to be in the middle," he said, glancing over at her.

"Where would she get the idea we were at war?" she asked

"Someone told her as much?" Angel suggested.

"Yes. Marat akUt'ar … akEr'tah … speak to Tuula Mir'ah. Words say do we'ir sharrah for Kep'tan Woh'kah."

"Why does it sound like the shiny man doesn't like me?"

"Maybe because he told her to feed you to the jungle," the handler said.

"Mir'ah no hear words of Marat akUt'ar," she said, jerking her head to nod. "At'ah'keet Kep'tan Woh'kah go akCha'nee."

"Of the Cha'nee? She is taking you to the Cha'nee tribe for something," Tash said.

"Kep'tan Woh'kah go Cha'nee make Mir'ah big tuula Ut'ar," she said.

"Tuula is queen isn't it?" Nuko asked, glancing at Tash to get a confirmation. She exploded into a belly laugh that startled Mir'ah clear back onto her butt.

"Boss, she's taking you home so you can make her the queen of all Ut'ar," she said. "I hope you ate your vitamins lover boy."

"Wait," he said, failing to see why she thought this was funny. "Can we go back to the part where some other guy in a PSE told her to kill me?"

"It might amount to the same thing in this gravity," Angel said, trying hard not to laugh, too.

"I'm serious. Why does some other human want us dead?" he asked.

"And why is she willing to stand up to him and keep us

172

alive?" Nuko added.

"Mir'ah akCha'nee tribe not all see Marat akUt'ar," she said. "No see keet. Kep'tan Woh'kah make see big keet. Make Mir'ah Tuula Ut'ar."

"Truth," Tash supplied. "See the big truth."

Turning her suit on, she rolled up to join them. "That makes sense. She needs to take you to her people to show you off as a trophy. To prove the shiny man exists, so they will believe and follow her."

"How far is it to her village?"

"A long day-walk for them," she said. "At the rate we're moving, two more."

"We'll all be dead before then," he said.

"Kep'tan Woh'kah no dead," she said. "Al'mor?"

"Al'mor?"

"Al'mor," she repeated, putting her fingers in her mouth. "Al'mor?"

"Eat!" he said. "We cannot eat Ut'ar food."

She looked down and swayed side to side again. "Marat akEr'tah must e'eet, yes." She waved her hand at the other humans lying on the ground. "Marat is small. I no mor'et we'ir sharrah at dawn."

"Their shine is small. I no … something … in the morning?" He glanced at Tash and shrugged.

"Kill and give the body to the jungle," she suggested.

"You don't want to kill the weak ones?" he asked, looking back at Mirah.

She nodded in her strange jerking way. "Yes. I no mor'et … kill … marat akEr'tah. Is big good yes?"

CHAPTER TWENTY-THREE

Ammo did know how to fly a shuttle. Her plan was risky, but if no one was looking out a window on the station, they'd be far enough away before they powered up the main systems that Watchtower's automated sensors might miss them. She launched them out of the *Olympus Dawn*'s hangar deck with a single burst of the main engine and then cut all power inside the shuttle. They coasted for several minutes, covering several hundred klick in freefall before she started applying gentle pulses with the manual steering thrusters to slow them enough that the planet would haul them down.

Apparently it worked, because when they hit the atmosphere like a meteor with no sign of pursuit, she finally started flying. Before that, they were a rock. An extremely fast, extremely hot rock, plummeting through the atmosphere barely this side of hell's incinerator.

By the time she pulled them around to a hard landing just outside the Rockpile, Quinn was more than a little green.

"Let's make feet," she said, pushing back from the console and laughing when she looked over at his sweat soaked face. The whites showed all the way around the edge of his eyes. "Or maybe you need to sit a second?"

"Yah," he said. His voice came out as a hoarse squeak that made her laugh.

"The ride wasn't that bad was it?"

"Nope," he whispered, clearing his throat. "It's probably

the drugs."

"Your first time doing a ballistic reentry isn't it?"

He nodded.

"Just breathe and you'll find your legs in a second." She heaved herself up and squeezed his shoulder as she headed to the back of the shuttle.

"It's more my stomach I'd like to find first," he said, grunting as he hauled himself up to a standing position.

Once they'd gotten deep into the atmosphere, she'd turned the gravity plating off so they were already at full planetary gravity. It wasn't as bad as she remembered, but they weren't physically active yet, so it would get worse.

She started pulling out their gear. They'd packed light since they didn't want to be carrying any weight they didn't have to, but everything felt awkward as she swung their bags up onto the rear passenger seat and started going through them to check it all once more.

"I do not know if there are Ut'arans in the basecamp, but it is possible," Marti said over the shuttle's internal comm.

"We can't afford the time to do much of a recon here," she said. "We'll get in and out as quick as we can and get your body back to the shuttle."

"If my automech's internal AA system realized that escape was impossible, it should have gone into standby mode to wait for retrieval. If so it will have adequate charge to assist."

"We'll get you out of there one way or another," Quinn said, scooping his bag up as he opened the door. "She's right though, we need to be moving. They've got a full day lead on us."

Ammo stepped up beside him. The sun was just rising to color the sky, but it was still too dark to see well.

Snagging a handbeam out of his kit, he snapped it on and scanned the area. They'd both studied the diagrams of the

Rockpile that Marti had created for them, so they knew where the entrance was, but it was still hard to pick out the cleft in the rock wall from a distance. "I think that's it," he said, holding his beam focused on a slit. "It looks like there are tracks in the grass around it."

She nodded, pushing out of the shuttle and dropping heavily down onto the ground a step in front of him. Tapping into her collar comm she added, "Lock the doors and keep an eye on the shuttle in case something comes out of the trees."

"You need to proceed quickly," Marti said. "There are several nocturnal predators that will find your presence interesting."

They trotted across the open ground and into the narrow crack that concealed the door. They didn't know where the Ut'arans had breached the basecamp, so they brought a pry bar from the shuttle, but when they got to the back of the slot where the opening was, it looked like a small explosion had blown it outward.

"Holy frak," Ammo whispered. "They did this with bare hands?"

"They do have rudimentary tools," Marti said.

"The metal of the inner door is shredded and twisted, and the stone that covered it is pulverized," Quinn said.

"They are also substantially stronger than humans," it said.

She pulled out her hand scanner to sweep the entry room and nodded. *All clear.*

Setting his back against the far wall, Quinn used a foot to push one of the larger shards out of the way so they could get inside. The metal groaned as he heaved against it, and he had to strain to make it bend.

She ducked inside and he twisted sideways to follow.

Several smaller jagged edges made it narrow for his bulk.

"It reeks in here," she said, gasping. "I'm getting no life signs anywhere in the Rockpile. Well, no larger ones. There are lots of smaller animals that have moved in already." She shined her light into a corner and a thing that looked like a hairy six-legged spider with a monkey glued to its back screeched and darted for cover behind a cabinet.

"It's probably a scavenger," he said. "I'm sure that's what most of the things in here are at this point."

"That's decidedly creepy looking," she said.

"My body is in a shielded closet along the right side wall in the next room," Marti said. "The video that Director Parker provided us shows that as where the majority of the fighting occurred."

"That's also where most of the monkey-spiders are," she said. "They don't seem aggressive, so we should be alright."

"Let's just get Marti's body and get on with things," he said. He was swinging his light back and forth making sure there weren't other creatures that might not be so timid sneaking up on them.

The main gallery looked like a bomb had gone off. Bodies, and pieces of bodies, littered the floor. A dried, red-brown goo covered the walls like a horrifying coat of paint. Some of the corpses had arrows through them, but the vast majority were crushed to a pulp. Or ripped to pieces.

When they swept the room with their handbeams, the spider things bellowed, leaping away like the light was painful. They were scavengers, and there were several other smaller animals also feeding on the carnage.

"Frak, what a mess," Ammo hissed, struggling not to shiver despite the relative warmth in the room. "This is unbelievable."

"Try not to look at anything that doesn't need your

attention." Quinn eased up beside her and pointed at the door. He took her hand and put it on the strap to his pack. "Nothing else matters. To us or to them. Just stay with me and focus on what we have to do. We need to get that table out of the way and then we can get out of here."

She nodded, following him across the room. Between them, they dragged the conference table far enough that they could get the locker opened. A body, pinned against the wall behind the massive table, collapsed onto the floor as they pulled it away, and several of the scavengers lunged for it. A sweep of Quinn's light sent them scurrying back with a wave of indignant howling.

Ammo grabbed the door handle and jerked it open.

"I am online," Marti said, its voice coming from inside the room rather than over the comm.

"Good, then let's get out of here," she said, already turning to dash for the door.

"The PSE locker area is through the other door in the entrance room," Marti said increasing the volume of its voice. She was almost to the exit, but stopped.

"You're not so good with violence are you?" Quinn said, coming out of the main gallery with Marti following in his shadow. He closed the door behind them. Firmly.

"I can deal with it," she said. "It's just that there's so much."

He nodded. "I'm arachnophobic, so as long as the scavengers have monkeys screwed to them, I can almost pretend they're not spiders."

"What's in the locker room that we need?" she said, jumping back to Marti's comment.

"The recording ended when the power went off, and that was the last known location of the captain and crew," it said. "Nothing has indicated that they were taken prisoner other than the word of Director Parker."

Pulling out his scanner, Quinn took a deep breath and walked up to the other door. "No life signs. Not even small ones."

"I can do this if it is easier for you," Marti said. Its automech face showed an expression of concern.

He shook his head and opened the door. Shining his light inside, he let out a slow hiss. "One body, mostly intact. And it's not one of ours," he said, pushing the door closed again and setting his hand in the middle of it while he hung his head and just breathed.

"Then let's get to it," she said. "How do we track them fastest?"

"We should be able to pick up their PSE power signatures." He turned away from the door and leaned back against it.

"Only from close range with the hand-held scanners," Marti said. "The shuttle would be able to detect them for several kilometers, but if the Ut'arans or any of the other creatures that live in the jungle see a shuttle, the reaction could be unpredictable and violent. Appearing with a blatant display of technology to rescue them might adversely affect their survival chances."

"I figured we'd have to track them on foot," Quinn said. "I used to hunt badgers in the back woods on the farm as a kid. A badger rarely leaves much to follow, so I know how to track fair."

"They have a full day head start," she reminded him.

"So we move fast, but according to what we saw on the recording, they're traveling with at least one person who has no PSE," he said. "That should slow them down a lot, and if the cap'n is hoping for a rescue party, he'll be doing everything he can to drag his boots. It will be in his mind to stay as close to ground zero as possible."

"That is logical," Marti said. "Additionally the Ut'arans will not travel at night under almost any circumstance. They have excellent night vision, but the jungle is not safe after sundown. You will need to travel only during the day as well, as all the known predators are nocturnal. Several of them are substantial."

"You're sure there's nothing to worry about during the day?" she asked.

"There are several smaller creatures that might be dangerous if cornered, but the only one you will need to worry about is the wakat." Marti's face disappeared and an image of one of the wakats they'd seen just before they entered the Rockpile took its place. "It is not a predator, but it is easily agitated, extremely fast, socially organized, and capable of lethal violence. It is comparable to an Earth chimpanzee in size. There are feral wakat, but some of them live symbiotically with the Ut'arans. They also have a rudimentary language that some of the natives speak and they appear to operate as spies or sentinels."

"They were all over the video of the attack," Quinn said.

"That means if one of them notices us, we're in trouble?" Ammo asked.

"Yes," it said.

"Then you shouldn't go with us," she said. "A shiny metal midget would definitely attract attention."

"I am approximately the same height as the native Ut'arans," it said, sounding insulted at the implied inadequacy of its stature.

"But you do shine," Quinn said, looking down at their slick synthetic coveralls and tugging on the fabric. "If we're going to get close enough to rescue our people without setting off the werecats, we should go naked. There's no way this won't attract attention."

"Even nude, I should point out to you, that unless you walk on your knees, you are nearly double the size of a native Ut'aran," it said.

"There is that," Ammo said.

"Momma fed me well, what can I say?" He grinned.

"You aren't serious are you?"

He nodded. "Only issue in my mind is that it will also make hiding our gear challenging."

"The Ut'arans wear utility pouches and shoulder packs," Marti suggested.

"You're not helping," she said, glaring at the automech. "Our utility belt and packs are as obvious as our jumpsuits."

"There are several examples of their pouches in the PSE locker room in a small display cabinet to the right of the door."

Quinn pulled it open and stepped inside. She heard plasglass shattering and he reappeared carrying two brown bags with long belt like straps attached to them. He held one out to her and swung the other over his shoulder.

"We're amped up on all these vaso-regulators, so our clothes are optional. If we don't smell and look synthetic, then we stand a better chance of getting closer before they spot us."

"Did you hunt baggers, or whatever you called them, naked?"

"Badgers," he said. "I didn't, but I had an uncle that did. He said it was easier to get close and it made it a lot more exciting."

"You've got to have the strangest family in all of human civilization, you know that don't you?"

"What? Are you growing a timid streak?" he teased, ignoring the insult to his heritage.

"No, but … frak, I guess it doesn't matter." She shook her head.

"At least this way, if we run across any werecats they won't freak out and kill us instantly," he said.

"They are called wakats," Marti corrected.

"I'm sure they'll still get bendy when we can't say hello," she said.

"There is a linguistic database in the computer here. Since you appear to have decided that I am a liability to your stealth, I will endeavor to get the power operational and download the information. I should be able to provide limited translation capability."

"You don't think an earpiece will upset the locals?" she said, shooting Quinn a glare that bounced off with no effect.

He was busy transferring the contents of his pack into the Ut'aran pouch.

Finally, she shrugged. He was right. As insane as it felt, if they could blend in, the chances of getting close enough to rescue their people would be a lot better.

Shoving her gear into the pouch he'd handed her, she peeled down her coverall and thinskin with a sigh. Facing a jungle, and who knew what else, naked was playing her senses hard. The vaso-drugs made the air around her feel much colder than it was, and she shivered again.

Tying the belt pouch around her waist, she slid it around to the front like an apron. "Is this how they wear them?" she asked, turning to face Marti

"Females wear them to the side and males wear them to the front," it said. "However you both appear to have the version worn by females since the belt straps are equal length."

"Wonderful," Quinn said. "Even nude, I get to go in drag."

"Can we just get on with this?" she said, walking over to the door and looking outside. "It looks like the sun is up, so we should be good to go."

Stepping up behind her, he smiled. "One naked man with a knife can do more damage in a night, than an army, though clothed and heavily armed," he said.

"What?" She waggled a finger in her ear. She was sure she hadn't heard him right. "Never mind, it's probably something your momma used to say."

"Yup. And she was good with a knife too."

CHAPTER TWENTY-FOUR

Ethan spent the night staring up at the sky with his suit powered down and his mind wandering restlessly, even as his body lay pinned to the spot by his own crushing weight. Just before sunrise, a fireball shot overhead. On its own, it would have been an impressive sight, except that as he watched it arc across the sky, it began to deflect off its original trajectory.

It wasn't a meteor. A pilot was flying it!

Nuko slept on the ground beside him and he flopped his hand over against her, rattling her awake. "Help is on the way," he whispered.

"How do you know?"

"I saw a shuttle on a ballistic reentry," he said.

She rolled her head in his direction and there was just enough light from the coming sunrise that he could see her face. "Too late for Toby."

A knife of guilt slashed through him and he swallowed hard. "But not for the rest of us, maybe," he said. "We've got to hang in there and they'll find us."

"Hopefully," she said.

"I saw it too," Angel whispered. "Why would they be doing a freefall dive? That's got to be like sending up a beacon."

"Apparently it got the Ut'aran's attention, too," Tash said as she sat up and powered her visor.

"Can you follow what they're saying?"

"Just that they're arguing about the shiny one not being

good with them," she said. "See how they're sitting back to back while she talks to them? That means she's arbitrating their disagreement. When she finishes listening, she'll decide which perspective is right and which is wrong."

"If they're connecting a shuttle entering the atmosphere with the shiny man, then it sounds like they know where the shiny ones live," Nuko said.

"We never do that kind of landing," she said. "We're careful to do all our approaches over the southern sea and come in slowly so we don't attract exactly this kind of attention."

"Alright, I'm tired of this," he said, sitting up with a grunt and turning to glare at her. "We know about the natives on the station. We also know that you were traveling back from Proxima with one. So you want to explain it to me?"

"I'm not sure what—"

"If you're going to tell me anything but the straight specs on this, then don't bother," he said. "Our lives depend on knowing what's really going on here. You have to know more than you're telling us."

"I don't know what—"

"If I'm going to get us through this, I need the truth from you. Either start talking or I'll have Angel hold your ass down, and I'm taking your battery pack and putting it in Rene's suit and leaving you here."

She opened her mouth to reply but just blinked several times. She glanced at Angel who had gotten up on her knees and looked ready to do as he'd suggested.

Nuko reached out a hand and put it on his leg. Her eyes begged, *Please, don't do this.*

Shaking his head, he looked back at Tash. "I'm done being lied to. I know you've got Ut'arans working as slave labor on the station."

"Not as slaves," she whispered. "They're containment accidents. We can't let them stay here after they've seen us. So we take them up to Watchtower and teach them enough to deal with our civilization."

"What about the implants?"

"What implants?" she asked, looking shocked. "I don't know about any implants."

"Tash doesn't know," Sandi hissed. She kept her eyes closed as she hauled in a pained breath. She looked a half step from death with her skin ghostly white and her teeth shining in a hard edged grimace as the gravity pulled her face drum-tight over her skull.. "Was ... Morgan's idea ... nobody else ... knows."

"What do the implants do?" he asked.

"Teach ..." she wheezed.

Ethan glanced over at Mir'ah. She was staring at him while the two members of her tribe were still arguing over the meaning of the shuttle. "That explains how she knows our language," he said.

"No... only ones ... up there ..." Her voice trailed off into a slow hiss. Ethan watched for several seconds before he saw her chest rise again in another breath.

"Then somebody needs to explain her," he challenged, flinging his arm toward Mir'ah.

Sandi's eyes flickered open and locked on his. "Can't," she mouthed silently.

"Marat akUt'ar ta'eka sho'te caros ena'che." Mir'ah's words sliced through Ethan's next thought as they echoed from across the encampment. She had her hand on one of the two who were arguing as if she was bestowing a blessing.

"She's passed judgment," Tash whispered.

"What did she say?"

"Something about the shiny man pouring down blood of the stars, maybe?"

"That sounds like a bad omen," Angel said.

Judging from the reaction of Mir'ah's people, the handler was probably right. They were all moving at once, packing up things and loading various objects into their wakat's pouches.

"Looks like it's time to move out," Ethan said, switching his suit's power on and standing up. His night vision arm swung into place and he blinked several times. Through the visor, the sky was brighter than daylight even though the ground was still dark.

The rest of the humans, except for Sandi, all climbed to their feet. Tash bent over her and started to pick her up, but she shook her head.

"It's … my turn," she said, groaning as Tash tried to pull her up by her arms.

"I won't leave you here," Tash said, her voice cracking.

Angel leaned close to the captain's ear and whispered, "If that was a rescue party and they track us on foot, leaving her here means they'll find her first. We've been holding the Ut'arans back, so we're probably a half-day from help getting here."

"You think they'll be tracking us on the ground?" he asked.

"I don't think they'll risk an aerial search." She shrugged.

"That assumes they care at all," he said. "Obviously this isn't the first contact the Ut'arans have had with us. Somebody's left footprints all over this civilization, and they don't seem to be overly worried about the natives seeing them. They risked a lot of exposure doing that hot entry."

"It's a hard call to make, but I think she's got better chances of getting help faster if we don't carry her further," she said, shrugging. "And if they do fly in, we can always lead them back to her."

Staring down at Sandi, he nodded.

He reached out and pulled Tash back to a standing position by her shoulder. "She's right. We know help is coming, so she's better off if we leave her here."

"We can't—"

"Yes. We can," he said. "They'll be tracking us on foot, which means they'll find her before they catch up with us. I need you and what you know about the Ut'arans with me."

"Kep'tan Woh'kah," Mir'ah said, startling him. She'd come up and stood outside the rope ring watching their exchange. "We go at new sun."

"She needs we'ir sharrah," he said, shaking his head. *The more we can slow them down the sooner we all get to go home.*

She looked down at Sandi and made a noise that sounded like a grunt. "Marat akUt'ar comes. Is no good at Mir'ah."

"No. She cannot go more," he said. "We must give her to the jungle."

"Mir'ah no hear words of Marat akUt'ar. Must make go, or stars blood is more."

"I think that's marching orders," Angel whispered.

"Mir'ah no hear words of Walker akEarth," the captain said. "Sandi is we'ir sharrah at the new sun."

"Is her end now?" she said, tilting her head to the side.

"Yes," he said.

"I'm next," Rene whispered.

Ethan shot him a look, but realized from the lack of glow that the engineer had deactivated his suit. He was standing upright on pure muscle. He might have missed it in the glare from the lightening sky, but Nuko stood with him and her suit was visible as fully powered.

Mir'ah looked at Rene and swayed back and forth. "He

we'ir sharrah, yes?"

The captain shook his head. "He goes with us."

"He is slow, marat gone. No good."

"Only she stays," Ethan said, swinging his hand toward Sandi.

She looked over his shoulder at the sky and blinked, her eye color changing from dark to pale blue. When she looked back at him, she blinked again and they returned to their original shade. She jerked her head up and down. "Words of Kep'tan Woh'kah akEr'tah good. We'ir sharrah at new sun."

She spun and walked away.

"Why don't you want to leave me here with her?" Rene asked, collapsing back to the ground in a barely controlled fall.

"Help is coming and we have to do everything we can to slow things down," the captain said, settling down beside him and killing his suit's power. "If we can make this we'ir sharrah take as long as possible, and then drag you along until we have no choice, we're buying time for the rescue party to catch up."

He nodded. "I can't say as I like being an anchor, especially since the more you have to carry me, the sooner you go down, too."

"It should only be a few hours," he said.

"You are risking Sandi's life on a maybe," Tash said.

"Seems to me you wagered all of our lives on a secret you've been keeping," he said, without turning to face her. "I don't trust you, but at this point I have no choice since I can't risk losing access to what you know. Otherwise I'd be feeding your naked ass to the jungle too."

"All I know is what I've already told you," she said.

"It might be best to just fold your chips while you're behind," Angel said, leaning in close and making sure that

Tash understood it was not a suggestion.

They sat in silence for almost an hour watching the Ut'arans going through their morning rituals. After the sun was high enough that the tops of the trees far above them were brightly lit, Mir'ah announced that it was time for the we'ir sharrah. Three others joined her and they waited until the humans had moved to the far edge of their enclosed area before they moved the rope to put Sandi on the outside. Rolling her over, they picked her up and carried her to the trees.

Unlike Toby, Sandi was wearing part of a hardened PSE exoshell. And although Mir'ah's knife made short work of the polymorphic liner, the mechanical augments were tougher than her blade. The oily ferrofluid that gushed out of the liner when she cut it, turned everything into a slimy black mess, and made the whole process even more challenging.

The captain wasn't sure if he should let them struggle with it, but the longer they tugged and pulled at the shell, the more Sandi cried out in pain. When it looked like they were on the verge of ripping her arms from her body, he had to do something.

"Tuula Mir'ah! Stop. No good," he bellowed, hoping to give his voice the right tone to cut through the chaos, but not sound like he was aiming for trouble.

She spun and glared at him. Apparently, interrupting the we'ir sharrah was a bad thing. Several of her people rushed toward the humans obviously intent on tearing them apart.

"Et'ah re'eshat!" she roared, bringing everyone to a standstill. She walked over to the rope ring and stared into his eyes. "We'ir sharrah can no be stopped. Sharrah Ut'ar must e'eet."

"I hear Mir'ah's words," Ethan said, nodding and looking

down at her feet where she stood. "I can help with Marat ... skin?" He rapped his knuckles on the hard shell over his forearm.

"Marat akEr'tah Kep'tan Woh'kah. We'ir sharrah Ut'ar?" she asked. Skepticism translated in her tone in spite of the language difference.

He raised his eyes but kept his head down. "Yes. I help do the we'ir sharrah for her."

She waved the other humans back and waited until they moved away before she bent to pick up the rope and place it behind him. Three of her tribe unslung their arrow throwers but held off until she gave them instruction.

Reaching into her pouch, she pulled out a knife. Looking at the blade for several seconds, she held it out to him flat in her palm. Although the ones watching could have ventilated him in undesirable ways, that she offered him a hand weapon showed a shocking amount of trust.

He held out his left hand palm forward and fingers down, in the same gesture he'd seen the ones do who were asking forgiveness.

She stared at him with her head tilted far to the side. "Mo'oh ke'esha. Kep'tan Woh'kah words good." Shifting the knife into her right hand, she reached out and turned his hand so the fingers were upward and bumped her left palm into his.

Tash gasped. "She made herself his equal."

Mir'ah snapped her head up and down once and then flipped the knife over and put the handle in his right hand.

CHAPTER TWENTY-FIVE

Kaycee sat alone on the ConDeck staring out the window and feeling helpless. It wasn't a feeling she experienced often. Since she was the only one aboard, there wasn't much to do other than wait until Ammo and Quinn had news. She glanced at the chrono every few minutes but all she could do was imagine what was going on down there.

She knew that Marti's humanform body was working to reconnect the power in the basecamp so it could get access to the language database, but other than sporadic reports that it relayed from the two of them, there wasn't anything to do but sit.

"Dr. Forrester is requesting permission to come aboard," Marti said, startling her. "He is at the outer airlock."

"Is he alone?" she asked, leaning forward to open a screen.

"Yes. He claims he needs to do a medical follow-up exam on you," the AA said.

"Do you think he's saying that for effect, or that he doesn't remember the truth?" She watched as the image opened and she shook her head.

"He appears to be exhibiting signs of physiological stress, so I would say it is likely that someone is monitoring him."

"Then I can't go down there and talk to him," she said.

"I can meet him at the inner lock with my Gendyne 6000 automech," Marti said. "I believe it would be sufficient visual deterrent in the event that he is seeking to gain access for others."

"Do you think it's safe to let him come aboard?"

"If he is alone, I do not think there would be much potential for problem," it said. "You could meet him in the MedBay and he may not realize you are the only one aboard. I can escort him there and make sure he does not explore beyond areas he has already seen."

"Do it." She pushed herself up from the captain's seat and headed down to the mid-deck.

Several minutes later, she sat on the edge of the diagnostic bed when Marti stopped outside the door and Forrester came in alone. He looked nervously around the room before he settled onto the stool beside the bed.

"I'm here to check on how you're doing," he said. "I have to say I'm surprised to have been met at the door by a robot. Where's your handler?"

"He and Ammo are on the ConDeck, I think," she said.

He nodded, looking around again. His eyes fell on the collar where Quinn had left it, and he studied it for a moment before he said, "So how are you feeling?"

"I'm doing fine."

"That's good. Your injury was pretty severe and I'm surprised to see you up and around," he said, rubbing the back of his neck where she had cut him to sever the failsafe. It appeared he wanted her to be aware that someone was listening.

She nodded.

"I'm also here to deliver a message from Parker," he said.

"Really? He doesn't seem the type to worry about my well being," she said.

"He's not." Forrester shook his head and looked down at the floor. "Parker wants me to tell you he's willing to get your people out of there, but he needs something from you first."

"I thought they planned to rescue them, anyway?"

"I don't think that's the plan at this point. Your crew is in grave danger, and they won't last another full day," he said, holding up his hand to stop her from reacting. "He told me to tell you that if you want them back alive, you'll have to do him a favor."

"He's holding them?" she hissed.

"I don't believe so," Forrester said. His expression told her that he wished he wasn't the one facing her. "But all he has to do is delay the rescue mission. If they don't get down there in time, the gravity or the jungle will kill them."

She nodded, biting back on her desire to kill the messenger. She could tell it wasn't something he personally wanted to have happen. "What does he want us to do?"

The doctor swallowed hard and then took a deep breath. "He wants you to haul a load of slaves."

"What?" She bounced off the edge of the bed with the sudden intent to go ahead with his execution. That idea was dangerously close to reality, but she stopped herself short of making it happen. Barely.

"You already suspected that's what he's doing," he said, pushing the stool back far enough to remain out of reach. "He's got a regular buyer for heavy world slaves, and he conscripts private haulers to carry them."

"You're serious?" She turned away from him and started pacing in small orbits around the MedBay. "If we even load them up, he's got us wedged over the bulkhead."

"That's true. But he's done this before to leverage indies into hauling slaves," he said.

"He's kidnapped other ships' crews?"

"No. Not that I know of," he said. Strangely, he looked shocked at the suggestion. "I think the situation in this case is just opportunistic of him, but he's used other ways to coerce freighter captains in the past."

She stopped and stared at him, shaking her head. "Slaving is one of the few capital crimes left in the Coalition. We'd be lucky to get a trial if they catch us."

He nodded. "Exactly. He knows he can bury you once you take them aboard."

"Well he'd be right on that point," she said. "What if I say no?"

"Then he'll let your crew die on the surface. You don't have any choice if you want them back." He looked down at the floor and shrugged.

If Ammo and Quinn can't rescue them, then he's right, she realized, slamming her fist down on the counter.

"What makes him think we wouldn't just turn on him?"

"It's that whole capital crime thing," Forrester said. "Unless being a hero is more important to you than being alive, you don't dare. He's got connections that will get you hung for it ... without a lot of extra unnecessary talking time. You'd never get a chance to state your case."

"If he's the master badass, why'd he send you to negotiate this?"

"Would you have let him on the ship to talk to you?"

"No."

"Which made me the logical choice, since he's smart enough not to do this on an open comm," he said. "Honestly, he doesn't think there's much to negotiate. He knows you'll comply."

"Frakking bastard," she said, sighing. "He's probably right."

He looked over at the cervical collar. Grabbing it, he hit the button and swung it over his neck. He gasped and shook for a second before he nodded. Clearing his throat, he said, "He also thinks I have to comply with his instructions."

"Why didn't you tell me about this before?"

"Because the implant blocked my memories," he said. "You have to believe me when I say I didn't know the extent of what's going on here. Since you helped me, I've been able to dig up things that the implant was keeping buried. Without the pain to keep me locked out of my own brain, I remember a lot more about what's happening."

She wasn't sure she should believe anything he said, but she had little choice.

"Parker's got eyes on the surface watching over your crew. As long as you agree, I have no doubt he can get them home safe," he said.

He picked a medical scanner up off her counter and opened it like he was going to use it on her. Instead, he snapped the lid closed and slipped it into his pocket. Reaching into his medical pouch, he pulled out a different one and set it down where the other one had been. "That should help once you get loaded."

"What is it?"

He shook his head. *Don't ask.* "Just don't turn it on until you are away from the station. If it logs in to the local network, he'll know."

He pulled the collar off and blew out a slow sigh. "I'm glad you seem to be doing so much better Dr. Caldwell. I'm sure you understand what you need to do next."

He spun and disappeared back through the door with Marti dropping in behind him.

Kaycee picked the scanner up and turned it over several times in her hand. She hoped, whatever was on it would be enough to unbend things when it came to that point.

Otherwise she knew she was about to make a very wrong decision, for all the right reasons.

CHAPTER TWENTY-SIX

After the first hour, Ammo wasn't as much conscious of her nakedness as she was aware of how intensely connected to the environment she felt. It was uncanny how her senses felt heightened. The world around her seemed to vibrate with waves of sensation as the fine hair over her entire body danced with each breath of wind. The smallest chattering or squeak of an animal scurrying high in the trees above her pierced her awareness, and even her sense of smell seemed to reach out to swallow everything around her.

It was the metallic coppery scent of blood that stopped her in mid-step. Squatting down, she held up her hand. "Something ahead," she whispered, glancing back at Quinn who followed a few paces behind.

Sliding up beside her, he dropped onto a knee. He drew in a deep breath and held it for a second. "Smells like blood?"

She nodded, reaching into her pouch and pulling out her hand scanner. She opened the faceplate, tapping the screen to activate it, and the jungle around them exploded into chaos. Startled by the sudden cacophony she dropped the unit back into her pouch.

"What the frak?" Quinn whispered as the sounds of angry animals gradually died back to a more normal level. "Looks like they don't like technology much."

"If tech freaks out the wildlife, how have the science teams been able to get anything done?" she challenged. "A PSE would make the jungle go insane wouldn't it?

"Maybe it's just the scanner that's doing it," he suggested. "Like a dog whistle."

"What's a dog whistle?"

"It's a little metal pipe you blow through to call your dog. It puts out a high frequency whistle that's above human hearing, but dogs can hear it just fine. Maybe the scanner whistles, figuratively speaking."

"I do not remember an instance of seeing one of the science personnel using hand scanners," Marti said over their earpieces. "If that is true, it might make tracking the prisoners by their PSEs' electromagnetic signature difficult."

"So far, tracking them isn't a problem," she said. "They've left an obvious trail."

"We've got to keep moving if we're going to catch them," Quinn said, standing up and stretching to look over a small wall of underbrush. "Uhm … that's a mess. There's a small clearing and something ugly off to one side. You might want to stay here while I check it out."

She shot him a glare.

"Or maybe not."

They edged forward and into the open area. It looked like a place where the Ut'arans had stopped. Off to one side of the clearing what looked like an explosion of blood covered a patch of grass and up the side of a tree. Ammo's throat tightened as she realized there were pieces of flesh mixed in the blood.

"That's a body I think," she managed.

The handler nodded, walking up and stopping before he got too close. "Yah, it's human too," he said, pointing over to where there were a few larger pieces of the body.

"Can you determine if it is one of our crewmates?" Marti asked.

"Give us a second," Ammo said. She stepped up behind

Quinn and tried to force herself to look at what was left of the body.

"I don't think so," he said, pointing toward a pile of what looked like blue and white rags. Something had scattered them. "That might be a coverall and a thinskin."

She nodded. "It looks like one of the coveralls the scientists wear on the station."

"You check it out and I'll see if I can figure out what happened to the body," he said. "It looks like something ate it."

"And we're running around out here naked," she said, looking toward the trees and trying not to shiver in spite of the warm air.

"It is important to remember that all the large predators are nocturnal," Marti said.

"Hopefully we won't be here overnight." Quinn reached out and squeezed her shoulder.

"If that becomes necessary, I can bring the shuttle in to give you shelter," it said.

"That's not a lot of comfort looking at this mess," she said, turning away to check out the clothes.

"It may be difficult to tell superficially if it is human or Ut'aran," Marti said. "The primary difference that the doctor noted was in the spinal column."

"I remember," he said. "I'm sure it's human. There is an intact hand and it's wearing a finger band."

Ammo knelt and examined the pile of fabric. "The coverall has been split with a knife, but other than some smears of blood that look more like an animal was nosing through the pile, it doesn't look like it was being worn when whoever it was died. The blood is well dried too."

Quinn nodded. "I'd say it happened last night. Probably one of those big predators. There are some serious bite marks on these bones."

"Are there any other identifying details?" Marti asked.

"There are command bars on the coverall collar," she said.

"And the ring," he added. "It looks like an engagement band, maybe. And it's a large hand, so probably male."

"That makes it likely that the victim is Commander Stocton," it said. "He and the mission medic are both commanders, but she wore no jewelry and from the partial record we have, I believe she was killed in the corridor outside the PSE locker room."

"At the end of the security recording he wasn't in an exosuit," she said.

"He was not," Marti said.

"Then he'd have been moving slow, or they'd have been carrying him," Quinn said. "Maybe the Ut'aran's killed him and left him behind."

"We're only five klick from the basecamp so they weren't making big feet for sure," she added. "You don't think this is where they spent the night do you?"

"If it is, they're not moving very fast at all," Quinn said, turning around and giving the clearing a cursory examination. "I'd also think they'd have left more evidence of spending time here. They aren't trying to conceal any of their tracks, and I don't see much that shows they made a longer stay of it. I'd bet they stopped to eat or something and then moved on."

"Marcus Elarah ate every five hours while he was aboard. If we assume that they follow a similar schedule then it is likely that they were roughly five hours from the beginning of their trek," Marti said.

"That's encouraging. They're making less than a klick per hour," Ammo said walking over and examining a spot on the ground where it looked like several bodies had spent time sitting. There was a trampled ring in the surrounding grass.

"But now they've unburdened themselves of one slow mover," Quinn pointed out. "They'll probably pick up the pace from here."

"Then we'd better make feet," she said. A set of deep gouges in the ground caught her eye as she turned to walk away. It looked like an arrow pointing down the trail with some words scratched into the dirt below it.

Day 1 Midday. Leaving Toby here. Sandi won't last long. That way. Slowly. NT

"Nuko says his name was Toby," she said.

"What?" Quinn asked, sounding shocked that she'd know that.

She pointed at the message in the dirt. "She left us a note. It says they were here midday yesterday, and that they went that way. One of the other survivors is Sandi, and she won't last much longer."

"I wonder if it's the same one that was on the ship?" he asked

"She was one of the guides on our expedition," Marti said. "And Tobias Stocton is the name of the Rockpile mission commander."

"She also says they're moving slow."

"That'll conserve power for their PSE, but we've got to keep moving," Quinn said, walking over to stare at the ground with her. "Fortunately, the arrow points downhill. Climbing a mountain in this gravity would be a bitch."

CHAPTER TWENTY-SEVEN

Director Parker's eyebrow raised the barest of millimeters as his face appeared on the ConDeck screen. "Dr. Caldwell, I'm surprised to be talking to you. Morris told me you would recover, but he said your injury was rather severe."

"I'm fine," she said, reaching up to touch the back of her head where she'd forgotten to cover the alleged injury. Fortunately, if she didn't turn, he couldn't see there wasn't a bandage back there. "Let's just skip the small talk. I understand you want to discuss business and I need to get on with it."

"I expected as much, although I anticipated it would be your load broker I'd be talking to, but it doesn't matter." He reached up and tapped something on his desk. "The fact that you're here means I should assume you got my message and are willing to accept my offer?"

He has initiated a recording of your conversation, appeared on the bottom of the screen as Marti advised her of what he'd done.

"Understand me you bastard, if I had any choice this would not be it," she said, holding her voice steady and nodding slightly in response to Marti's notification.

"That's probably true, but you're smart enough to realize you've got no choice," Parker said, shrugging off her opinion of his parentage.

"I sure as frak don't want to be hauling—"

"Remember we're over an open comm here." He cut her off with a tone that made sure she understood to mind her words.

"At this point that's more your concern than mine," she said.

"Trust me it's mutual, so watch your mouth." His glare punctuated his words with a far more personal threat.

Shocked at how easily he drew out her rage, she bit back on her visceral reaction to the director's tone. "I'll take your cargo on, but you need to get my people out of there."

He smiled. "Tonight, it won't be a problem."

"I meant now," she said. "Obviously you aren't burdened by a conscience, so breaking some rules shouldn't be a problem for you."

He shook his head. "Your people are safe. I know exactly where they are, but we will load the cargo before I lift a finger to get them back."

"You know where they are?"

"Like I said, they're not facing any immediate risk at the moment." He leaned back in his chair and laced his fingers behind his head. "You need to understand that their situation could change. I don't need to remind you that Dawn is an inhospitable world and the Ut'arans are a dangerous people."

"You really are a bastard," she snarled.

He laughed. "I've been called a lot worse by people far more powerful than you."

"I'm sure you have." She let out a slow breath before she went on, "I have one condition if you want me to take this job."

He leaned forward and glared at her for several seconds. "You're pretty arrogant if you think you can set any of the conditions, especially given the tenuous security of your crewmates."

"I don't care what threats you're making. You deal only

with me on this. My handler and load broker are not going to be involved."

"That's a damned thin wall for them to hide behind," he said.

She shrugged. "Maybe so, but it's my decision alone. What they don't know, might keep them from being hung for this."

"That's noble of you," he said. "Pointless, but noble. If you do your part and deliver the cargo, nobody's hanging for anything. You aren't the first carrier I have worked with and you won't be the last."

"Then let's get on with it," she said.

"I'll have my crew begin loading immediately."

She shook her head. "You won't load anything until I know where we're taking your cargo, and exactly what we're doing with it."

"I'll be aboard in a few minutes to work out the details."

"You'll come no further than the cargo container. That's where the load goes and you've got no business we can't discuss there."

"You sure screech like a beast for somebody with no legs, but I'm on my way." He slapped his hand down on the desk to cut off the comm.

Remembering to make a quick detour by the MedBay to grab a small surgi-seal dressing for the back of her head, she had Marti apply it before she went down to meet Parker on the cargo container catwalk.

He stood just outside the inner airlock waiting impatiently. Marti's Gendyne automech walked out behind her and took up a position blocking access to the ship. It extended its legs fully and both heavy manipulator arms sported live-fire projectile rifles.

"Your robot doesn't intimidate me much," he said.

"Everybody knows robots have blocks against firing on human targets."

"That is a factual statement, Mr. Parker," Marti said. "However you should be aware that my Gendyne automech is under the control of a registered artificial awareness, and is not independent. As such, I have the cognitive authority to determine what is an acceptable use of force. Additionally, even if I were inclined to follow the robotic directive standards, the cargo you are bringing aboard is not human and therefore not protected under that inhibition." The two fine dexterity arms locked rounds into the firing chambers on both guns simultaneously and it made sure they were pointing at the center of Parker's body.

He took a half step back reflexively and Kaycee smiled. "Let's call this insurance. You may have me over a bulkhead for the sake of my crew, but you need to understand that we play square, or it ends now."

"You aren't the only one with that kind of mindset, Doctor." He tilted his head toward the far end of the container as two guards appeared just inside the airlock. He held out a thinpad. "That will serve as a bill of lading for you and your ship. For security reasons, it does not have your destination and timetable. I will give those to you after you're loaded and ready to leave the system."

"I want to know where we're going," she said.

"Not happening. The less you know right now the easier it is for you to keep it secret."

"You're worried about me turning on you?"

"Of course I am," he said. "I'd be a fool if I didn't have safeguards in place. For example, you need to look at the last screen on that thinpad." He smiled as she flipped through to the end. "Do you recognize what that is?"

It was a piece of heavy artillery mounted on the bottom

of the station and aimed at the underbelly of the *Olympus Dawn*.

"It may be antiquated, but in case you're unaware of how much damage a rail-gun will deliver at close range, if you choose to back out there's more than enough hit potential to guarantee there won't be any pieces left of this ship big enough to survive re-entry," he said. "Ordinarily I like to think of that as a motivational tool, although since you like to point guns at people, too, I think you can see the bigger picture here. What I've got aimed at you is along the same lines of what's in your guard dog's hands, except a lot bigger. I think that makes my dominance in this little game we're playing clear enough. Don't you agree?"

She nodded.

"So if you're done pissing on the deck, I have 300 sleeper cabinets and an independent power supply to get mounted before sunset down on the planet. As long as you and your robot stay out of the way, you should be ready to leave about the same time we are launching the rescue mission."

CHAPTER TWENTY-EIGHT

Ethan walked untied from the line, but he stayed with the other humans as they trudged through the jungle. They had reached the edge of a wide, slow-moving river before they stopped for their midday meal. Instead of setting the rope ring in the center of their camp they set it against the edge of the water. Possibly so that the prisoners could drink.

As soon as they'd stopped marching, the wakat hoard dove into the river and swam out several meters into the deeper water. It wasn't until they began throwing creatures up on the shoreline that he realized they weren't playing, they were fishing. The Ut'arans grabbed up the writhing snakelike creatures and with a twist of a bare hand broke their heads off. They passed the fish out and everyone began eating ravenously. They appeared to prefer recently killed food over the preserved rations they carried in their pouches.

Ethan refused to eat the still squirming food and chose to stay inside the ring. Mir'ah had made it clear she now trusted him enough not to keep him a prisoner, but when he decided to join the other humans, she didn't question his desire to be with his people, and instead opened the rope border for him.

He crashed to the soft dirt beside Tash and powered down his suit. He'd been stumbling along on muscles for about half the day but hadn't shut his liner down at all, so he was sore, but still not crippled. When the liner powered off and the gravity pulled his blood supply toward his lower body, a wave of dizziness washed over him and he collapsed flat onto his back.

Rene and Angel were already in that position.

"Is it safe to drink the water?" he asked, glancing at Tash.

She shrugged.

"If we don't drink some, dehydration will kill us before the gravity does," Angel said.

"There are parasites in the water," she said.

"How long will it take for them to kill us?"

"We haven't found any in the local environment that will kill us. With the right medical care they can all be dealt with easily," she said. "The problem is they can make you sick for weeks, and that can be deadly without treatment."

"I don't think any of us expects to be here for weeks," Nuko hissed. Her patience with the situation had reached a ragged end.

"Then I'm going to risk it," Ethan said, rolling over onto his belly and sliding down to the edge of the river. "I don't think I'll have another day to worry about it if they don't catch up with us soon."

"What about those carnivorous fish?" Angel asked.

"They're all small. If you don't put your face in the water your suit will protect you enough to keep them from being a problem," Tash said.

He shoveled up a handful of water in his gloved hands and with only a moment of hesitation sucked it down. It was shockingly cold and tasted faintly sweet. He nodded, scooping up another handful to rinse his face. It was an inefficient way to drink, but it was worth the effort.

Nuko helped Rene roll over and get close enough to the bank so he could get a drink too. He looked painfully weak.

"How are you holding up?" Ethan asked after the engineer had gotten several handfuls of water into him.

"I'm done," he said, breathing hard and resting his head

on the wet dirt as he looked at the captain. "My suit liner is dead and the only time I'm not shit-blind dizzy is when I am lying down."

"I can keep carrying him," Angel said, she was kneeling on the bank, scooping up water and letting it run down over her head.

Rene shook his head, making squishing sounds as it rocked in the mud. "This would be a smart place for me to stay. If you cross the river, you'll need someone to point the rescue team in the right direction. It's hard to track footprints in the water."

"Nothing says we're going across," the captain said.

"Doesn't matter, it's still better to leave me here. I have water and …" his voice trailed off. He'd run out of ideas to try to sell them on abandoning him here.

"He's right," Angel said. "If he can keep his liner intact, he can float in the water and take some of the gravity stress off his body. All he has to do is hold his head up to keep the killer tuna from eating his face off."

"I hadn't even thought of that," he said. "My plan was to go up a tree and try to get them to leave my suit intact. I figure if nothing else, the liner would help seal in my stink. The less I attract the attention of the critters, the better my chances."

Tash sat cross-legged on the grass more than a meter back from the bank. She hadn't dipped her hands into the river. "I think the clothes are an oddity for the Ut'arans. Cutting them off has to be improvising on their usual ritual, so if we strip him down first, there's no reason for them to shred his liner."

"How sure are we that help is coming?" Nuko asked. She looked like she was fighting to accept that they might have to leave Rene behind.

Ethan was too, but he forced himself to focus on what they had to do instead of what they felt right doing. "I'm sure that was a ship this morning. The only thing we're wagering on is how fast they can catch us."

"Before nightfall?" she challenged.

Tash nodded. "If this is the river I think it is, we're about eighteen klick from the Rockpile. A Windwalker team can cover twenty before midday."

"Then they could be close by this point," Rene said. "I'll be alright."

Ethan rolled onto his back and with a grunt propped himself up onto his elbows. "They'll have brought down some command personnel too. A medic and some security types, so they won't be quite that fast."

"And nothing says they didn't spend some time at the basecamp figuring out how shit went sidewise," Angel added.

"The Rockpile has an integrated surveillance system. They probably already know what happened," Tash said. "At least until the power went off."

"Even if we add a couple hours for getting their bearings, that means they're still only a few hours away," Rene said. "I think this is where I have to make my exit from the party."

Nuko shook her head. "That's a lot of assumptions to be wagering your life on."

He struggled for several seconds to roll over before Angel grabbed his arm and pulled him onto his back. Tash grabbed him by his feet and pulled him up so that the back of his head could rest on dry ground. "I'll do what I can to stretch my survival time, but you all have to march on. Help me get undressed and then just don't let them hide the liner. As soon as you move on, I'll get back into it and go for a swim."

"Do you even know how to swim?" she asked.

"Nope. But I can use a vine to tie myself off to

something. All I have to do is keep my head above water."

CHAPTER TWENTY-NINE

Kaycee paced along the length of the command deck corridor between the ConDeck and the lift cage. It wasn't as disturbingly empty as the mid–deck lounge or the crew deck, and it kept her from feeling like she was completely alone. She'd been on the *Olympus Dawn* for most of a year, but this was the first time she felt the size of the ship. It wasn't huge by any real measure, except when it was empty.

She had made the only choice she could, given the options, and although she had talked it over with Marti, she still chewed herself up with doubt. The AA's measured logic gave her no reassurance in a human sense. Stopping at one end of the hallway, she leaned her head against the bulkhead beside the ConDeck door. "Marti can you get a message to Ammo and Quinn without the station picking it up?"

"You can speak to them directly if you wish," it said.

"That would be better." She palmed the door open and took Ethan's normal seat on the ConDeck. "This might be a stupid question but, don't the PSE have comms? Why can you talk to them, but not the crew if they are still in their exosuits?"

"The PSE use low power transmitters and have a much shorter range than our space-rated systems," Marti explained. "I use encrypted pulse signals to my body on the surface and I can convert these signals to audio RF through the shuttlecraft transceiver. With that, they can receive that transmission via their comm earpieces. They are almost ten kilometers from the basecamp, but I can keep the broadcast power level low enough not to be detected above the planet's ionosphere."

"Good, I don't care how you do it, but I need to talk to them."

"Stand by," it said. "They are currently moving quickly in a dense jungle understory and I want to make sure your voice doesn't distract them. The environment is hazardous enough without an unexpected voice in their ears."

"Good thinking," she said as the sound came up on the comm speakers. She could hear both of them breathing hard and grunting with occasional snapping sounds as punctuation.

"Go ahead, Kaycee," Ammo said. "I think Quinn needs a breather, anyway. He's been running point for the last couple hours."

"Sounds intense. How are you holding up?"

"We're both swinging in spec," the handler said. "Blood's still making it to the brain so far."

"We're tracking them," Ammo said. "We're hoping to find them before dark, so we're pushing hard and fast."

"Just watch each other close. You could stroke out if the drugs burn through your system too quickly," she said. "The harder you work, the more likely that is to happen."

"We're not quite jogging, but we figure if the Ut'arans maintain the pace they've set so far, we can catch them," he said.

"Marti's kept me posted. So you're on foot?"

"And naked as the day I hatched," Ammo added.

"Nojo?"

"All-our-bits-swinging-in-the-wind, style of naked," she said.

"That's insane." Kaycee shook her head. "I'm not even going to ask why you made that decision, but you need to be careful."

"More careful than walking naked in a jungle full of wild animals and angry natives?" she asked.

"Yah, probably. We've got an exit strategy," she said. "Once they get the cargo loaded, Parker said he can get them back."

"Cargo?" Quinn asked.

"Yah, it's what I had to agree to, in order for him let us leave," she said.

"Should we stop and let him get them?" Ammo asked.

"I don't trust him to keep his word. He says he's got people with eyes on them now."

"Then why the frak hasn't he gotten them out already?" he snarled.

"He's using them as leverage," she explained. "Problem is, once he's bent us the rest of the way over, he's got no reason to hold up his end of the deal."

"You think he'll go sidewise?"

"Maybe," she said. "Considering what he's doing up here, if they catch you there's no doubt in my mind he'll twist it."

"How's he putting the pegs to us?" Quinn asked.

Kaycee thought about if for several seconds. "If I tell you this, I don't want you to explain it to Ethan before I have a chance to talk to him. Understood?"

"Stand by," Ammo said.

Almost a minute passed with no answer. "What's going on down there? Did we lose them?"

Negative," Marti said. "They are discussing the propriety of withholding information from the captain."

"Where do you stand on it?" she asked.

"I accept the necessity of the situation, and the desirability of having more than one path to rescuing the crew. I am uncertain if the risk level is commensurate with the potential return, because of the uncertainty of either option producing the desired results. However, not revealing details about the payload until we have secured the captain and the crew does not seem unreasonable."

"I just don't want Ethan flying off before we get away from those guns." She shivered as her mind once again showed her in vivid detail what that might mean.

"In my observation, the captain does tend to react before being aware of all the facts," Marti said. "Such an action could have detrimental consequences regarding our collective survival."

"That was what I thought, too." She drummed her fingers on the edge of the console while she waited.

"They have concluded their discussion."

The sounds of the jungle came backup on the speakers. "Alright, we agree," Ammo said. "But you need to understand you're asking Quinn to swallow his sense of loyalty and it's not going down easy."

"I understand that. It's not going down easy up here either," she said. "I'm having to do something dangerously far over the line, but I've got no choice."

"Doc, just toss it out on the table so we can get on with business." The handler's tone was dead flat.

"They're not just using Ut'arans on the station, they're harvesting slaves to sell off world," she said. "They're loading 300 sleeper cabinets in the cargo container now."

Ammo gasped. "You are joking aren't you? Not about the slaves, but about loading them."

Kaycee cleared her throat. "Parker made it clear that he would let the crew die if I refused."

"We're down here to get them. You could have told him to go fuck himself," Quinn hissed.

"I really couldn't. He's holding the *Olympus Dawn* too."

"Director Parker has a set of railguns locked on the ship and threatened to use them if we failed to accept this arrangement," Marti added.

"He left no doubt that he'd shred us and dump the remains into the atmosphere," she said.

Silence hung long enough that Kaycee thought they'd disconnected from the comm again. Finally, Ammo said, "If we get caught, that's the end of all of us. They still execute slavers."

"That's not the kind of exit strategy I'm thinking makes sense," Quinn said.

"I know that," she said. "Marti and I are still working on the next part of the plan, but we have to get everybody home safe first."

"I'd like to know what you're thinking," Ammo said. "If we're all going to hang together, I think we've got a right to know what we're trying to do."

"Forrester gave me something that he says will help us get out on the back end," Kaycee said. "I don't know what it is yet, but I've got it locked down for now and once we clear out, we'll figure out how to use it."

"Doc, you're not helping to make me feel fuzzy about this," the handler said.

"I get that," she agreed. "Right now, you stay after tracking them down and I'll focus on the long game."

"Fine," Ammo said, her tone sounding more than a little icy. "You said that Parker has eyes on them. What should we expect?"

"He said he knew where they were and that they were safe. For now," she said. "I assume that means he's got people on the ground already, but it might not."

"If he does, they don't give a frak about people dying," she said. "We found a place where it looks like they stopped and the remains of a body. Mostly eaten by animals."

Kaycee's heart turned to granite in her chest. "Is it one of ours?"

"There wasn't enough left to identify, but Nuko left us a note in the dirt that confirmed it was one of the basecamp staff." She drew in a noisy breath and let it out. "All we had to go on were the remnants of a jumpsuit and some leftover scraps of meat."

"The big animals come out at night," he added. "It probably happened last night and we're making the best time we can. Problem is if we haven't caught them by sundown we'll have to shelter in the shuttle."

"Parker said once they get the cargo loaded, they'll send down a rescue party to get them out of there. Hopefully you'll find them before then," Kaycee said. "Have you gotten any readings of them yet?"

"Technology tends to freak out the animal life. If we don't want to give their captors a warning that we're following them, we need to travel close to nature," Quinn said.

"Which is how he talked me out of my clothes in the first place," Ammo said. "We're hoping to blend in with the natives."

"It might not convince the Ut'arans, but if he has eyes on them it might get us past the ones watching," he said. "There's no way they'd expect naked humans out here in the jungle."

"There is that," Ammo said. "I just wish I knew how close we are to catching up."

"You can't use even the handheld scanners?" Kaycee asked.

"Every time we pull them out it sounds like someone is lighting monkeys on fire," he said. "And at any kind of range

I don't think a handheld scanner will differentiate a human from the locals."

"We were hoping to track their exosuit's EM signatures, but with another set of eyes around them, we'll have to walk in blind," Ammo said.

"Which brings us back to the point. We need to keep moving," the handler said. "Especially if there is another layer of crap to cut through."

"Just be safe."

"I think we're well past that point now." Ammo said.

That was undeniably true.

CHAPTER THIRTY

Quinn trudged along the trail in front of her, looking down at the ground but still aware of his surroundings. It was clear that the change in their situation had upset his sense of propriety with the universe.

"Do you want to talk about it?"

"Not really." He shrugged. "We're hammered no matter how this plays out."

"We need to figure how it changes things." She'd reached the same conclusion he had and was struggling not to give up.

"I'm trying to wrap my head around that," he said. "What bothers me most is that we should have seen this."

"Sometimes it's hard to see the forest—"

"Until you're beating your head against the branches." He took a swing at a convenient limb that hung over the trail. "Frak, we really got our eggs handed to us."

He hauled himself up onto a tree that had fallen beside the trail and sat. They needed to take breaks more often as muscle fatigue started to take its toll on their legs. That meant they were slowing down, but hopefully not enough that they wouldn't find their crewmembers in time. It was a physical wall that neither of them could push through.

Knowing that when they finished here, their troubles would only get worse once they got back to the ship, didn't help their motivation.

"We should have seen it coming," he said, pulling out a waterbag and handing it to her.

"Kaycee did," she said. She settled onto a rock and took a small sip before she handed it back. "The rest of us were just slow on the pickup."

He shook his head. "This isn't slow. The minute we tied off to the station, Parker had us. If he's got guns ready to rip the ship apart, you know he did that while we were all sitting on our asses."

"We expected them to be a science station full of science types."

"I get that, so we're out here trying to rescue our captain and most of our crew because we were stuck to the deck." He pounded the side of his fist against the log he sat on. "He's at least a step ahead of us every time we try to get a handle on what's going on."

"I can't argue that," she said.

"Now we find out he's got someone on the surface keeping track of the situation," he said. "We might have been able to overwhelm a bunch of natives, but if he's got people down here too, you can count on the fact that they'll be a lot harder to get past. They've got to be better equipped than we are."

He was right, but unless they wanted to give up now, they had no choice but to see it through. It made her feel a lot more naked.

"You know, being in our skin might be more effective against them," she said, grinning as her mind reached for an idea. "They sure as hell won't be looking for a naked rescue party. They might just dismiss two sunburned idiots walking through the jungle without a second thought."

He laughed. "There is that. We might be more invisible to them than to the natives. At least if they don't look too close."

"And if they do, then it will take them a long second to

fit it into their reality," she said, watching the spark come back to his face.

"The element of shock is always better than the element of surprise."

She grinned. "Your momma said that I'd wager."

He nodded, standing up and offering her a hand. "I think she got it from weird Uncle Bob. The badger hunter. This one time he came in from a hunt covered in—"

"Quinn, honey, I don't need to know."

"But it has to do with an alligator and …" He winked as she shook her head.

They'd covered another two hundred meters when the trail opened up onto a clearing. He stopped at the edge of the trees and ducked down to scan the area with his eyes. Blinding sunlight flooded through the opening in the canopy above them. He held a hand over his brow and squinted.

"We've probably got another body," he said. "I don't see it but there's a pile of hardware that might be a PSE and a bunch of rags blowing in the wind."

Ammo had hidden on the opposite side of the trail and leaned against the base of a massive tree. She closed her eyes for a second and then nodded. "If it's clear, let's go see who it is," she whispered.

"I don't see a body but the whole area is trampled flat," He stood backup and stepped out into the open. "The grass is taller here, so it looks like they didn't move out too long ago. Otherwise it would have stood backup."

They edged around the perimeter of the clearing toward the pile of suit pieces.

Fortunately there was no spectacle of blood and gore this time. Only a body, naked, and facing up. As they got closer, Ammo recognized it as Sandi. "At least it's not one of ours."

Quinn stopped well back, from where she lay. "She was

one of the passengers we brought in with us," he whispered.

She nodded. "She was the one that Nuko said would be next."

"I'll check her out and you can look around to see if she left us another note?"

"It's alright. I'm not that squeamish about dead things. At least not ones without catastrophic disassembly issues," she said as she stepped around him. We should start with the body then do a fast once over on the rest of the clearing together."

Kneeling down beside Sandi's body, she almost missed the knife that came up out of the grass in a feeble swing. It was weak and slow and Quinn kicked it away. Her arm fell limply back to the ground above her head.

Ammo jumped up. *She's still alive!*

Her eyes flickered open. "Pra mor'et at'esha," she whispered, her voice so weak as to be almost inaudible.

"No. Kill. Help," Marti translated.

"We don't want to hurt you." Ammo looked around to make sure there weren't any other weapons hidden in the grass.

Her eyes opened wider and she shook her head. She obviously wasn't firmly feeling reality. She looked like she was close enough to dead to see the afterlife from where she lay.

"You know us, we're from the *Olympus Dawn*," Quinn said. "We're looking for our crew." He'd fished a waterbag from his pouch and was tearing the top open as he knelt on the other side of her. He tilted her head up and dribbled some on her lips.

Rolling her eyes to the side, she struggled to fit their nakedness together with their sudden appearance. Clearly, that wasn't happening for her yet.

"What happened to you?" Ammo asked.

"We'ir Sharrah," she croaked out, licking her lips and staring at the waterbag as he dropped more onto her mouth.

"Giving to the jungle," Marti translated again.

"They left me … to die," she whispered.

"When?" he asked. Easing her head back to the ground, he handed the water to Ammo and dug in his pouch.

"This morning." She took another sip. "I was weak … so they abandoned … me."

"What about our crew?"

The water seemed to be infusing her with strength, but she still looked like someone had beaten her with a hose. "They were all in PSE," she said. "But Rene's suit was almost dead. When it quits, he'll be next."

Quinn pulled out one of the injection pens and jammed it against her leg. She made a little squeak as the medication shot into her system.

"What's that?" she asked. Her eyes rolled back in her head but then seemed to clear up.

"It's a vaso-regulator," he explained. "It'll get your blood moving in the right direction again."

"I can feel it," she said, nodding.

Making a decision, Ammo stood up. "Marti, bring the shuttle to our location and stay here with her. We've got plenty of open landing zone."

"Can't let them … see the shuttle," Sandi said, strength coming back to her voice.

"Marti, ignore that. Just do it," she said, glaring down at her. "Get her aboard and then keep it here. I think we're catching up with them."

"I am en route now, ETA forty seconds," it said.

"We've been trying to slow the Ut'arans down," she said. "I don't know how long I've been here, a few hours maybe."

"When did they leave you?" he asked.

"No more than an hour after sunrise," she said, reaching out for the waterbag.

"Then they can't be that far ahead of us," Ammo said, feeling a shot of optimism feed her in an almost physical sense.

A screeching chorus exploded from the jungle just before the shuttle shot over the edge of the trees and dropped like a stone toward the ground. Marti was standing in the open door and jumped out before the engines had completely shut down.

"I will get her aboard and tend to her medical needs," it said. "As I was on approach, I detected a very weak power signature approximately four and a half kilometers to the northwest. It may be from an exosuit."

"I think that's the way they headed," Sandi said as the automech bent over and scooped her up in its arms. "There's a river about that far down the trail. The Cha'nee village is downstream from there. Mir'ah told us that's where we were headed."

"How far away is this village?" Ammo followed Marti toward the shuttle.

"From here I don't know for sure. Twenty-five klick maybe. Another full day at the speed we were traveling," she said. "I don't think any of them have the power to make it that far though."

Quinn reached out and grabbed Ammo's arm. "If they get that far, there's no way we'll be able to get them out."

CHAPTER THIRTY-ONE

"What the hell is that?" Kaycee growled as she walked through the airlock and sidestepped to get around a huge piece of machinery they were anchoring to the center of the catwalk. It sat a few meters inside the cargo container on the ship end of the center catwalk.

"It's an insurance policy," one of them said. He was wearing an engineering service patch on his coverall but was driving a heavy steel pin into the deck plating to hold the device in place.

"It guarantees that the cargo maintains power until you arrive at the destination," Parker said. He was supervising the installation.

"It appears to be a power plant," Marti said. Its Gendyne automech had stopped outside the airlock. It could not squeeze past the hardware without trampling the workers who were installing the gear, since they'd removed several of the modular deck plates to limit access.

"That too," he said. "It's a three terawatt antimatter reactor."

"That is substantially higher output than is necessary to support the independent operation of the sleeper containers," the AA said.

Parker nodded. "It is."

Marti extended its sensor head up and around the unit. "It also appears to have substantial modifications to the original design."

"That is true too," he said, crossing his arms and leaning

back against the roll-along that they used to cart the reactor into place.

Kaycee glared at him. "Why did you bring your own power plant? We've got the power hooked up to the container from our end."

"Do you know what a deadman switch is?" he asked.

"A failsafe device used to provide a specific response to an undesirable change in situation," Marti said.

"Exactly." He grinned in a way that sent a shiver down her spine. "In this case, we've modified the reactor to overload if you don't deliver the cargo, or try to dump the container before it reaches its destination."

"A three terawatt antimatter detonation would cause an explosion of 10,800 billion joules," it said.

"That sounds like a big number. What is that in human terms?" She knew she didn't want to know, but she had to ask.

"Approximately equivalent to two-and-a-half megatons of high explosive," it said.

"So you've just mounted a bomb in the cargo container to destroy the evidence if I try to cross you." She shrugged.

He laughed. "And your ship with it."

"What triggers the overload condition?" Marti asked.

The engineer stood up and wiped sweat off his forehead with the back of a sleeve. "Any fluctuation in the ground plane connection between your ship and the container. As long as you keep the power connected to your ship, you've got no worries."

"Change your mind and you can't get far enough away before it goes off," Parker added.

"Get that out of here now." She took an involuntary step back. "I didn't agree to you putting a bomb on the ship."

"Nope. It's already armed." He reached out and patted

the reactor affectionately. "Truth is, that it doesn't matter what you agreed to. In case you didn't notice, we do things my way."

"Once we deliver the slaves, how do we get rid of this … thing." Her mind ran into an emotional wall and bounced to a stop.

"My agent on the receiving end will disconnect it after the sleeper units are unloaded. Before that, trying to cut it lose from your grid would be bad." He stood up straight and made sure she looked at him before he added, "If you stop somewhere else along the way, and then decide to go on to your destination, a second transition to cruise will also set it off."

She nodded. "That means we go straight to the delivery." He was making sure they didn't have a chance to roll over on him. If they didn't show up, they couldn't get the bomb out of the ship without his help, and they were dead.

He smiled at her again. "On the plus side, once you get the load delivered we'll transfer the balance of your payment to your ship's account."

"Wait, what?"

"Right after you arrived we put a deposit for your return load into your account. You'll get the rest when you get there," he said. "We don't want this to look like something unusual is going on. You know, we need a financial trail and all that."

"That also makes it look like we are willing participants in the whole thing," Marti added.

"You know for a freighter brain, you're pretty smart," Parker said, glancing over at the automech. "Now, if you'll let us get on about our business, we're ready to connect the cabinets. Once we finish that, we'll load the real cargo and we can get you on your way."

"Not until you get my crew out of there," she said.

"Ah yes, of course. Once we get your crew back," he said. "We've got about five hours of work if you don't interrupt me again. If it goes longer than that, we won't be able to get down to the surface under the cover of darkness. Dr. Ansari will never let me take a shuttle down if I can't make a night landing. I'm sure you understand why that makes it imperative that you leave me the frak alone so I can get this done, yes?"

"Fine," she said, spinning around and pushing her way past the engineer and back to the ship.

As soon as they'd closed the airlock, she turned to Marti and shook her head. "We have to figure out how we can disarm that thing as soon as they're out of the container."

"I will research the possibilities," it said. "However we may need to accept that it could be impossible."

"I know," she growled as the inner door opened. "Otherwise I'm tempted to set it off right where we sit and take Parker and the fucking mess right along with us."

"That would be undesirable," it said, following her inside.

"If we don't get Ethan and the crew back …" She stopped herself short of letting the helplessness she felt push her over a line she knew she should never cross.

CHAPTER THIRTY-TWO

"There's the PSE," Quinn said as they both dropped over the dirt ledge and down toward the river.

Ammo pulled out her hand scanner and bending over it, opened the lid and tapped the screen. The jungle went insane above her but she watched the readout for several seconds before she nodded and closed it down again. Eventually the screaming overhead died back down to its normal level of chaos.

It was the source of the power signal. "It's weak enough I'm surprised the shuttle sensors picked it up at all."

"I wonder if it's Rene's suit?" he said, walking over and picking up a piece of an arm shell. He held it up to his own arm to compare size and shrugged. The whole arm barely went from his elbow to the tip of his fingers.

Joining him, she picked up another piece and checked it against her own anatomy. It was only a little smaller than her arm. "It looks about his size. Or Nuko's," she said. "But where's the liner?"

"If the power was dying, maybe he tried to go on without the exoshell," he said dropping the piece back onto the pile.

"Why would anyone keep just the liner on? If it was dead it'd just make it harder to walk wouldn't it?" She pitched her piece down too.

"I've never worn one so I don't know," he said, walking up to the edge of the river and staring across at the far bank. "They keep the circulatory system working, so maybe it was still powered enough to help?"

"It looks like they might have stopped here for a while and then gone into the river," she said, pointing to some scuff marks in the mud near where he stood.

"I wonder if it's safe to swim?" He reached down and scooped up a handful of water and sniffed it. "Smells clean."

"If you say so," she said. "I didn't think water had a stink except if you had a bad recycler."

He nodded, looking back at the far side. "If they crossed here, we might have trouble tracking them. Especially if they went downstream."

"How would they get across?"

He shrugged. "Swim."

"That assumes any of them know how to swim," she pointed out.

He shot her a strange expression. "Of course, they know how to swim. Who doesn't?"

She stared at him for several seconds before he realized why she'd asked. Most of them were born in space colonies. Even Mars had little enough water that swimming was a rare skill to have.

He lowered his head and his shoulders sagged. When he turned back around to study the far bank again, Ammo realized he looked tired. Bone weary with a load of frustration piled on for good measure.

"Maybe we need to take a break," she said, walking up beside him. "We're both fighting the gravity, and we haven't slowed down or even eaten."

He shook his head and glanced up in the direction of the sun. "We've only got a couple more hours before the sun drops on us. We've got to find them before then."

He was right, but reality might crush out that possibility. It was hard to stay motivated when everything kept pulling them down, literally and figuratively. Time was running out and the dead exosuit they'd just discovered only drove that point deeper into their awareness.

"You look around here and I'll try to figure out if they crossed," he said. "If I get lucky, I might be able to see where they climbed up on the other side."

"You're going to swim over and look?" she asked. Obviously, he missed the hint that she couldn't swim.

He shook his head and pointed to a tangle of big tree branches that stuck up a dozen meters and overhung the river. "I'll just climb up there and see if I can see anything. Maybe they had a raft or something."

"Yah, whatever that is," she said with a sigh.

Heading back over to where the PSE was sitting, she watched him grab a branch and pull himself up toward where he could see across the river. She was barely standing at this point and he still had the energy to climb.

She knew it was emotional fatigue starting to tear her down too. Nine hours of hiking at two-g was enough to kill anyone's enthusiasm, but other than the small shot of hope they got when they found Sandi, there wasn't much else to keep them motivated.

She nudged the pile of exoshell parts with a toe and then paused. She looked at the two pieces that they'd picked up, and using the indentations in the ground put them back in place. Whoever laid them here set the pieces in a pattern.

An arrow.

Pointing almost at where Quinn was climbing the branches.

"Look sharp. These things are pointing in your direction," she said, hollering up at him.

"What?" He leaned around the side of the tree trunk to see what she was talking about.

"Yah, right at you there." She pointed at the exosuit and

then swung her arm along the line of the arrow.

He looked around and down at the base of the tree before he cocked his head to the side. "Is that vine tied to the tree or does it just look like it from here?"

She couldn't see which one he was talking about in the tangled underbrush. He'd eased himself back down to the ground and by the time she got to him, he was pulling it out of the water. "It looks like we've got something here," he said.

"Frak! It's Rene," she said as she recognized the limp form he was hauling up to the river bank. She ran out into the waist deep water and grabbed him under the arms to pull him in.

He opened his eyes and blinked several times in surprise. "I didn't expect to see you," he whispered. "And maybe not so much of you either."

"You're alive," she said as she heaved them both back toward the shore.

"I think so. Otherwise I have to say this isn't quite what I expected the afterlife to look like." He grinned and glanced pointedly at the decidedly female parts of her anatomy that hung close over his face.

"Obviously you're hallucinating, so shut up and let us rescue you."

He nodded and closed his eyes while they hauled him the rest of the way out of the water.

"Bring the shuttle. We've got Rene," Quinn said. He untied the vine from around the engineer's chest and helped roll him over onto his back.

"Stand by. ETA ninety seconds," Marti said.

The utter shock as he opened his eyes again and looked up at Quinn made Ammo double over in laughter.

"Yah, this is definitely not the right afterlife at all," he said. "Why are you both naked?"

"It was his idea," she said, tilting her head at the handler. "It has something to do with hunting baggers with no clothes."

"Badgers," he said as he knelt to untangle a collar of small branches that wrapped around Rene's neck.

"This has to be a hallucination," Rene said.

"We have that effect on people," she said. "Sandi reacted almost the same way."

"You found her?" His face wrinkled up strangely. "We had to leave her this morning and she was in a lot worse shape than I am."

"She's on the shuttle now," Quinn said. He handed Ammo a waterbag.

Rene nodded. "So they let you two come along."

"Parker doesn't know we're here." She tore the top off the water and handed it to him. Rene was in much better shape than Sandi so he took it and sipped at it slowly.

"He and Ansari insisted they had to wait until tonight to rescue you, and he wasn't going to let us come along," the handler said, his tone carrying a load of contempt as he spit out their names.

Quinn handed Ammo one of their vaso-regulator doses and she slapped it against Rene's leg. He grunted in surprise as the medication readjusted his circulatory pressure. Letting out a slow hiss he said, "Sandi would have been dead as soon as the sun went down. Me too probably. There are some big predators in the jungle."

"We know," she said. "We found some of their handiwork this morning."

"Toby."

"Probably." She glanced up as the sounds of animals rolled out of the jungle like a wave. "That's your ride."

The shuttle arced out over the river and dropped toward the water before it pushed in under the canopy of trees to settle on the muddy bank.

"Marti should be able to get you loaded," Ammo said, standing up. "We need to keep moving."

"Which way did they go?" Quinn asked as he picked Rene up and handed him to the automech. "Did they cross the river?"

"They went downstream on this side," he said. "But before you go, you need to know there's something going on."

"Yah, we know," she said. "They're slaving the natives."

"That explains why the one running things speaks our language," he said. "They're probably using her to harvest them."

"It also means they'll be doubly dangerous," Quinn said. "There's no telling what knowledge they've uploaded to her."

"Uploaded?"

"They're putting implants into them and uploading things directly to their brains," he said.

"Mir'ah's the one in charge," Rene said. "She's smart and ambitious, but she seems to be in awe of us. She calls us shiny."

"Shiny?"

He nodded. "They can see in infrared and our exosuits give off heat. In the dark that makes us look like we glow. The reason she didn't kill us with the others in the Rockpile is that we were suited up and she mistook us for someone she'd seen before. She called the other one Marat akUt'ar."

"It means shiny man," Marti said.

"She calls Ethan the Marat akEarth, and she seems to like him," he said. "He's been leaning into that to keep us alive."

"Anything else we need to know?" she asked.

"Night time is when it gets dangerous out here."

"We figured that out already," the handler said.

"You need to watch out for the wakats," he said. "They're almost as smart as the natives and they seem like they have a common language. As far as I can tell they work like guards and they can move through the trees faster than you could possibly move on the ground."

"Marti warned us about them too," she said. "What I'm more worried about is the ones that Parker has watching you. They've been keeping an eye on you all along."

"Keeping an eye on us?" Rene's eyes flashed in pure rage.

"He told Kaycee that they knew where you were all along, and that they had someone keeping an eye on you," Ammo said. "I don't know if it's true or not, but we have to assume he still has people on the ground somewhere."

"The Windwalkers," he hissed. "They're the ones who provide protective escort to expedition teams. They're good, and almost invisible."

"The Windwalkers had an entrance on the roof of the Rockpile," Marti said. "When I was restoring power to the basecamp so I could access the language database, I determined that their entrance had not been forced, but was the point of access for the Ut'arans."

"Do they wear PSE?" Quinn asked, pulling his hand scanner out and raising an eyebrow.

"Normally," he said.

"Then they aren't invisible to us," she said, grinning and looking down at her bare chest. "But odds are we'll look like a hallucination to them."

"There is that distinct possibility," he said. "You might sneak past for sure, but Quinn, not so much."

"Yah, he's a freak of nature even by earthly standards."

She nodded in the handler's direction where he'd walked over to look for the trail. "We figured in his case we'd rely on shock value."

Rene glanced over at him and closed his eyes. Shaking his head he whispered, "Next time he should get a longer loincloth."

CHAPTER THIRTY-THREE

Kaycee sat in the mid-deck with her head on her arms. She had been riding emotional waves as they'd recovered Sandi and then again, as they discovered that Rene was alive, and in fair condition too. Now she was just trying to keep from collapsing.

Although she knew Parker had outplayed them, she felt responsible because she was the one who had accepted his terms. There was no easy way out.

The more she racked her brain, the deeper she felt buried. Undeniably, they were humped.

"They appear to have completed loading the cargo container," Marti reported. "Director Parker is asking to speak to you at the outer cargo container airlock."

"I don't suppose I can just ignore him?"

"He says he has our orders."

Orders? I guess that's right. He owns us until that reactor is off our backs.

With a sigh, she pushed herself onto her feet.

Parker was waiting just inside the cargo container with three guards when she got there. All of them looked to be human for a change.

"You're loaded," he said when she walked up. Marti had managed to pick a path around the reactor so followed several steps behind her as a visual deterrent and bodyguard.

She nodded, looking around at the sleeper cabinets they'd pinned to the deck. 300 Ut'arans slept in glass cylinders packed into racks. *It looks like a morgue.*

"Here are your orders." He held out a single data stick. She took it and handed it over to Marti.

"Where are we taking the cargo?"

"You will make delivery to the Maxima Six Mining Station in Lyra Prime," he said. "It should take you 120 hours. Unless you have problems. And then, well that would be bad."

"Who do we contact?"

"You don't. My people will watch for you and make contact once they detect that you've entered the system. That's all on the stick."

"Of course," she said.

"It's been a pleasure doing business with you, Doctor." He turned to walk away and she reached out to grab his arm.

"We're not done. When do we get our crew back?"

He jerked his arm away and one of his guards shifted to put his hand on the butt of his sidearm. Marti swung one of his heavy manipulator arms around, bringing his rifle to bear on the man's chest. Its second arm brought another gun up to target Parker.

He locked eyes with her for several seconds before he nodded. "We will launch in an hour. Once the sun sets."

"I've heard that before. I want to know specifics."

"You don't seem to understand the topography here do you?" He glanced over at the guard and shook his head. The man stood down and moved his hand away from his weapon. Marti didn't move. "I do things my way. You're lucky I like you or I'd be telling you to be on your way now. There really is no reason for me to go out of my way to do you any favors."

"And you really don't understand how desperate I am to get my people back either," she said. "Almost insanely desperate you could say."

"I feel your frustration, Doctor, I do," he said, shrugging it off.

"I don't think you do." She stepped forward and lowered her voice. "How would it change your topography if I disconnected this cargo container from the ship's power right now? A couple megaton blast would take most of the station with us, wouldn't it?"

Parker eased back but his eyes flashed wide for an instant before he shook his head. "You're bluffing."

"Try me." She leaned in a little closer to fill the gap between them. "You obviously haven't done your homework."

He swallowed and shook his head. She could tell he was trying to reinforce his faith in his superior position.

Tilting her head to the side, she opened her eyes wider for effect. "If you'd checked into me, you'd know that in the last year I lost my family in the Starlight Colony disaster, and most of my entire fortune along with it. Now you're holding hostage the only people left in my world. I have no more fraks left to give about anything anymore."

She leaned forward more and bounced on her toes as she flung her arms out beside her. "I'm sure you picked up on the fact that the captain thinks I'm batshit insane. Do you really want to find out if he's right?"

She glanced around at the other guards with him. They were all sweating. Obviously, they were feeling her insanity rather vividly.

"Marti, how long will it take the reactor to overload once I disconnect the power to the box?" She didn't turn to look at the automech.

"Five microseconds."

She spun and took several steps back toward the ship before she pulled a medical scanner out of her pocket and looked at it like it was a detonator. "Deadman switch is such an ugly word isn't it?"

"You've got bigger eggs than I would have guessed, Doctor," he said. "Especially for a rich bitch."

"You know, I hate that phrase," she hissed, flipping the scanner open. She didn't turn it on, but she held her finger over it like she might.

He held his hands up and took an unconscious step back. Not that it would make a difference if she wasn't bluffing.

"Now I want a real frakking answer from you. When will you get my people back?"

"Ansari won't let me do anything until sundown. Seriously, that is outside my control." He turned his arm to look at his wrist chrono. "That's in fifty-six minutes. Flight time is about ten and then another ten or so to make contact."

"That wasn't so hard was it?" She smiled and closed the lid on the scanner.

He tried to hold his face steady, but she could see relief in his eyes.

"Then as long as you do your part, we'll be on our way." She let the smile melt off her face. "One last thing, you might be smart to point those railguns somewhere else. I know you won't use them, because you've just shown me that it's you who's lacking the eggs to blow us all up."

"You'll be leaving in two hours," he said, spinning and heading back through the airlock to the station with his guards almost stumbling over each other as they retreated with him.

"Insanity is an effective deterrent," Marti said.

She watched them pull the door closed before she dropped the medical scanner back into her pocket and let out a slow hiss of breath. "Even if it was a bluff."

"You played it well," it said.

"Lock them out of the ship. They don't need access anymore and you need to take a closer look at that power plant to see if we can get around the failsafe."

"I have locked the access codes on the airlock controls," it said, pivoting and heading over to begin its analysis of the reactor.

"I need to give Ammo a heads up." She followed Marti back toward the ship and stopped several meters away. Knowing that she was looking at an antimatter bomb still made her nervous, in spite of the fact that she's just threatened to use it herself.

"Secure channel open," it said.

"Yah, Kaycee what's swinging?" Ammo said over her commlink.

"You've got about seventy minutes before they supposedly show up to rescue the crew."

"Supposedly?" Quinn asked. "Is something telling you they're not planning to follow through?"

"I know he wouldn't hesitate to kill them and force me to make the run without a crew. He's shoved an antimatter bomb up our ass to make his point."

"What?"

"Yah. He's got us bent way over," she said. "Marti and I are working the problem though, so you focus on getting the crew out of there and leave this one to me."

"Got it," Ammo said. "We're pushing as hard as we can."

CHAPTER THIRTY-FOUR

The sun was almost on the horizon and long orange streamers of light split through the trees along the river. Ammo leaned over a log on the side of the trail and stared off into the distance. Her legs were shaking from the continuous strain but she knew they had to keep moving so she tried to ignore it.

"We've got two groups of PSE signatures ahead," Quinn said, flipping his scanner closed and waiting for the screeching in the jungle to echo down to its normal level. "A group of six and a group of two and a half or so."

"What does that mean?"

"The smaller group had two strong EM signals, one weak one, and one so faint it's almost undetectable." He put the scanner back in his pouch and leaned down beside her. "I'd assume the weaker signal is from our people. The others would be Parker's team."

"Where are they?"

"The larger group is eight hundred meters that way." He pointed through the trees and uphill from the river. "The other group is about five hundred meters further downstream."

She squinted into the setting sun. The glare was making her eyes hurt. "Could you tell what they were doing?"

He shook his head. "They're clustered together about twenty meters above the ground in the trees. They might be setting up an observation post since the Ut'arans don't seem to be moving."

"That would be the Windwalkers that Rene was talking about." She turned her back on the log and leaned against it. "We're sure nobody else is out here?"

"There are lots of other life forms around the crew. Dozens. Maybe more," he said. "But I didn't detect any others in PSE. My thinking would be to take out the Windwalkers first."

"We're running out of time," she said. "You won't sneak past them as big as you are. If I can keep their eyes on me, how long would it take you to get into position behind them?"

He shrugged. "Eight or ten minutes, depending on how hard it is to cut through the underbrush. It's a lot more dense than the path they took."

"I'll give you five minutes head start then I'll take the trail and see how distracting I can be," she said. "Hopefully they'll look twice at a native girl shaking her ass."

He stood up and pointed downstream to where a large outcropping of rock jutted into the river. "Don't go past that point. If you're going to put on a show, those rocks should be a good place for them to see you."

She nodded. "I'm not liking the idea of splitting up, but I don't see that we've got much in the way of options."

He pulled out his stunner pistols and chambered a round to both, then checked his extra clips. Eight in all. "I'll take the high road and you take the low road."

Keeping one of his weapons in his hand, he pulled himself up onto the small ridge that paralleled the river as an upper bank. He vanished in seconds, leaving her standing there counting down the minutes until it was time for her to move out.

"What the frak am I supposed to do to get their attention? Naked yoga?" she whispered to herself as she shuffled down the trail.

"Yoga could be dangerous at two-G," Marti said over the comm.

"Nojo," she said. She'd forgotten that they still had the AA as a backup if things got sidewise. It made her feel a lot better knowing that it was only a few kilometers away. With a shuttle, that was only a matter of seconds.

She started to haul herself up onto the rock outcropping, trying to make sure that if someone was looking, he was getting an eyeful. Normally, she could pull off seductive without a worry, but rock climbing naked wasn't one of her usual approaches. Nor did she think she was particularly graceful at it in this gravity.

By the time she reached the top of the eight meter high ledge, she felt a wave of fatigue grab her body. Forcing her legs under her, she faced toward the river and walked slowly toward the edge. Suddenly the exhaustion turned to dizziness. "Marty can you ask Kaycee what it feels like when the drugs burn through? I'm feeling exhausted and like the world is spinning."

Spreading her feet for stability, she stopped well back from the edge and slipped her hand into her pouch, feeling around for one of the injector pins. Quinn carried the extras with him, but she had two of her own. She didn't want to use it unless she had to, but she was definitely feeling out of spec.

"Are you alright?" Quinn whispered.

"I'm sure I will be," she said.

"The doctor says what you are feeling is likely the drug cocktail starting to wear off," Marti said. "She advises you to sit down before you give yourself a booster shot."

"Got it," she said, dropping onto her butt with a smack. Glancing over her shoulder to see if she could tell where the black-hats were, she realized that it didn't matter, anyway. She pulled the pin out, pressed against her thigh, and hit the button.

She gasped as her blood flow normalized. "Frak that's a rush." The world around her went from spinning to vibrating.

"Dr. Caldwell said that the boosters she prepped for you both had an adrenaline compound that was not in the original medication she gave you," it said.

"No shit, I think I'm glowing," she said, bouncing up on a wave of artificial energy. She twirled around several times, trying to get the feeling to burn off, but it clung to her like fire coursing through her body.

"She advises that your response to it is probably because you were unaware of how depleted you were before you medicated yourself."

"I can see where they are," Quinn interrupted over the comm. "Problem is, I can't get them without going hand to hand. They've rigged some kind of thermal drape around where they're hiding, and there's only one on the outside. He's standing guard, but whatever you're doing, he's watching you for sure."

"What are we going to do?" She stopped spinning and without looking in the direction she thought they were, she started running her hands over her skin. It felt like sparks were leaping from her fingers. It would have been a sensation she would have enjoyed exploring, except she was still acutely aware of the danger around her.

"I can make some noise and drop them as they come out to investigate." He grunted as he apparently moved in.

"If you think you'll have to dance with these guys, you might be smart to give yourself a kick, this is a hell of a rush."

"After I'm done, maybe," he said. "Just keep doing what you're doing until you hear the party start, then say a prayer that I'm faster than they are."

Less than a minute later, she heard a loud crashing sound from the trees in the direction where she assumed they were. A deep thud followed, and more than a few animals shrieked their displeasure.

Even in an exosuit, a fall of twenty meters at two-G was enough to punctuate someone's existence. She slid down the rock face and dove into the underbrush, trying to get into position to back him up.

"One," he said, announcing that he'd dropped the guard.

Three hissing cracks echoed overhead as he fired off a short burst of stunner rounds, followed by three more strings of noisy crashes as his victims tumbled to the ground. "Four."

The commotion kicked into full as the two remaining members of the party realized what was happening and started to fight back. She tracked in on them by the sounds. Overhead she could see the branches of a tree swaying as Quinn struggled to subdue both of them at once.

As another body tumbled down, she realized that it wasn't a fair fight. She was still too far away to see who had fallen, but when the sounds of the battle died abruptly, she had a moment of panic.

"Quinn, are you alright?"

"The other one got away," he said after several seconds of silence. "I lost him but I think he was headed toward our people."

"That's not good," she said, stepping up over a rock ledge and stopping short to avoid slipping on a squishy mess that had once been a person. She eased to the side and edged past the bloody pile of flesh, pressing on toward the tree where the fight happened.

"We can track him from his PSE," he said.

A faint hissing groan came from behind a thick tangle of vines just beside her. "I've got a live one down here," she said, jumping back and pulling out her stunner. She pointed it in the direction of the sound.

"On my way."

She could hear Quinn grunting as he worked his way down the tree, but she didn't take her eyes off the source of the noise. She couldn't see anything in the dense underbrush, although she knew from what she could hear that she probably didn't want to.

Swinging down from a branch overhead, he crashed to a stop at her side. She jerked her head toward where the sound had originated. He pushed into the tangle and stopped suddenly, sucking air through his teeth. "He's not going to last long." Pointing his stunner at something, he snapped two quick rounds into the vines.

"He'll be better off that way." He turned back in her direction and she could tell from his face he was trying not to think about what he'd just done. "We should make sure none of the others will be a problem."

She shook her head. "Judging from what I saw back there, I'd bet he was the lucky one. And we don't have time." She glanced to the west and realized that the sun was no longer visible at all. "We need to get back to the trail and try to catch them before we lose the rest of the light."

He pulled out his hand scanner and flipped it on. The screeching seemed much closer this far off the trail and he glanced around before he looked at the screen. "Looks like he's running right toward the camp."

"That will be a problem," she said, raising her voice and leaning toward him to be heard over the din, "but I don't like the thought of being eaten, more than I'm worried about the one that got away."

"At least we can see where he is with this," he said. "It means he won't sneak up on us."

"Yah, but we won't sneak up on frakking anything as long as you've got it turned on."

"Exactly," he said, grinning at her. "That gives us two tools to use against him. If he's smart, he'll be listening to the voices of the jungle."

CHAPTER THIRTY-FIVE

Ethan sprawled flat on his back staring up at the darkening sky. His PSE was dead. Completely and utterly. He'd powered down his exoshell almost three hours ago and his liner flat lined more than an hour before they stopped walking. He was in good shape so he'd managed to muscle it in, but he could feel his circulatory system refusing to push his blood to his head. After lying down, he propped his feet up on a rock to help keep his brain powered, but it was giving him more than a trivial headache.

He knew tonight would be his night. In the morning, he wouldn't be moving well enough to travel further.

He rolled his head to the side and looked at Angel. She was lying face down and looking almost as bad as he felt. Her power had only lasted an hour longer than his, but her liner had stayed active until she hit the dirt. "How are you doing?" he whispered. He couldn't muster even enough energy to talk in a normal voice.

"Better than you I bet," she said. "I know you walked half the afternoon with no suit."

"Yah, I'm a bit uncomfortable." He craned his neck to look around at Nuko and Tash. They sat near the edge of their rope ring, whispering to each other.

Nuko glanced in his direction and rocking up onto her hands and knees crawled over to him. She stayed above him and hung over his face. Her suit still had power and just watching her hang in that position made him tired.

"Something's up," she whispered.

He raised an eyebrow but didn't respond.

"Look over my shoulder up into the trees." She shifted a little to make sure he had a clear line of sight. "About thirty meters up. Do you see him?"

Ethan shook his head, but then a slight motion caught his eye. "It looks like Isaiah. Maybe that's the rescue party."

She shook her head. "I don't think so. Tash says he's being sloppy. She noticed him when he knocked a branch down and it hit the ground just outside the zo'mar ring. She swears he'd never make that kind of mistake unless he was rushing."

"If it's not a rescue party what's he doing?"

"He looks like he's fixated on something back in the direction we came." She dropped down beside him and turned over to look up into the trees. "He's barely looked down at us. It's like he's worried about something behind us."

"Angel, are you scanning this?" he asked, turning to face her.

She'd rolled onto her back and nodded. "I see him now. He's in a position that leaves him overexposed to us but not visible to someone coming from up the river."

Tash had eased up next to Angel and was watching the Ut'arans. "Look at the wakats. They're acting strange, too. There's something out there that's got them spooked."

Ethan tilted his head up and dragged his arm under it to keep it propped in a position where he could see the rest of the natives. Most were doing their usual evening rituals and getting ready for the night. But Moktoh, the wakat he recognized as Mir'ah's personal companion, was walking in circles around her while she talked to one of the others. Even being alien, it was obvious he was agitated about something.

"Something's coming," he said.

"Maybe it's the rescue party?" she said.

Angel shook her head. "If it is, why's he hiding from it?" she asked, pointing her chin at the man in the tree.

Tash bit down on her lip. "When Mir'ah attacked the Rockpile, we thought they got in through the top egress hatch. The Windwalkers bunkrooms are up there. You don't think they let them in do you?"

"It doesn't matter, but from how he's acting I don't think he's here to help," Nuko said. "We'd be safer assuming that his arrival means trouble."

"At least until we know—"

The rest of his thought vanished as an explosion of chaos erupted in the jungle just beyond their protective ring of stones.

"What the frak?" Angel growled as everything around them leapt into motion at once.

"Is it one of those predators?"

Tash shook her head as she stood up. "It would have to be a whole pack of them to create that much commotion. Korah are lone hunters."

"Stay down," Angel roared. She sacrificed what little battery she had left to power up and yank her back to the ground. "If it's a rescue party, the shooting is about to start."

Ethan looked back into the trees to see what Isaiah was doing but he'd vanished. It wasn't until a cascade of branches and leaves caught his attention that the captain realized the Windwalker was tumbling out of the tree toward the river. He heaved himself over in time to see him crash down into the water in a tangle of mangled limbs. From the way he hit, it didn't look like there was any way he'd survived the fall.

Twisting to look up into the canopy, he saw a single Ut'aran hanging out into the air by one arm while he fished frantically in his pouch for something. He pulled out a pistol and started firing into the camp.

"Somebody's armed the natives!" he hollered, pointing up into the tree as the closest wakats started screaming. More than a dozen rounds found targets but most of them climbed back to their feet. It took a second stunner hit to leave them face down and twitching.

The noise in the jungle made it hard for the Ut'arans to identify where the shots were coming from, although after another wave of wakats started dropping, Mir'ah caught on to the fact that the attack was coming from above. Barking orders like a seasoned warrior, she got control of the chaos and pointed up at the enemy position. A swarm of the enraged beasts launched themselves toward the base of the tree.

Ethan watched as the attacker realized that retaliation was moving in his direction, and rather than retreat, he swung down to land on a lower branch. Jamming his back against the trunk of the tree, he crouched low and pulled out a second pistol. As he dropped into his new position it was obvious that, although the person was not wearing a PSE, or even armor, he was definitely too big to be Ut'aran. He had to be human.

Then he realized he was too big to be human, too.

Quinn?

"Holy fraking shit! It's Quinn!" Ethan yelled as adrenaline surged through him and he shoved himself to his feet.

Nuko stared at him like he'd lost his mind, but he pointed to the branch where the handler was firing at the approaching wakat hoard. Bodies were piling up around the base of the tree, but it looked like the tide of alien flesh was gaining ground.

"He won't hold them all off," Angel hissed, pushing

herself to her feet and scanning the area around them for something she could use as a weapon. Her suit was running on borrowed time and he could see in her face that she was moving by pure force of will.

"Is he naked?" Tash asked as she spotted him.

"I think so, but I don't really want to know." Ethan shook his head and tried to make sense of the chaos.

Nuko launched herself toward the tree, intent on doing as much damage as she could with her augmented strength. She was the only one who still had the reserve in her suit to run it at full output. Grabbing the nearest wakat by the arm, she spun once around and flung the creature head first into a tree stump. It didn't even twitch as its skull exploded and it crumpled down in a lifeless heap. She turned, looking for another victim as two of them launched themselves at her.

Angel dove for one wakat, snagging it by the foot and crashing onto it with her full weight as it toppled forward. They plowed into the dirt face down and she slid up its back before it could react. Bringing her arm around into a choke hold, she hung on as it pushed up and dragged her away toward a tree. It thrashed backward with flailing fists but never had a good enough angle to land a hard blow. She clung to the wakat's back, squeezing harder until its thrashing weakened and it dropped.

Ethan knew he couldn't move well enough to join the fight, but the adrenaline accelerated his mind and he caught flashes of shocking violence in vivid detail.

He stared for an eternally long second at Nuko. Blood covered her and his heart skipped a beat. Or two. She had an odd shaped club in her hand and was using it to beat on another wakat. It took him several swings to realize that it wasn't a club at all. It was an arm. She'd ripped it off one of the creatures and was beating another one to death with the bloody end.

He turned as another sound sliced through his shock. Another layer of confusion erupted on the opposite side of the camp as a second Ut'aran charged into the battle, also brandishing a pair of pistols. This time the new wave of violence centered on their captors and not their companion pets.

As he watched in amazement, the newcomer cut steadily through the camp. The light of the setting sun had grown too dim to make out details, but he could see silhouettes of motion in the crackling sparks of stunner pellets erupting against Ut'aran skin.

Whoever it was, stood head and shoulders taller than the tallest of the Ut'arans., This person wasn't a native either, even though she wore nothing but a belt pouch. *She?* His mouth fell open as he recognized Ammo charging in his direction.

He snapped his head back and forth several times. *This can't be real!*

The sounds of fighting echoed further into the back of his mind. He suddenly felt disconnected, as the moments stretched into a blur of indefinite time. He realized that his vision seemed to fade with the dying light and he stumbled backward toward the river, unable to keep his feet under him.

Fortunately, the water cushioned his fall, even as its shocking cold forced a strange gurgling scream from his lungs. He bobbed in the water as reality swirled in odd ripples around him. The sky spun overhead. Faint orange streamers of the setting sun glowed against the violet clouds of night.

He blinked his eyes.

"Ethan stay with me," Nuko said, her voice strangely

muffled across the distance.

A shadow hung over him, blotting out the stars. A head and shoulders. A face too dark to see. It was her. She was holding on to him. He could feel her trembling.

"Marti, bring the shuttle now," another voice said. "We've got them but the captain's down."

"I'm in the water," he whispered. A metallic taste filled his mouth. Strange, hot and salty.

"ETA ninety seconds," Ammo said. She appeared over the shoulder of the shadow.

"He's awake," Nuko said.

"Kaycee wants us to give him a dose of juice. She says the adrenaline will keep his heart beating."

"Quinn?" he asked, this time he recognized the taste. It was blood.

He blinked again. Somehow, in that instant, when he opened his eyes, Naked Ammo had replaced Nuko. Daylight flooded the entire area. *No, not daylight, it's moving.* Bright arcing lights and long shadows danced on the edge of the jungle.

"Are you really naked?" he whispered.

"Yah, blame Quinn," she said, grinning sidewise at him. She had something in her hand and was fiddling with it. "This will be interesting. You two hold him still in case he bounces." She glanced up at someone above his head and nodded. He tried to look at them, but the light was so bright he had to close his eyes again.

There was a stab in his thigh. Then he exploded.

Every nerve in his body screamed in agony and he heard something howling. When he stopped to drag in another breath, he realized it was him. A horrific pain in his chest and shoulder sliced through his reality and he thrashed his arms wildly trying to clutch at it.

"What the holy fuck?" he roared, trying to shake free of the pain and whatever had him pinned to the ground.

"Ethan, be still, you've got an arrow through you," Nuko said, reappearing above him.

He shook his head, but with his vibrating nervous system, moving even that much threatened to wrench another scream from him.

"We must get him on the shuttle," Marti said. "A landing party has just departed Watchtower Station. ETA six minutes."

"Get me up, I can walk," he said, not realizing the insanity of his words.

Ammo set her hand in the middle of his chest and held him down.

In the distance, he heard another hissing crackle that his brain identified as a stunner round. "We've got to move," someone said. It was the handler, but he struggled to put his name to the voice. "I'm down to ten rounds and they're all starting to wake up. These are some tough little bastages. Especially the boss lady. She just won't stay down."

"She speaks our language," the captain hissed as Marti's glowing artificial face flooded his vision and it slipped its cold arms under him. "We should take her with us. She knows things."

"Of course she does," Ammo said. "She's been implanted."

CHAPTER THIRTY-SIX

"They were not Marat akUt'ar. They were not Marat akEr'tah." Mir'ah squatted with her head down, not looking at Parker as he glared at her. He held a small upload stick in his hand and watched as the file loaded to her implant.

She shouldn't be able to speak to him at all until the transfer was complete, since the language file didn't remain in her long-term memory. She had to be linked to his controller to understand human language.

At least that was how it was supposed to work.

"What happened to Walker?" he asked, deciding not to wait until the file finished to ask questions.

"Kep'tan Woh'kah mor'et ... dead," she said, glancing up at him but not rising. "Arrow kill him and korah e'eet. We'ir sharrah. He die in river. I see it."

"What about the others?"

"All run to sharrah. Korah e'eet, yes."

"How do you know?" he glanced down at the upload stick. The *completed* indicator light blinked green. The file was in her implant, but would not transfer to her brain until he toggled the activation switch.

"I know sound, big loud. Yes. Korah. Loud in sharrah. See?" She snapped her head toward the tree where it looked like a war had happened. There were several dead wakat and several more that looked to be dying.

"Boss, a moment?" His tactical team leader stood off to the side looking at a small screen in her hand.

"Mir'ah, do not move." He held off on finishing the

activation as he walked over to get the officer's report.

"Can you tell what happened yet?"

"A small invasion," she said. "Or maybe a tribal war?"

"You think it was other Ut'arans?"

"Not really. There are enough stunner casings under that tree to look more like an invasion than other natives," she said.

"Stunner casings? That means it has to be humans," he snarled.

"I'd say that's likely, but I don't know who."

"It's got to be someone from the ship."

She shook her head. "Not unless they have twenty handlers in that ship that we don't know about. As far as I know, all but three of them came down for your little safari. There's no way the other three could have pulled of this kind of attack."

"It would actually have to be two people, because I know the doctor is still up there. But why do you say that?"

"Your pet here has almost fifty in her war party. Plus the monkey-dogs. The video shows she took no losses when she attacked the Rockpile. Zero. Except for one wakat that discovered electricity is bad magic and the one that got body slammed by Captain Walker." She stopped and turned to face the carnage below the tree. "Do you really think two humans without battle armor and artillery could have done this?"

It was a good point, but Parker was a terminal skeptic. "The prisoners probably helped."

"In dead PSE? After a two day death-march, they'd be lucky to stand upright on flatlined batteries."

"How do you explain the casings then?" he challenged.

"Either the Windwalkers turned over and helped them, or another Ut'aran tribe got inside the Rockpile and found the armory."

He shook his head. "The natives are clever, but to assume they learned how to use stunners and then attacked here is implausible at best."

"So is a two person rescue party doing this much damage." She rolled her eyes. "Especially while fighting uphill against two-g, without exosuits."

"Do we know they didn't have PSE?"

"You've got a witness and she knows what a suit looks like," she said. "It's why she calls you the shiny man."

Parker turned and stared at Mir'ah for almost a minute before he nodded. "I'll talk to her, and you see if you can track down Isaiah and his people."

"Yes sir," she said, pivoting and walking toward where her team was waiting for instructions. He watched her giving instructions and could tell that none of them were happy about her orders to search the jungle at night for their missing men.

Unfortunately, he knew it was a blind chase since there was no way the Windwalkers could have turned. All of them had volunteered to take the implant as a term of their posting to the planet. But they needed to at least find the bodies.

"Tuula Mir'ah, join me," he said, walking toward the riverbank.

She slid up beside him, never raising her eyes. He did not turn to face her. Instead, he stood listening to the murmur of the wind in the trees and the almost inaudible hiss of the water on the sand.

After several minutes with no words she asked, "Is Marat akUt'ar not good Mir'ah?"

He glanced at the stick in his hand. Still holding on the transfer. "Did Walker teach you to use my words?"

"No Marat akUt'ar. Is my knowing. You show Mir'ah. Small words stay inside me."

That is unfortunate. We'll have to wipe her memory now. He felt a fleeting moment of remorse for her loss.

"I need to ask you again, Tuula Mir'ah," he said as the moment passed. "Were the ones that took Walker shiny, too? Were they Marat?"

She looked up at him making long, steady eye contact. It was something she'd never done before. "Is keet … true. No Marat." She swayed from side to side.

The commlink in his ear chirped. "We've got several bodies out here." Parker didn't recognize for sure which of his people it was.

He tapped the stud to reply. "Is it Walker and his people?"

"It's hard to tell," the man said. "Something mangled them pretty good. It looks like they were trampled to death."

"And eaten," one of the others said.

"How many are there?"

"Five … ish," the first one said.

"That's about the right number," he said. "Bag them and bring them in."

"No sir," the second one said. "Whatever did this is still around. I'm not going to get myself eaten to bring in a puddle of goo."

"Fine, get some images and then report to me."

He let out a slow hissing breath and shrugged. *That will make the doctor unhappy, but at least if she sees what happened she can't say I didn't try.*

"You were right. The jungle got them," he said, realizing Mir'ah was still watching him.

She lowered her head and let out a slow breath. Raising both hands above her head she spread her palms up toward the stars and raised her voice to announce, "We'ir sharrah Kep'tan Woh'kah Marat akEr'tah. Ut'ar Sharrah."

Mir'ah's people all stood and raised their hands as she had. "Ut'ar Sharrah!" echoed through the night.

The jungle replied with a million voices and Parker shivered.

He looked down at the stick in his hand. Hesitating only a moment, he hit the button to transfer her upload. The information surged into her brain, and even as her eyes lit up with the fire of knowledge, he saw for the first time that glow of who she was fade away into the darkness.

CHAPTER THIRTY-SEVEN

Kaycee sat in the captain's seat wanting to chew her nails but instead she bounced her leg up and down like a pneumatic hammer. Anything to burn off nervous energy, while she waited for Marti to set enough bandwidth aside to open a secure channel to the shuttle. She knew they couldn't risk letting Parker know they were down there, especially not while they were still close enough for him to retaliate.

The AA had reached its comm limits with running its automech and teleoperating the shuttle simultaneously. She didn't understand the technical side of data control and communications, but she took Marti's word for it.

So she waited for the comm blackout to end and burned nervous energy with a twitchy leg.

"The shuttle has reached sufficient range from the rescue location that it is no longer necessary to maintain close terrain avoidance," Marti announced. "We are now able to restore manual control and establish a secure commlink."

"We're on our way home," Nuko said. "I'm trying to get us far enough out that they can't catch us when we pop up on their sensors."

"How's Ethan?"

Even over the commlink, Kaycee could feel the pilot emotionally regrouping so she could report factually on his condition. "Bad. He's still losing blood. Whatever it was that Ammo gave him, kept him alive, but it's damn close to his heart."

"He keeps reaching for the arrow," Quinn said. "I'm

having to hold him down."

"Just don't let him move it. Leaving it in place until I can get him into surgery will keep the bleeding from getting worse," she said.

"Copy that," he said. "We've got him laid out on his side since the business end of the arrow protrudes fifteen centimeters out of his back. It's a serious hole on both sides. The exit wound looks like it brought pieces of his shoulder blade with it."

"All you need to do is keep him alive until you get home and I can glue him back together. What's your ETA?"

"I don't know how we're going to get back to the ship without them seeing us," Nuko said.

"We didn't think that far ahead when we put the plan together," Ammo added. "And the rail gun is a surprise."

"Director Parker is on the comm from the surface," Marti interrupted.

"Stand by a minute. I'm receiving a comm from the ass gasket in charge down there."

"Yah, do what you need to, I'm driving," Nuko said.

What the hell do I say to him? She took a deep breath and let it out slowly. *When all else fails, I guess I fake it.*

"Parker, do you have my people?" she asked, trying to sound worried, which wasn't too far out of her way given the truth of the captain's condition.

He cleared his throat before he spoke. "There's a problem with that."

"No problems Parker, do you have them or not?"

"We were too late," he said.

"Too late?" she asked. *Of course you were, bastard.*

"Apparently, they tried to escape. If they'd waited for help, they'd have been fine." Even if she hadn't known he was lying, he wasn't making much effort to sound concerned.

"What happened?"

"It looks like they were killed by a korah."

"What?" she asked, trying to make her voice sound like she was in shock. "You said they were safe."

"We've located where they were, and unfortunately nobody's alive."

"What about your people?" she asked. She hadn't heard from Quinn and Ammo about what they'd had to do to them, but she was sure it wasn't pretty.

"We're looking for them," he said. "We don't know for sure what happened but we know it was ... violent."

"Frak. What the hell am I supposed to do now?"

"I'd suggest you go ahead and pull out." His voice took on that tone that told her it wasn't a suggestion as much as an instruction. "You've got a cargo to deliver and once you do, you can afford to hire yourself a new shipmaster and crew."

Yes! Oh wait, he has to believe I'm devastated. She bit down on her lip until it hurt to keep from laughing. "I can't leave. They are my family. I need to take their bodies home at least."

"Have you ever seen what a person looks like who's been eaten? Well maybe it would be better to say crushed. A korah weighs six tons and they tend to trample their dinner first." He paused, probably for dramatic effect. "There isn't enough to recognize as a body. It's just a wet mess."

"I don't know..." she let her words trail off. She really didn't want to protest too hard, but if she didn't push back enough, he'd suspect something was up.

"Being an indie, I'm sure you have an inheritance clause in your contract with Walker. Looks to me like you've got yourself a ship." His tone was edging toward impatience.

"I've got to have something to show for it. I'll have to have some kind of proof of death," she said.

"Dr. Ansari and I will take care of that, and I'll send it ahead to the authorities," he said. "We'll clean up the mess down here. You just focus on getting my cargo to Lyra Prime."

"I don't like this." She let out a loud sigh.

"I don't give even a miniscule frak what you like. Consider yourself lucky that you weren't down here with them." The deep growl in his voice told her he was through with her pushing back and expected her to suck it up and move on. "You need to wrap your feeble brain around the concept that your continued health is directly proportionate to how effective you are at getting my cargo delivered. Is that clear enough?"

"Perfectly," she said. "We'll push off now."

"He has disconnected the comm channel from his end," Marti announced.

"Do you think he suspects we slid it by him?"

"I do not," it said. "I would assume he is involved in trying to assess what happened on the planet and that situation is where his focus lies. If he discovers that it is his people's bodies and not ours, he may reevaluate your conversation."

She nodded. "I wasn't very convincing was I?"

"If the range of your performance exceeds the range of the station's rail guns, then your believability was adequate."

"I guess that's what matters," she said.

She pushed back in the seat and stood up. "Are we still on with the shuttle?"

"For another ninety seconds. They are dropping over the horizon and I will lose my link at that point. If we do not move away from Watchtower Station to keep a signal lock, we will need to use standard communications channels."

"Then put me back through to them."

"They remained online during your conversation with Director Parker."

"Yah, we're still here," Nuko said. "Railguns and cargo?"

"It's a long story," she said. "I'll fill you in, when you get aboard. You and Marti coordinate the details of getting you back, and I'll get set up for Ethan's surgery."

"Understood," she said. "One battle at a time."

"Exactly."

She turned and headed toward MedBay trying to focus on the immediacy of keeping the captain alive, but the whole list of future fights loomed large in front of her. Closing her eyes, she leaned against the back of the lift cage as she rode down to the mid-deck.

Taking several deep breaths and pushing them out slowly, she tried to drive the distractions to the corners of her mind.

"Dr. Forrester is asking permission to come with us," Marti said, gouging a hole in her efforts.

"What?"

"He is in the airlock asking to come aboard. He believes that if we do not take him along, Director Parker will know he assisted us and will have him killed."

"That's his problem." The railing opened in front of her and she just couldn't force herself to move. "We don't need another crisis on this ship."

"There may be several reasons to bring him with us," it said.

"I'm not seeing an advantage at the moment."

"He does have an intimate familiarity with the situation and those involved," it said. "This may be useful when the time comes and we are dealing with the authorities. Regardless of what the medical scanner that he gave you contains, having a witness to the events here will give credibility to our defense."

"There is that," she agreed. "What else?"

"He is a qualified surgeon, and as you are the only uninjured member of the crew at this point, his assistance with medical support may be invaluable."

She nodded, pushing herself out of the lift. "Let him in, but make sure he knows that there is no guarantee that when Ethan recovers, he won't lock him up until we get this straightened out."

CHAPTER THIRTY-EIGHT

Ethan woke up the following morning with a newly printed scapula and a dermal regenerator clamped to his shoulder. He felt like he'd been beaten, pounded, and dragged naked through the jungle.

Wait? Naked? In the Jungle?

Flashes of memory came back to him. He remembered most of the ordeal, but the last night seemed to be lost in an impossible surreal dream. None of it made sense. He stared up at the ceiling plating trying to piece things back together.

He could tell he was in a MedBay, but he was too weak to move his head enough to look around. "What happened?" he whispered. His vocal chords felt sandblasted.

"Ah Captain Walker, you're awake," a man said. He stepped into view and Ethan blinked.

"Who the hell are you?"

"I'm Dr. Morris Forrester." He smiled. Reaching out, he adjusted the regenerator and Ethan felt the tingling sensation in his shoulder change. "You're lucky to be alive I think."

"Where am I?"

"You're on your ship, Captain," he said.

Ethan shook his head and pain shot through his chest and neck like a laser burn. *Don't do that again.* "Where's Kaycee?"

"I believe she's taking care of your engineer at the moment," he said. "He's far less critical than you are. Should I call her for you?"

"Is everyone alright?"

"Yes, for the most part," he said. "You were all suffering from exposure and various degrees of other injury, but no one is facing anything life threatening, at least not now that you've recovered enough to be awake."

"I'm awake?"

"Yes, you are," he said. "For the moment anyway." He reached up and adjusted a control somewhere above Ethan's head.

A heavy dark blanket began to settle over him and he fought to stay awake. "Wait. Is the ship safe?"

"Yes. We're on our way to Cygnus Localus."

"Cygnus Localus? Why?"

"Enough questions, Captain. You need to rest."

He shook his head again, but instead of stabbing pain the room spun dizzily and he closed his eyes.

When he opened them, he sat propped on a bed. The lights were much more pleasant. Dim, and more like a bedroom. The hardware previously attached to him was gone, and he looked around. He was in his quarters on the *Olympus Dawn*.

The vivid band of rainbow streaks visible through the window above his bed told him they were moving.

"How do you feel, Boss?" Nuko's voice came out of the near dark and startled him.

"I'm not sure." He shrugged and the muscles around his right shoulder pulled like an electrified net held them. He flinched in pain. "What happened?"

"Kaycee said you might not remember much," she said.

"I feel like I've been asleep for a week." Trying to push himself up in the bed, he groaned.

"Close." She stood up and walked over to fluff his pillows and then sat on the foot of his bed. "Actually it's been over forty-eight hours."

"What happened?" he repeated.

"Ammo and Quinn got us out of there." She grinned. "It was all rather heroic, even if it was strange."

He nodded. "Probably not as strange as my dreams. I really don't …" He struggled to push back through the fog that blanketed his memories, but the images from his dreams were vivid and refused to get out of the way. "I dreamed that Quinn and Ammo jumped out of a tree naked and started shooting wakats."

"It was only Quinn. Ammo wasn't in the tree."

"Ah yah, right, she came running in along the river bank," he said, feeling the gears in his brain grind to a halt. No matter what he did, they refused to mesh back into motion.

She sat staring at him and he couldn't tell if she was playing with his reality. He didn't feel drugged anymore, but he couldn't be sure. Finally, he decided she was screwing with him. "That was my dream."

"No, that's a memory." She held up a hand as if to swear an oath.

"But they weren't naked," he said.

She nodded. "They were. Quinn said it was so they could sneak in close enough to rescue us. Apparently it worked. They took out all six of the Windwalkers and then took on Mir'ah and her party."

"Naked? I could barely stand up in that gravity."

"Yah, really. Kaycee pumped them full of drugs and they both managed to hike twenty klick and still have enough juice to kick some Ut'aran ass. Like I said it was pretty heroic."

"I need some of those drugs. I don't think I could kick my way past the edge of my bed."

"She said you could get up and move around today if you

feel up to it, but only if you want to." She reached out and squeezed his leg. "I know the rest of the crew and our passengers would all like to see that you're doing better."

"Passengers? Where are we?" He rolled his head upward and looked out the window to make sure they were moving, and that it wasn't just another dream fragment that refused to let go.

"We're about six hours from the Cygnus Localus threshold," she said.

"What's there?"

"Help, I hope," she said.

A rapping at the door cut him off before he could ask another question. He still felt like it took an act of will to keep the lights on in his brain, but he wasn't willing to turn loose of the certainty that he wasn't getting the answers he needed.

Kaycee stood in the doorway to his bedroom. She carried a medical scanner in one hand and a large coffee mug in the other. Her expression told him it probably wasn't the drink he'd want, once she'd given him the answers he needed.

She walked over and handed him the mug and then pushed herself up onto his dressing cabinet to sit. They stared at each other for several seconds before she took a deep breath and asked, "Are you feeling better?"

"At the moment," he said. "I have a feeling that's about to change though." Glancing down into the cup, he realized it wasn't coffee. It looked more like used industrial lubricant. He remembered that enzyme sludge Quinn had tried to push on him once, and he put it on the bedside table. Downwind.

"I should go," Nuko stood up but Kaycee shook her head, her eyes pleading for her to stay. She obviously wanted reinforcements.

"Enough of this, let's just get it on the table." He pushed

himself up on the bed again. "What's wrong? Did somebody die and you're not telling me?"

"No, nothing like that," Nuko said.

"Everybody's good," Kaycee added.

He shot a skeptical eyebrow in her direction.

She nodded. "Really. Everybody's alright. Better than you, in fact."

"Then what's swinging? Why are we going to Localus?"

"Because we're carrying cargo back."

"From Watchtower?" He felt a fist of pain in his chest as his heart charged forward, faster than his brain, to a conclusion he didn't want to make.

"I had to negotiate with Parker to get us out of there alive," she said, pulling a thinpad out of her jumpsuit and handing it to him.

He glanced down at the open screen. "Those are sleeper pods," he whispered. "Slaves?"

"It's a load of sedated passengers from the planet," she offered. Her face wrinkled in a slow motion cascade of emotion. Swallowing hard, she added, "They've been sold."

"Sold? That makes them slaves." He brought his hands up and ground his fists into his eyes.

She shrugged. "It's probably a matter of semantics."

"Slave trading is one of the things in the Coalition that is punishable by hanging." He swung his feet off the side of the bed and pulled himself to the edge so he could stand up and choke her to death. "You can't be that … insane. Why would you agree to transport slaves?"

"Ethan, wait," Nuko said. "She had no choice. They loaded an antimatter bomb into the cargo container and tied it to the ship's power grid on a deadman switch. She couldn't refuse."

"And it was the only way Parker would agree to get you

back," Kaycee said.

"He didn't get us out of there." He shook his head and stood up. Violence was still the top item on his personal agenda.

"Ammo and Quinn were supposed to be Plan-B," she said.

He wobbled on his feet and reached out for the wall to brace himself. He wasn't going to sit back down until he had an answer that made sense, or until he'd carried out his fantasy of strangling her.

"Can you just look at it like we're freeing 300 slaves bound for Lyra Prime?"

He glanced at the pilot and frowned. "I thought you said we are approaching Localus?"

She nodded. "We're stopping there first."

"Why? It's two days out of the way."

"So we can get this to the authorities," Kaycee said, holding up the medical scanner she'd been carrying. "Dr. Forrester documented as much of the operation as he knew about, and we're hoping to get it into the right hands to do something with it ... before they find out what we're carrying."

"Forrester?"

"Yah, he was the Medical Director at Watchtower, and is the one responsible for implanting the Ut'arans they were harvesting," she said. "He also helped patch you back together."

The anger started to drain from him, as something far less pleasant pushed ice water through his veins. He eased back down on his bed. "If he was part of their operation, why would you trust him?"

"He'd been implanted before he got to Watchtower," she said. "He had no way to resist working with them until I cut his connection."

"You're saying this is bigger than just what was happening at the station?"

She nodded. "There's a lot on the scanner's storage drive. Hopefully it will be enough to end their operation."

"If it's not, then we're all screwed," he said. "I don't know if I can swallow all this right now. You've wagered everything on whether we can dig ourselves out faster than the Coalition will be looking to bury us."

"I know," she whispered. "I had no choice and I had to do the right thing."

"There's no way this is it," he said.

"Exposing their operation? How is that not right?

He sighed. "But you've done a lot of wrong things to do it. I don't even know how many laws we're breaking just having them aboard."

"Haven't you gone against the rules to do exactly that in the past?"

He glared at her. "That's a cheap shot."

But it was valid.

CHAPTER THIRTY-NINE

Cygnus Localus was a farming colony. Small, agrarian, and low on the technology index. Only seven parsec from Earth, it didn't need much in the way of heavy industry. In fact, other than the gas mining operations on one moon of the ringed giant, there was almost nothing of value in the system. That meant the Localus government had no need for major security forces.

Considering what they were carrying, that suited Ethan just fine.

They'd shut down their transponder just before they entered the system, and waited in the darkness on the outer edge of the system, hoping that nobody noticed them. The less attention they attracted, the better their chances of not dying with a noose around their neck.

They were already a day late on making the drop off at Maxima Six and by now, Parker had probably sent out a warning to his network that something was moving sidewise. He was shrewd enough to have his own Plan-B, as well as several other alphabetically arranged backup schemes, with progressive degrees of ugliness.

Ethan sat on the ConDeck alone, staring at the distant sun and trying not to chew himself to death while he waited for things to break loose. He knew it was pointless, but still he chased down all the ways that they might play out … and all of them ended badly.

Rene rolled onto the back riser of the ConDeck and parked his mobility seat behind his normal monitor station.

Kaycee had confined the engineer to a wheelchair for several weeks since he had dozens of small stress fractures in the bones of his lower legs. He stood up with a groan and swung into the other seat.

"Give me some good news," Ethan said, swiveling to face him. He'd ordered the engineer to assess their options to disarm the reactor overload trigger.

He let out a long sigh and shook his head. "The only thing I can come up with is to build a phase lock controller for the ground plane. If it works, it should delay the reactor going off if we disconnect."

"That means we can cut the container loose. And then what?"

He shrugged. "Leave it and run like hell before it blows up."

"There are three hundred Ut'arans in there."

"I'm not sure it would work anyway, but it's the best I can do." The engineer drummed his fingers on the edge of his console. "Whoever designed this thing is a master—"

"Captain I am detecting a ship approaching," Marti interrupted. "They just dropped to sublight over the nearest threshold beacon. ETA twelve minutes."

"What is it?" Ethan spun to face his console and opened up the sensor display.

"It appears to be a Percheron class freighter."

"A freighter?"

"Pirates?" Rene suggested, opening his screen and calling up the data. "They're running hot, but it looks to be all engines. I don't see any weapons active."

"Can we run?"

He shook his head. "Sublight only. That kill switch Parker told Kaycee about lit up when we dropped out of cruise. As soon as our coils kick up to threshold levels, it'll trigger an overload in the reactor."

"Just to be safe, let's arm the repelling lasers and prepare for boarding parties," Ethan said. "Get Kaycee and Nuko up here."

"Yes captain," Marti said.

"This isn't the kind of trouble I expected. Security, yah, but pirates?" Ethan growled. "Can't we ever catch a break?"

"Doesn't look like it," Rene said, pointing at the screen in front of him. "There are two wings of ships leaving the mining colony. They're probably security."

"They appear to be Defender class patrol gunships," Marti confirmed. "Range and velocity put them at just over four hours to our current position."

"So we survive the pirates, only to get arrested afterward," he said. "All we need is FleetCom to show up for the party to get things really swinging."

"That comes later," Kaycee said, appearing on the ConDeck with Nuko a step behind.

The eyeball that Ethan shot her almost knocked her through the wall. She froze so fast that Nuko was three steps up her back before she bounced to a stop.

"I assume that help is here?" she said, sheepishly.

"If it's disguised to look like a pirate raider and a flotilla of security gunships, then yah, help is coming."

"Pirates?" Nuko dropped into her seat and logged into the control screens.

Ethan nodded. "A Percheron class freighter at ten minutes. They're not charging guns. At least not so far."

"Have they hailed us," she asked.

"Not yet," he said.

"Do you have a visual on them?" Kaycee asked.

He rolled his eyes. "They are still almost five light minutes out."

"Can we open a comm?" she asked.

"Yes, your ladyship," he said, rolling his eyes and biting on his lip. "Would you like to drive too, while you're giving orders?"

"I don't think it's pirates," she said, ignoring his sarcasm. "I think it's the cavalry. Marti can you check the transponder on the ship, or is it still too far away?"

"There is an error," Marti said. "The identification code identifies it as CSV-1070, *Olympus Dawn*."

"Excuse me?" He shot a side eye at Nuko. "It's running a jigged transponder?"

"That is correct," it said.

He glanced back at Kaycee who was nodding.

"Its transponder identifies the ship as us, clear down to the keel serial number," Rene added. "That's going to take some explaining."

"Can we get that comm now?" Kaycee asked.

Ethan nodded. "Spin it up and let's see what's swinging."

Nuko opened the comm. "You're on."

"*Olympus Dawn* to … *Olympus Dawn*. Standing by for visual channel," he said.

The image of the other ship's ConDeck materialized on the forward viewscreen. Elias Pruitt and Jefferson Cordwain stood on the riser behind the captain and her pilot. *An alien technologies engineer and a legal advisor?*

"Actually it's the *Elysium Sun*," the other captain said. "At least it will be in a few minutes."

"Captain Walker, I'm surprised to see you up and about already," Pruitt said, jumping in and drawing an eye roll from the other pilot. "Kaycee said you were pretty badly injured."

"She did a good job of gluing me back together," he said, shrugging with his good shoulder. The other one still wasn't happy about life but he had hopes that it would have time to get better before they hung him.

"Elias, I didn't expect you to be here," Kaycee said, she was obviously pleased to see him.

"I brought a few toys with me in case we couldn't convince our passenger he needed to play along," he said. "I figured I might be able to help out."

"So did it work?" she asked.

"He has agreed to cooperate," Jefferson said. "In exchange for certain considerations."

"Who?" Ethan asked.

"His name is Sho-chen Addams," Elias said.

"He came aboard of his own free will," the advisor said.

"That might be because when we showed up in Lyra Prime he mistook us for the *Olympus Dawn*." Elias grinned.

"The fake transponder." Ethan nodded. He wasn't sure why it mattered.

"He volunteered to help us out?" Kaycee looked relieved.

"For the most part," Pruitt said. "That's probably why he still has most of his body parts."

"I'm still blind. Who the frak is Addams and why is he important?" Ethan said.

"He's the person who designed the failsafe detonator on the antimatter reactor you're carrying. He's agreed to deactivate it as long as we give him a running start on the law… and Mr. Parker," he said

"I think he's more afraid of his employer than of any legal problems he might face," Jefferson said.

"The transponder lured him out of his hole. He had a crew with him to help unload the cargo, but when they realized it was a trap, they bailed on him faster than roaches in a solar flare," Elias added.

"From there it was simply a matter of convincing him

that his only hope of survival was to disappear, and that we had the resources to help him with that," he said.

"Or we could feed him in several pieces to a recycler." Pruitt smiled in a chilling way that told the captain he was a lot more than just an engineer.

"Alright, that solves the bomb problem, but what then?" Ethan asked.

"We'll take the files on the medical scanner that Dr. Forrester gave you, and use them to negotiate with FleetCom authorities," Jefferson said. "If there's enough there to take down the whole operation, it shouldn't be any problem getting you off the hot seat."

"What are we supposed to do in the meantime? We're sitting on a cargo container full of—"

"Yes, you are," he said, cutting him off. He pointed at his ear and nodded at the captain sitting in front of him. "The security forces en route from Localus Trinity Mining will make sure you're safe until we return. Just sit back and wait."

"But no matter what, don't let them aboard," Elias said.

"FleetCom has jurisdiction in this matter. As long as you don't make any threatening gestures, they have no rights to board or search your ship," the advisor said. "Of course, if anyone else shows up, they would be obligated to protect you."

"Captain another ship just dropped over the threshold," Marti said. "It looks to be a private cruiser."

Jefferson glanced at his wrist chrono and smiled. "Perfect timing. That would be Coalition News Service. They got an anonymous tip that someone had taken down a slave trading ring and that if they wanted the exclusive story, they had to be here before it all goes public."

The captain of the *Elysium Sun* twisted in her seat to face the advisor, but he ignored her reaction.

"CNS?" Ethan asked.

"A free media can be your friend, if for no other reason than because people in power don't dare cross any lines when there are witnesses with recording gear and a loud voice," he said.

"I'm not a fan of being in front of an optic," Captain Walker said.

"We'll handle all the media engagement," Jefferson said. "You just keep them off the ship until—"

"Right, until you get back."

"Now, Elias and Mr. Addams will be aboard in a few minutes," he said. "You need to give their pilot the documentation that Dr. Forrester gave you, so we can rendezvous with the *Nakamiru* before it gets here."

Rene shook his head. "I didn't even know the *Nakamiru* was out of spacedock yet."

"It's on a training mission about three parsec from here. It just so happens that the Wing Chancellor for FleetCom is aboard as an observer, so we will present the evidence to her in person," he said.

"FleetCom doesn't announce training missions publicly," Nuko said.

"Smythe isn't only a biomedical company," the advisor said. "You could say we're not really public as far as that goes."

"So your plan is to fly into a FleetCom training theater, in a ship with a hotwired beacon, and hand Chancellor Parada what we've got on the Watchtower operation?"

"As soon as we rendezvous with you, we will reset our transponder and have you go live. From the range of the approaching ships it shouldn't be possible to tell we traded names," the other captain said.

"Well that takes one item off the list of criminal acts."

Ethan leaned back in his chair and shook his head. "That doesn't change the fact that pushing this down her throat is going to take some big titanium eggs."

"If it all goes according to plan, they will review the evidence and decide they want to take charge of your payload. Hopefully this means you are less than a day from getting this mess off your back."

The advisor sounded confident, but it was still a shipload of wishes as far as the captain was concerned.

"If he can convince the chancellor." Nuko shot Ethan a skeptical eye roll that confirmed she shared his opinion.

"We won't tell them where you are and what exactly you are carrying, until she agrees not to prosecute," Jefferson added.

"And if she doesn't?"

"Then you can always take them back to Watchtower," Elias said.

"Yah, I can see Parker letting that happen." Ethan laughed out loud at that mental image.

"It looks like you've packaged it cleanly to me," Kaycee said.

Ethan was far from convinced, unfortunately it seemed to be their only way through and out the other side.

"There is one last thing," the advisor said. "I will need you all to imprint a Power of Agency for me." He pulled out a thinpad and tapped a screen to send the documents.

"We're receiving the files now," Marti announced.

"These are so that I can represent you and your crew in negotiating your legal settlement," he explained.

"Settlement?" Ethan asked.

He nodded. "Watchtower Station is a Coalition Science facility. The reckless endangerment to you and your crew that occurred while under the care and protection of the government, gives us a very strong legal position for pressing a case for damages."

"We're going to bring a suit against the Science Wing of the Coalition?" Rene's face ratcheted through several expressions as he tried to process that reality. "We're sitting on a boat load of … ahem … cargo, and you want to go full frontal on them?"

"A strong offense is often the best way to keep an adversary off balance," Jefferson said. "However I think the threat of legal action will be sufficient for them to admit liability and make an offer commensurate with their exposure."

"Are you angling to use this as a bargaining chip to keep them from prosecuting us?" Ethan asked.

"If they assume that to be true it would only operate to our advantage, but I don't intend to let it play out that way," he said. "When they see the filing I intend to make on your behalf, they will consider it in their best interests to settle."

"What are we talking here?"

"Let's just say the settlement should be substantial."

CHAPTER FORTY

Ethan Walker stood alone on the shipyard observation gallery of Cochrane Station One, staring out at the matched pair of Percheron class freighters. Less than a year ago, he'd been struggling to make his lease payment on the *Olympus Dawn* and today he paid cash for the *Elysium Sun*.

He reached up and fingered the small slash that stretched horizontally below his captain's bars. *Fleet Captain*. It was only a commercial merchant designation, but since he had never hoped to have more than his own ship, it floated his spirit in a profound way. Even if it was only two ships and a couple dropships under his license.

Of course, he knew it wouldn't have happened at all, except that the settlement Jefferson had landed from the Science Wing of the Coalition, was obscenely huge.

The government administrator who ended up holding the glueball of responsibility, turned out to be more than accommodating when he realized how far they had him bent over the bulkhead. The fact that a government employee was running a slaving operation out of a Science Wing Facility worked well as a hammer to shape the negotiation in a favorable direction. Keeping the details from public scrutiny was more important than protecting a lot of credits sitting around in a government bank account.

The Coalition had deep enough pouches that when they opened them up, fortunes changed. The *Elysium Sun* was proof of that.

His thinpad beeped in his pocket, snapping him out of

his euphoric cloud. He pulled it out and read the message: *If the Lord-Admiral can quit eyeballing his new baby, he needs to remember his crew is waiting for him to show up for dinner. Quinn is about to launch another rescue party for you, and unless you want to see him prowling naked through the station, I think you should show up soon. Nuko.*

On my way. Tell him to keep his pants on … at least until I get there and we all get more alcohol into us. He pried himself away from the window and turned toward the upper lift platform.

Grabbing the first overhead carriage, he punched in the name of his destination and was surprised as it swung out over the lower decks and whisked him toward the station's high-cred district. He looked down at the display on his thinpad to confirm the address.

How did a place named Badger Bob's end up on Promenade-Two?

When he stepped off the tram and bounced down onto the landing platform, he looked around in awe. It was undeniably above his paygrade, no matter how many chits he had under him now. A shimmering wall of light and mist stretched in both directions to the edge of the deck and blocked the entire end of the promenade. His destination was a polished metal arch that penetrated through the center of the mist.

A woman stood outside the arched doors, scowling at the entrance as he approached. Behind her, what appeared to be her two husbands stared at the ground and tried not to attract her looming wrath. She wore a gown that looked like a cloud of dancing ice crystals. As he got close enough to get a good scan of her he realized that the translucence of her dress was an illusion, and what she actually wore was a holographic projection from a jewel encrusted headpiece, and not much else.

"Two hundred thousand in papercred for this dress and that LEO Colony scuzzwhistle won't let us through the door," she hissed, glancing toward Ethan as he walked past her. "What do you think? He's a flatbrain isn't he?"

Frak!

He turned and smiled politely. "Were you talking to me, ma'am?"

"I was," she snorted, looking down at his basic duty uniform. "But what would you know, you probably crawled out of the same recycler he did."

He bit down on his first response, and the next several, that popped into his mind. Finally, he shrugged and leaned to look past her to husband number one. "Perhaps one of you gentlemen should take her home and see that she gets her meds rebalanced?"

He spun and walked on toward the door as both husbands snorted in unison.

"How dare you?" she shrieked. "I know the owner. They don't let people like you in there."

He nodded, but didn't turn in her direction. He half expected her to hurl a shoe in his direction ... except he was pretty sure she wasn't wearing those either.

He reached the doors without a projectile accompaniment, and the proximity scanner swept over him once. He smiled as the face of a real person appeared on the display.

"Captain Walker. Welcome to Badger Bob's. Your party is waiting for you in the Hole in the Sky lounge." The doors opened silently, leaving more than enough audible headroom for him to hear her stunned gasp.

As soon as he cleared the inner edge of the arch, it was his turn to gasp. He swung his head in a slow scan of the area, trying to absorb the reality of what he was seeing. It looked like he'd suddenly transported down to Earth.

In spite of knowing better, he glanced back at the doorway he'd just come through to make sure that wasn't what had happened. For an instant, the howling lady in the cloud bank dress was still visible before the doors sealed shut behind him.

The walls and ceiling had to be screens, but it was the finest projection job he'd ever seen. A slight breeze in his face, matching the gently swaying trees that had replaced the walls, enhanced the illusion.

He was still shaking his head as a large man walked up and stuck his hand out. "Captain Walker, I'm Bobert Primm. Welcome to the Badger."

"Primm?" Ethan raised an eyebrow as he shook the man's hand. He was over two meters tall and bore more than a passing resemblance to an older version of Quinn.

"Yah, you know my nephew Quintan," he said, winking and holding an arm out in the direction he wanted them to head. "He's told me a lot about you."

"Hopefully not the bad stuff," he said, dropping in a step behind the man. It was disconcerting to walk on a hard floor when the projections made it look like they were on a rickety wooden deck sticking out over a sandy beach.

"He speaks highly of you," Bob said. "It's why he wanted to bring you here before you head out again. He said you are quite the captain."

"I don't know about that. I'm just lucky I think."

"Favorable odds are a desirable consort. Many never climb above the machinery of fate to win her favor."

As they followed the deck further out toward the ocean, the beach dropped away and the platform they walked on rose on massive wooden pilings. They paused beside a large potted areca palm sitting next to a gap in the railing. Quinn's uncle pushed his hand against what looked like open air, and a door swung open ten meters above the sand below. The illusion of opening a hole in the sky was so convincing that Ethan's mind resisted the reality. Voices he recognized carried out of the impossible space beyond.

Bob winked at his reaction. "Do try the lobster tonight. That is, if you fancy ocean meat. It is wonderful with our house brew."

"Lobster?"

"Yes, we brought them up from Newfoundland this morning."

Ethan nodded. Not sure what exactly a lobster was, Quinn had taught him to not to ask a Primm about food. It was probably better not to know.

"Enjoy your evening, Captain. The room is all yours for as long as you want, and the food and spirits are on me."

"Thank you, but that's really not necessary," he said.

"Nonsense. Family always eats on the house." He waived toward the room as he turned to leave. "I will send someone by to present the appetizers and whatnot."

Ethan had to force himself to step across the half meter gap, tapping his foot lightly to make sure there was a floor under him. "That would be a hell of a drunk trap," he muttered as he managed to make the step across without leaping.

Looking back at the wall he'd just come through, it had disappeared, along with everything but the floor and a railing. The sky above was velvet-black and shot through with stars, while the world beyond the edge of the deck was an endless ocean. The moon hung just above the horizon and sent flashes of light across the surface of the undulating water.

Angel, Ammo, and Quinn leaned against what looked like an antique wooden bar that sprawled like a mahogany monolith along what had to be a wall. The rest of his crew reclined comfortably around a circular table that dominated the center of the deck. Jefferson and Elias had joined them and they were all talking animatedly about something.

"Evening boss," Quinn said as he walked up to order a drink. "Was that Uncle Bob?"

He nodded. "It's pretty obvious too. You look a lot like him."

Ammo's mouth dropped open. "He's the one that used to hunt—"

The handler nodded. "Yep. Papa gave him the nickname. Probably better than using the one momma gave him."

Angel scrunched her eyes closed and shook her head. It was clear she was trying to hold back on asking.

Ethan jumped in fearlessly for her. "What was that one?"

"When she was feeling mannerly, she called him Naked Bobby." The handler grinned. "She had others, but I don't think I should be repeating them in polite company."

"That'd be a lousy name for a top deck place like this," he said.

"So he really is your uncle?" Ammo asked.

He held his hand up like he was swearing an oath. "He's my double uncle. He's my mother's brother, but he's married to my father's uncle. That makes their kids their own half cousins once removed, and he's his own—"

"Quinn, I don't think we need to know that much about your family bush," the captain said. "Grab your beer … or whatever fancy umbrella juice that is … and let's sit. I want to talk about where we go from here."

He walked over and dropped into the open seat between Rene and Nuko. He looked across the table at Jefferson and

Elias. "I want to say thank you to both of you for pulling off what has to be the biggest Miracle Mike in history."

Nuko grinned and nodded. "I didn't see any way we wouldn't be spending the rest of our lives locked up."

"I have to admit that I am surprised at how fast they rolled on this," Jefferson said. "We had a winnable case, but I don't think I got a good understanding of what happened behind the front face. They were pushing back like I'd have expected, but then I got a summons to the Science Chancellor's office. She made a fast reverse and we were looking at a lot of zeroes."

"What would have caused that?"

He shrugged. "It was like a higher authority told her to let it go."

"There is no position of authority above the Wing Chancellors," Marti said. The humanform automech walked up to the table carrying a small glass of something fruity looking.

"God, maybe?" Rene suggested.

The AA stared at him for several seconds before it drew the corner of the mouth on its projected face up slightly. "Debating the existence of a creator awareness is a null value endeavor, even as I sit in the presence of what could be called the people of my own gods."

"Don't be too quick to give us that label," Ammo said, shaking her head as she slid into the chair beside Marti. "I was watching the newswave a couple hours ago and they were covering the arrests of Parker and Ansari. They were definitely not being godly."

"I'm sure they weren't," Ethan said. "Have we heard what will happen to the Ut'arans we brought out?"

"I've been told they'll have their implants removed and will go home to be repatriated," Jefferson said.

"How much will they remember?" Nuko asked.

Kaycee shifted uneasily in her chair before she looked down at her hands on the table. "I don't know. Probably some of it. A lot, maybe," she whispered.

"What about Mir'ah akCha'nee? Will they hunt her down and remove her implant?" the captain asked.

"I don't know that, either."

"You know she believed the shiny man was a god," Rene's expression showed that the idea didn't sit well with him.

"Her god has abandoned her," Angel said. She and Quinn stood behind their empty chairs, looking like they were each slaying emotional dragons of their own. "She committed atrocities in his name. When the implant is gone, if she remembers, how will she deal with that?"

"We've done it, too," Ethan said.

"But have we ever come to grips with it?" the engineer asked.

Ammo shook her head. "Not really."

After the silence hung for almost a minute, one of the tenders walked up and poured a round of alcohol into the tall crystal glasses that sat in front of each table setting.

Ethan picked up his glass and stared at it. Small bubbles rose to the surface and exploded in miniscule sparkles of vapor. He raised it higher and waited until everyone had lifted their own glasses.

"To the day when Mir'ah akCha'nee can accept that no matter how shiny, her gods are still made of clay."

Rene nodded, glancing over at Quinn.

"And to longer loincloths."

THE END

Get the prequel to *Wings of Earth*. The complete *Shan Takhu Legacy* trilogy in a box set. With a bonus short story published for the first time in this set.

It waits in the darkness.

Beyond Neptune, a routine prospecting mission explodes into chaos and throws Commander Jephora Cochrane and his crew into a crisis that will test their experience to the limit.

After crash-landing on the surface of an icy asteroid Cochrane's crew discovers an ancient artifact that may hold the key to stopping a battle destined to shred civilization. Yet an attempt to rescue the crew of the *Jakob Waltz* brings civil war to the edge of the Solar System, and catches Commander Cochrane between an emerging authoritarian regime and a desperate fleet of resistance forces.

Understanding the power of the ancient Shan Takhu technology may be the only hope for the future of humanity, but first Cochrane must defeat the warships that will stop at nothing to control the power of the alien structure they've discovered.

With no choices left, they have to keep the exploding war from burying the Legacy of the Shan Takhu back into the ice from which it came.

Come along on the journey and discover how eleven unlikely heroes will have the strength to change the destiny of humanity.

Read the complete trilogy of the *Shan Takhu Legacy* and enjoy a special vignette published for the first time in this set.

Thank you for reading *Wings of Earth: 3 - Chains of Dawn.* If you enjoyed the story, please take a moment and consider leaving a review.

Reviews feed the creative souls of all authors and are invaluable in helping readers discover new books to experience.

Thank you. EMC

ABOUT THE AUTHOR

 Eric Michael Craig is a Hard Science Fiction writer living in the Manzano Mountains of New Mexico. He is the former Director of Research for a private consulting laboratory in Phoenix, where he experimented with inertial propulsion and power generation technologies.

Fascinated with the "cacophony of humanity," he dedicated much of his life to observing society and how people relate to each other and the world around them. Ultimately this drove him to write full time.

When not writing, Eric is active in Intentional Community Design, plays guitar and bass, occasionally dabbles in art of various forms, and designs websites. He also owns way too many dogs.

Eric is a founding member of the SciFi Roundtable. The SFRT is an active online group dedicated to supporting indie and traditional authors by networking them with other writers and professional resources.

Connect with the Eric at: ericmichaelcraig.com
Facebook: facebook.com/ericmichaelcraigauthor/
Twitter: @EricMCraig
Amazon Author Central: http://author.to/emc
BookBub:https: bookbub.com/profile/eric-michael-craig

Sign up for Eric's newsletter to keep up on new releases and special features about his science fiction worlds and technologies. http://ericmichaelcraig.com/subscribe

ACKNOWLEDGEMENTS

Thank you, to all the readers who have enjoyed my books so far. Continued thanks to Jennifer Amon, my proof reader and Ducky Smith, my editor and cover artist. You both make my books shine.

Made in the USA
Middletown, DE
06 September 2019